The Sinners

Raven River Academy

Ruby Vincent

Published by Ruby Vincent, 2020.

Prologue

What happened?

I cringed. Thinking made the pounding in my skull worse.

What was going on? I was with Hiro. Then... we went to Caesar's Garage and... and...

Slowly, I peeled my eyes open. The light was a sharp spike to my foggy brain. Through the pain, I made out multiple blurred figures.

"Ember?" One of the figures moved, coming toward me. "You're awake. Let me apologize for the rough treatment."

Rio materialized before me—agreeable smile nowhere to be found. His apology poured from bloodless lips and nothing reflected in his eyes but coldness.

"It's abhorrent to handle a young lady in this manner but circumstances have brought us to this."

I blinked at him, not comprehending what he was saying. Movement flickered out of the corner of my eye. I looked away from him and choked on a gasp.

Cassius and Clay had been taken down and tossed on the office's threadbare couch. Hiro was placed between them and all three had been beat to shit. Blood wept from cuts on their faces and Hiro cradled an arm that was surely broken. They might have gotten up and done something about this if the three men with Rio weren't standing before them, guns trained on their forehead.

Cold seeped into my back. I was sitting on a metal chair and—

Cloth bit into my wrists as I strained against my bindings.

—and I wasn't going anywhere.

"Relax, my dear."

Rio shifted to the side, giving me a view of Royal a few feet behind him—unscathed, unrestrained, and unthreatened by the men and their guns. He looked at his friends bleeding on the couch, face unreadable.

We were in a small room with nothing to say for itself but a desk, couch, file cabinets, and hooks on the ceiling.

Rio followed my gaze up. "Things get much more civilized from here," Rio said. "As long as you cooperate."

I just looked at him, feeling the wetness running down my temple and dripping off my chin.

Rio motioned to the couch. "While you were out, my men here were explaining their well-intentioned but misguided attempt to reward your saving their sister by claiming your debt and paying it off with my own money—"

Clay opened his swollen mouth. "Rio—"

His assigned brute backhanded him with the gun, startling a scream out of me. Clay's head snapped to the side. He swung back, lips peeled back as he glared unyielding defiance.

"As I was saying," Rio continued, "I understand their gratitude, but I'm afraid it doesn't work that way. My son pleaded on your behalf when you did not have my mother's money by the deadline. He assured me you'd make regular on-time payments and the matter would be settled. Instead, Cassius brings an envelope filled with the bills I marked for him and his brother, and he claims it's from you."

Rio stepped away. My attention glued to him as he walked over to Royal. "How this happened under my son's watch is a question for another day." Rio circled his blank-faced son like a hawk does its prey. "He assured me he had this under control, but here I am, forced to deal with the matter in person. At this point, my patience is at an end."

"I can still take care of this, Dad," Royal said, voice placid. "If you had let me know about the payment, I would have taken care of the triplets and made sure the next was—"

"Shh, shh, shh," Rio crooned. He clasped the back of his neck, bringing their foreheads together. "It's okay, my boy."

Despite his words, Royal visibly tensed. Seeing the two of them together, their resemblance was obvious. I should have known the moment Rio stepped out from behind the tires. The raven locks, the strong jaw, the air of promised danger.

"Even the strongest of leaders face betrayal," he said, "but the most important lesson we must learn is"—Rio withdrew a gun from his overcoat—"there are no second chances."

He punctuated each word with a tap of the gun on Royal's chest.

I bit through my lip, keeping in another scream. It leaked through my teeth as Rio turned on me.

Pull yourself together, Ember. Don't give the shadow man the fucking satisfaction of seeing you cry! This man has proven himself to be exactly what you thought he was and you will see him carried off in handcuffs if it's the last thing you do.

Sucking in a breath, I held it long, willing my galloping heart to slow. I would get out of this. That morning would not be the last time I saw my brother.

"I gave the lovely Miss Bancroft a chance," Rio went on. "All I asked for was the hundred grand for your grandmother, but now..."

Rio gripped the desk chair and pushed it in front of me. He sat down, gun trained on me, and looked me in the eyes. "Now, I'll have it all."

"A-all?" I croaked.

"Everything your parents stole, dear."

My blood ran cold.

"Twenty-five million would go a long way to getting you into my good graces and possible forgiveness for your friends over there." He mo-

tioned to the couch. "I'll have it right here and right now. Tell me where your parents are hiding."

Part of me felt I should have known this is where we were headed.

I started to speak. "I—"

"Before you make the mistake of lying to me," Rio cut in, "you should know I've been following your parents' case very closely since I discovered my mother was one of their victims. I know about the message they left you and I requested a copy of it from a friend of mine on the force." Rio's gun remained on me as he pulled a slip of paper from his pocket.

My eyes widened. No, no, no.

"Ember," he read, "surrender an offering onto the goddess. Tell your brother we love him. From, Mom and Dad." He met my eyes over the paper. "That first line is a hidden message if I've ever heard one."

I licked my lips, tasting copper blood. This was an entirely different situation from the FBI's interrogation.

"It is a message," I said carefully, "but it doesn't lead to their location as I've tried to tell everyone for the last few months. It's just an"—I cast about for the phrase—"inside joke," I finished. "It's a joke between us."

His perfect brows shot up his forehead. "A joke? Please share. I love a joke as much as the next guy. Don't I, gentlemen?"

The brutes he brought with him murmured their agreement.

"Well, Miss Bancroft?" Rio pressed. "I'm listening."

The explanation rose in my throat and lodged. Every fiber of my being rejected the notion of giving in. Of telling him what my parents truly wanted me to do. Of sharing the secret of the music box.

Tears filled my eyes despite my resolve not to cry. What else could I do but cry when the only thing I could say would certainly get me killed?

"I won't tell you." My voice was small, but strong. "It's got nothing to do with my parents or the money, and I won't say it no matter what you do."

"Ember," Royal said. His face was no longer blank. A clear emotion shown in his eyes and it wasn't anger. It was fear. "Just tell him!"

"No!" I bore into Rio. "No."

"You should rethink this, my dear," he said softly. "I will not hear no again."

I leaned as far as my restraints would let me. "No," I hissed in his face.

All of a sudden, Rio was on his feet. "Damien, Saito if you please."

One of the brutes seized Hiro and ripped him off the couch.

"What are you doing!?" I cried.

He threw Hiro in the middle of the room. The boy fell hard on his bad arm, crying out. He pushed himself to his knees, wincing in pain, and froze before the barrel of the gun.

"Dad!" Royal surged forward.

"Don't fucking move, boy," Rio hissed, peeling back the mask of civility. "This ends on her word, not mine."

Rio looked at me as he flicked off the safety. "What does the message mean?"

All pretense was gone. Hot tears gushed from my eyes. I wrenched at my bindings, twisting and jerking in the chair. "Stop! Don't do this! Please!"

"What I do is entirely up to you," said Rio. "I will not ask again. What does the message mean?"

Hiro did not beg or plead. Resignation shone in his eyes. He knew he was about to die and accepted it.

"Ahh!" A scream ripped from my throat. For thirteen years my horrid, painful shame stayed buried. I couldn't speak of it now or ever.

I can't. I can't.

"I can't!"

"I see," Rio said. "I'll have Clay next, Damien. Let's see if she has a softer spot in her heart for him."

Rio raised the gun.

"No!" shouted the triplets.

"Dad!"

"*The message was for my sister!*"

Rio stopped, finger twitching on the barrel. "*Your sister?*" *He rounded on Royal, and the gun flew away from Hiro.* "*What sister?*"

Royal shook his head. "*I don't know.*"

"*You don't have a sister,*" *Rio growled.* "*And I'm through playing games.*"

"*Wait,*" *I shrieked as he set Hiro in his sights again.* "*I do have a sister... or I did. She was— She was—*"

You have to get this out. It's time.

I swallowed past the lump in my throat. "*She was my twin sister,*" *I rasped.* "*Her name was Aurora B-Bancroft.*"

Silence gripped the small space.

"*Rory loved her name,*" *I said.* "*Dad told her it meant goddess of the dawn and that pleased her to no end—being a goddess. When we played pretend, she was always the goddess and I was her devoted servant because every deity had to have one.*

"*I didn't like playing along but Dad did.*" *A tear dangled off my nose. I sucked it in as I took a sharp breath.* "*He'd come in our room with our snack and bow before her saying 'please, goddess, accept my offering.' It would make her giggle like nothing else.*

"*After she died, we'd visit her grave bringing flowers and Dad would say the same thing as we placed them under her name. An offering to the goddess.*"

I glowered at Rio. "*There. That's it. In my parents' final note to me, they told me to tell my brother they loved him and put flowers on my sister's grave. Are you fucking happy now?! Leave Hiro alone!*"

Rio's eyes narrowed. "*No.*"

"*What?*"

"*No,*" *he repeated.* "*If the message was that innocent, you wouldn't have hidden its meaning all this time. You clearly do not take this seriously.*"

A bang ripped through the quiet. Hiro toppled over clutching his arm. His groans could hardly be heard over my screams.

Clay, Cassius, and Royal tried to run to him. Cassius and Clay were roughly thrown back. Royal knelt beside his friend. The feeling in his eyes as he looked up at his father told me everything I needed to know about their relationship: hatred.

"The next one goes between his eyes," Rio promised. "Tell me the real message."

"That is the real message, you fucking insane thug! What else would it be! If it was a message telling me where they were, why would I have stuck around here? Huh? How's that for proof I'm telling the truth!"

"If that is true, why did you hide it?" he demanded.

"Because—"

"Because what!"

"Because I killed her!"

Rio dropped the gun. A lesser man would have let the shock show on his face. His gave nothing away, although I sensed his surprise all the same. "Excuse me?"

"I killed my sister," I sobbed. "I didn't mean to but... I did."

Clay, Cassius, and Royal watched me in disbelief. I dropped my head. I couldn't bear to see their faces.

"My sister and I were playing on the front lawn a little after our fifth birthday. Grandpa gave us the best gifts. A music box for me and a porcelain doll for Rory. She was jealous," I whispered. "She had a bunch of dolls but she didn't have a music box. I took my box outside to play with the treasures I put inside.

"Rory came out of nowhere and snatched it from me. She said she wanted the music box and I could have one of her other toys. I said no and tried to get it back from her. Rory got angry and th-threw it."

My voice—my heart—cracked on a sob.

"I heard the splinter as it broke apart, and I was so mad, I took her doll and flung it as hard as I could. Rory ran after it, racing into the street... just as the car came."

"Holy shit," Damien breathed.

I paused a minute, getting myself under control. "After the funeral," I continued dully. "My grandfather returned the music box—fixed good as new. The only thing fixed. The way my parents felt about me after that day. The look I'd see in their eye every now and then. That wasn't fixed. I haven't spoken her name since Mom drove me to Grandpa's house saying she couldn't stand to look at me. I wasn't allowed back home until I was six.

"And you all ask me why I don't want to talk about it? Why I won't tell the FBI, the town, and the entire world the worst thing I've ever done. The reason why my parents left me and didn't look back. I won't let Rory be another thing you bastards throw in my face."

Raising my head, I held Rio's gaze. "I'm here where I am because of me. But I kept the music box and our matching baby shoes as a reminder of your lesson. There are no second chances."

He nodded. "I understand. What's more, I believe you. Which is rather unfortunate."

"What? Why?" I asked.

"Because if you can't lead me to your parents or repay what my mother lost." The gun flew up, fixed on me. "You're no good to me. I do pray you meet your sister again, sweet Ember."

I didn't have a chance to beg or scream. Rio set his aim and pulled the trigger.

Chapter One

"**N**o!"

Royal shoved his father's arm up, careening the bullet over my head in a whoosh of air that jostled my strands.

Terror struck me speechless. *He would have killed me.*

Rio's expression as he beheld his son was terrible to behold. "What do you think you're doing, boy?" he hissed low.

"You can't kill her." Royal shielded me, crossing the line of fatal defiance by blocking the bullet's path. "We need her, Dad. We— We can still get the money."

"Oh? And what do you suggest?"

Rio advanced on him. Royal retreated, bumping into my knees and staying between me and his father.

"Ransom her."

"Ransom?"

Through my fear-fogged mind, I picked up his interest. Rio was listening.

"This is about Gran, right? Eighty-four thousand dollars. She can't lead us to her parents or the money they stole, but her aunt and uncle are right here and they have plenty." Royal spun on me. I shook as he brushed the tears from my cheek. "We tell them we got her, and if they don't hand over the money, they'll never see her again."

Rio made a harsh sound. "Interesting idea, but you're well aware the Horsemen don't deal in kidnapping and ransom. Too many things can go wrong. Too many variables to account for. And police search harder for those who kidnap pretty rich girls than they do for car thieves." A hand gripped Royal's shoulder. "Move aside, boy."

My heart jumped in my throat.

"Let me handle it," Royal said, planting his feet. "I'll get in the Estate to deliver the message. I'll stay on them and make sure they don't call the police. One hundred grand is nothing to people like them. They probably have that much in their sock drawer. The Bancrofts will dump it in a trash can at Oleander Park, I'll pick it up, and this will be done."

"Why Oleander Park? They can make the drop at a park in the Outer Borough."

Rio changed his tune from the guy who didn't want in on this game.

"They have to know this is a simple, pain-free transaction or they might do something stupid," said Royal. "Raveners are afraid to go into the OB. Her aunt and uncle will think it's a trap or something. Plus, they'd stand out." He shook his head. "It makes sense for them to drop it in their park and I'll bring it out."

"They can just as easily set a trap for you," Rio argued.

"Not if I make it clear I'm watching them and any hint of the cops will get her killed." Royal's touch was gentle on my goose-pimpled skin. "Her little brother was just beaten for ignoring a blackmailer. By now they know people aren't messing around."

He grunted. "I'd be just as pleased to have the full amount. If we're taking this route, why wouldn't I charge Frank and Lenora Bancroft to transfer that money into *my* offshore account."

Royal turned on him. "Because if those shits cared about their children, they wouldn't have abandoned them to us. The aunt and uncle took them in. They care enough to keep her off the street. They'll care enough to keep her alive."

I couldn't see Rio's face. I imagined it reflected little as he considered his son's plan.

It's my hope that he's considering.

"You say your patience is out on being forced to handle business yourself," Royal went on. "But you're the one who dragged us down here for no fucking reason. You want me to step up, Dad? Get out of the way. I will deal with my crew and I will get Gran's money. If I fail, you can shoot me."

My eyes bugged. What the hell was he saying?!

"Is that right?" Rio laughed. "Don't be ridiculous. No one will hurt you. My boy. My only son." He grasped the back of his neck. "But I will concede I did not give you the chance to correct the matter yourself." Rio's gentleman persona was sliding back into place. "Go to the Estate. Make clear the situation. Tell me the time of the drop. We'll be there."

Royal didn't move. "When it's done, Clay and Cas will be forgiven."

"I will agree to that," Rio replied.

"And Hiro goes to the doctor. Now."

Rio came fully into view, moving to the side. "Damien."

I heard movement. A grunt. Then the door opening and closing.

"There," said Rio. "Any other requests?" His father sounded amused.

"No one touches her while I'm gone."

"Who are you speaking to? Young Ember will remain untouched while you handle the matter. I'm stepping out of your way, son."

I inched my foot forward, touching my boot to his heel.

"One last thing, Ember's done with the Horsemen after they make the drop. I'm taking her back to the academy and then we'll pretend none of this ever happened."

Rio's eyes sharpened. "You have some attachment to this girl?"

"None," he said clearly. "Do you agree?"

"Yes," he responded after a beat. "Go on. I expect word by tonight that our money is incoming."

"Right."

Royal lingered. He pushed back on me ever so slightly, and then he left.

My eyes shut on the click of the lock.

I was going to die.

Royal bought me time and nothing else. My aunt and uncle would not pay. Their first call would be to the police and their second would be to their conscience to let it know they were satisfied in doing what they were required to do.

I was threatened and Uncle Harrison wasn't moved to release my money. Eli was beaten and neither one called to ask if he was okay. Short of kidnapping and ransoming Aunt Violet herself, my uncle would not be giving the Horsemen a cent.

I jerked as fingers brushed my wrist.

"I'm certain you won't be any trouble." Rio's velvety voice tickled my ear. "Let's do away with these."

Freed, I bolted out of the seat and ran to the triplets. "Clay. Cas. Are you okay?" Rio's man didn't react as I pushed him out of the way. Straddling Clay, I gently cupped his battered face and kissed the only part of him not swelling. "I'm so sorry," I whispered.

"Don't be. It's not your fault."

Clay placed his hand over mine, pouring waves of comfort into me though he was the one hurt. He warned me no one could know they were covering my debt. I never imagined this would be the retribution.

His healing split lip cracked, dripping blood as he offered me a grin. My heart ached for so many reasons on top of that smile. Since the day the Angels came into my life—the day Clay Walker stole a kiss—electricity singed my blood like I'd stuck my fingers in a socket. Wild. Dangerous. Reckless. But sleeping with Cassius, being near Clay, and battling Royal awoke a soul that died thirteen years ago.

Unheeding of those watching, I pressed a feather-light kiss to his weeping lips. A touch so gentle and it rattled my being. Clay claimed the last of my strength, drawing it through our kiss, relinquishing me to trembles and a begging need to cry.

"What was that for?" he asked softly.

I would die today. My last request from this world was a kiss from Clay. It was the least heaven owed me.

"Do I need a reason?"

Moving over to Cassius, I cradled him against my chest. "Are you okay?"

He burrowed into my bosom. "Better now."

The urge to laugh, cry, and smack him battled for dominance. I settled for holding him closer. "You look even worse than Clay. I don't have to ask if you mouthed off."

His chuckle rumbled my chest.

"You," I said to one of the brutes. "Get me a first aid kit. There has to be one around here."

The man didn't move, of course, cutting eyes to Rio.

"Give it to her, Jay," said Rio. The gang leader swept off his coat and draped it over the desk. "We'll be here a while. Might as well get comfortable."

Jay rescued the kit from the desk drawer and handed it to me without a word. Rio's men stood silent and intimidating, watching over us with guns aloft as I treated the results of their handiwork.

"Where else?" I asked, pressing the gauze to the cut above Cassius's eye.

"I'm fine, Em."

"No, you're not." I probed his torso. "You're favoring your left side."

"Jay deals a solid punch to the ribs," he admitted. "But I can take a beating."

"Are you sure it's not broken? Hiro—"

"Hiro said some choice shit to Rio when he tied you to the chair. He got worse for it."

I quieted. Hiro warned me of the consequences of disrespecting Rio and the sharp-tongued, fiery-eyed Angel broke them for me? And for me he was beaten, offered up to die, and shot.

Please let him be okay.

Reaching for Clay, I was stopped by a hand on my forearm. He took the gauze from me and dabbed my temple. He cared for my wound and then pulled away when I tried to do the same, jaw stiff and eyes blank as he firmly closed the lid.

Clay had been the one to take care of everyone since he was seven. Protector. Fighter. Weathering the cost without protest.

I settled between the boys and laced my fingers through theirs.

"Interesting." Rio zeroed in on the hands clasped on my lap. "I suspected Cassius and Clay's lapse in judgment had to do with this."

"It was about nothing more than Camila," I snapped. "You'd think someone who loves his mommy as much as you would appreciate where they were coming from. They paid you with money they *earned*, and you threatened a grieving, harmless teenage girl. We can spread the poor judgment around."

Jay bore down on me and the triplets surged forward, snarls leaking through their teeth.

Rio stopped it with a wave of his hand. "Calm down. I agree unfortunate circumstances brought us here, young Bancroft. My son intends to put it right, I'll allow him to do so while we wait in silence."

Rio leaned back, crossing his feet at the ankles, and closed his eyes. He was the serene father of Adonis—relaxed in the face of the acts he committed that day and those still to come.

I decided not to test Rio's demand for silence. The triplets and I were glowering ornaments on the couch—radiating resentment for the leader of the Horsemen and the hulking masses of brutality ready to do his bidding.

The office was windowless and a scan revealed there wasn't a clock. All the same, I felt the hours passing in the stiffness of my joints and the ache in my stomach.

My phone sat unused in my pocket. The knowledge that they didn't bother to take it from me burned. From the outset Rio didn't fear I'd use it to call for help. He knew he'd kill me before I touched the screen.

The need to text Eli pulsed a rising yearning in my heart. I'd be dumped in the trash somewhere. Far from Horsemen territory, but with the mark of savagery that revealed my killers. Rio's gang sought to own the entire OB and they killed the other gang members that dared to oppose them. Somehow, I had ended up on that side. The lone girl to deny Rio what he deluded himself into thinking was his. And he'd repay by throwing me out like trash.

"Jay." Rio spoke without opening his eyes. I thought he was sleeping. "Go out and get dinner. What would you like, Ember?"

I licked dry, cracked lips. "Serving up my last meal?"

"Why would it be your last?" The statuesque mold of power and man neither stirred nor raised his voice. "Is it my son you lack faith in or your family?"

My throat closed. I hated to say it was my family. That once more they'd push me onto the ledge and Royal would be my sole hope of coming down. I hated to say it because this time he would fail.

"How are you Royal's father?" I asked instead.

"I'm certain you're well-versed in human reproduction."

His men snort-laughed. Rio was quicker, smooth, and unburdened by conscience or the range of human emotions. I was not about to trip him up.

"Did you make him what he is? A knife-wielding car thief chained to a ruthless gang when he could be anyone and go anywhere." I should probably shut my mouth, but with my death incoming, what was there left to be afraid of. "I'd be an idiot to dismiss you as a mindless thug. You're a smart man and you must see he deserves more than this life."

Rio finally moved a muscle and it was the one that served his smirk. "I thank you for the compliment, but it reveals you are woman in body and child in mind. We deserve nothing. We are owed nothing. My son will build his life on what he's fought for. Bled for. And ripped away from those too weak to hang on. I would have it no other way."

"Do you love him?"

Slowly, his eyes opened. "What a question."

"My parents didn't love me. That's obvious to the world by now but I've known long before they abandoned me. I was broken by my sister's death and reformed in their hatred. I can't deny their actions shaped my life as inevitably as my own. You're wrong that children don't deserve anything. Royal is building his life on the cards you're dealing him. You, Rio, are laying his path, and to choose another, he'll have to fight you. Make *you* bleed. And one day, you'll be the one too weak to hang on.

"Aurora deserved more than me. Eli and I deserved more than my parents. And Royal deserves more than you."

Rio was expressionless through my speech. "I owe you an apology, Ember. You are far from a child. You're burdened by inexperience, immaturity, and naiveté, but not, it's clear, by lack of intelligence. The longer I'm in your presence you prove yourself worthy of the title—the first Horsewoman."

My stomach growled on rising bile. Three guns and two men between us and still I considered making him choke on that title.

"Tell Jay what you'd like, dear girl. You must be hungry."

He almost sounded like he cared.

Well, if he's content to play this game, so am I.

"I want the portobello mushroom carpaccio from Rosario's. Hold the arugula and get the dressing on the side. Also, the frozen hazelnut souffle from Chez Lacroix and to drink, Jamaican cream soda." I smiled. "I'll let you figure out where to get that."

Jay frowned, glancing at his boss.

"Excellent taste," said Rio. "I'll have the same."

Jay wasn't prepared to argue with him. He left and it was just the two of them against us three.

But is it? Clay and Cas have their reasons for being in the gang and their beating doesn't change them.

That they cared about me couldn't be denied, but there was a more than strong chance I stood opposite Rio alone.

Rio closed his eyes, signaling the end of our chat. He asked me if I had faith in his son, but I wondered if he did. Was he securely awaiting the call saying everything was handled, or preparing himself to put a bullet in my skull once and for all?

No clock to back me up, but the ravenous gnawing in my stomach told me hours had passed since Jay went off for food. My fault for sending him all over town. Rio let me leave the room once, escorted by his final man, to go to the bathroom. I returned and resumed the quiet vigil, waiting for the phone to ring.

Jay eventually stormed in, irritation etched in his face, tossing takeout bags on my lap and greasy wrapped burgers at the triplets. He wiped the annoyance away as he set out his boss's food on the desk.

"Do you want some of mine?" I asked Cassius and Clay.

It was insult to injury to hand them limp meat and soggy buns after what they put them through. Jay couldn't be bothered to get them a drink. They didn't deserve to be punished in the first place, so why should it continue?

"I'm good, baby," said Cas. "Chino makes the best burgers in the OB." He nodded at Jay. "Thanks, man."

The guy grunted in reply.

He was thanking him? A plain function of the gang's dynamic and one I couldn't understand. Cassius said he could take a beating but who would be doling them out besides the gang. He may even give them back just as hard. Was everyone in this room really going to go on about their lives after today like nothing happened?

Except for me.

My favorite meal was sawdust on my tongue. The mushrooms were chewy gum paste. The crunchy, chocolatey hazelnuts gagged me. I barely tasted the mingling of flavors. If anything, this meal was making me sick.

I sucked it down anyway. Eating took my mind off the internal clock ticking away the seconds of my life.

Eli is going to be stuck with my aunt and uncle for four years— No, he'll be stuck in the academy for four years with them taking full advantage of the year-round option. Then he'll be on his own until his trust fund comes through.

I should have found a way to prevent this. At some point since I became entangled with the Horsemen, there was a right turn to take me away from all of this and I didn't take it. I could blame Rio, Royal, the Angels, or my parents all I wanted, but it wouldn't change the fact that Eli depended on me and I wouldn't be there for him. I'd carry the shame of that until I died, which wouldn't be long now.

Setting my empty containers on the floor, I leaned onto the thin cushion and adopted the same position as Rio. I was out of distractions. Let the demons pour in.

"Ah, here we go. Good news for me, son?"

My eyes snapped open. Rio spoke into his phone, sipping nonchalantly on my favorite drink.

"Hmm. I see. Why would I do that?"

I slid off the seat, body drawn to the phone and the boy on the other end, relaying my fate.

"I will be there," he said. "Let's not start that up again. You've proven yourself capable." Rio latched on to me and held me frozen. "I'm told I'm responsible for the man you've become and, if that's the case, I'm proud. I can think of no one else who could have pulled off what you did today."

Proud? Capable? No one else could have pulled it off? Did that mean—

"Up, my dear." Rio got up and hooked our arms like when I first entered the auto shop. "Time to go."

I threw a look at the triplets, half out of their seats and wearing heavy looks that must have matched mine. "I don't understand."

"Your uncle saw it was in his best interest to agree to our simple transaction. He's got the money and will drop it at Oleander Park just as it closes," he explained as he led me out of the office and across the concrete floor. "Royal is there now to ensure he doesn't make an unwise decision to call the cops and try to move them into the park before the drop."

My head was spinning. Harrison Bancroft, my uncle, had agreed to pay the ransom and Rio was taking me to the Estate instead of the alley that would be my resting place?

Digging my heels, I pulled him up short just outside of the garage. The sun abandoned the town of Raven River hours ago, leaving us to fend off the creatures that went bump in the night. "This is a fucking trick to make me get in the car quietly," I bit out. Yanking on his hold, I screeched, "Get off me!"

"Easy." The flickering bulb showed and hid, showed and hid the gun held on me in the gloom. "If that was my aim, I could have easily shot you in the garage and had your body carried out. This is not a trick. Feel free to call my son and confirm." The barrel stuck in my ribs. "Only my son."

I got my phone and dialed Royal. He answered before the second ring.

"What's going on?" I asked before he could speak. "Are my aunt and uncle truly paying the ransom?"

"One hundred grand. Oleander Park. Nine thirty tonight," he said. "You're good, Cherry, so don't make it worse. Rio's bringing you to the park, the money will be put in the trash, and I'll get it. Once it's in his hand, he'll let you out of the car and it's all over."

"But—"

"No buts. And whatever you're thinking of doing—don't." I'd never heard him so serious. "You can handle me, Cherry, but you can't handle Rio."

"Your father," I hissed. "How could you not tell me?"

"I said there were a lot of things you didn't know about me."

The bastard hung up.

"A knife-wielding car thief wasn't enough," I flung at Rio. "You also had to raise him to be fucking infuriating."

Rio laughed, gripping my hand again like we were a couple taking a stroll. "I must admit you're not what I expected, Ember Bancroft. It would have pained me to kill you. Thankfully, we can set that unpleasant business aside."

Reasonable intelligence and the lack of a death wish kept me from socking him in the jaw. His refined gentleman act set my teeth on edge for the costume it was. Rio was desperate to portray himself as no different from a Ravener, but thousand-dollar watches and expensive coats couldn't mask the deadly, albeit clever, beast inside.

We didn't speak on the drive to the gates. Rio's car was simple, black, and understated on the outside. A car whose description wouldn't stand out to the police. On the inside, it boasted the sleek finishes of the best tech, touch screens, and plush seats that cradled me in false security.

Rio rolled to a stop next to the guard station. His gun was stashed in the pocket on the door and his affable smile slid in place in time with the falling window. "Gregory, good to see you. How are the kids?"

"Eating me out of house and home." The guard's girth jiggled at my eye level. This was my chance to yell, scream, bring the cops down on Rio's head like a grand piano in a Saturday morning cartoon.

"Ember Bancroft and Rio Cruz."

I let the chance pass. Royal's warning and the knowledge Rio could easily shoot me and Gregory and beat it out of here before the cops came, pressed my lips together.

"Good evening, Miss Bancroft," said Gregory.

"Evening."

"Back from the academy to visit your aunt and uncle?"

"Yes."

"Very nice. You both have a good night."

That was it. Part of me hoped Gregory would question why I was in this man's car.

A rich community like this wouldn't employ a man to ask questions.

"Who do you know in the Estate?" I asked as we drove through the rumbling gate. "Is it the same mystery person who put Royal on the list?"

"You assume I don't have a home here."

"I assume nothing," I replied. "You don't live in the Estate. Everyone knows everyone around here, and a man like you would not escape notice."

"Men like me blend in far better than you believe, sweet Ember."

It wasn't an answer to my question, but I long since accepted Rio did not give those. This man could be waterboarded, racked, dipped in honey and covered with fire ants, and he'd still share nothing more or less than what he wished.

Oleander Park was a short drive from the gates. The park we passed on the day Eli and I moved into my uncle's mansion. This beautiful patch of green was open later than normal community parks. This one was known for the manmade natural path trailed with fairy lights, leading to a cozy gazebo at the end for lovers to curl up under the moonlight.

It was in that gazebo my aunt and uncle renewed their vows on their tenth wedding anniversary. I knew this from the pictures in their drawing room. My family—when we still were a family—wasn't invited to the ceremony.

All of that went through my head as Rio pulled into the emptying parking lot. Those two didn't want me here as they celebrated one of the happiest days of their lives, but here they were risking everything to pay off a debt that wasn't theirs or mine to bear.

A peek at the clock read nine twenty. Couples young and old were dragging their feet, hanging on to the last vestiges of their dates. I saw why Royal chose this time for the drop. Swarming with people it would be easy for police or security to blend in. Whereas at closing time, if we saw someone other than giggling yuppies getting handsy, Rio would know to beat it out of there.

I pierced through the shadows searching for Uncle Harrison, Violet, anyone. "Where's Royal?"

Rio didn't answer.

"Will you truly keep your end?" I pressed. "You get the money for your mother and I never hear your name again."

"Shh." His shush was a soft croon sealing my lips. "Pay attention. Should something go wrong, you'll want to see who is to blame for destroying your last chance."

I swallowed through needles. I marveled at Royal's ability to menace with little fanfare or description. I thought he was the only one who could deliver a terrifying threat as blandly as a waiter asked for your order. Evidently, he was merely the apprentice learning at the knee of the master. With two sentences Rio laid out that he was firmly in control of this situation and my life.

The twenty-nine blinked out and three zero glared at me in harsh red light. Behind the swings, a writhing mass emerged from the trees.

Not a mass. A man.

It could only be a man from the expanding build, hunched shoulders, and hoodie pulled low over his brows. Hanging off his arm was a black duffle bag. The man skirted the edge of the lamplight, sticking to the darkness. I didn't need to be told his destination was the trash can a couple of feet from the park's sign.

Rio and I had it fixed in our sights, watching as the man dumped the bag in the trash and continued on without a hitch in his step.

In the space of a breath, Royal was there. I knew him for the simple reason that he didn't hide. Sans hoodie, ducked head, furtive glances, and no scurrying out of the light. He just walked up to the trash, fished out the bag, and approached the car.

Rio lowered the window for his son to toss the bag inside. "The weight feels right," Royal said. "It's all there."

How does he know what one hundred thousand dollars weighs?

"We're good, Dad," Royal stated, not asked. "I came through. The triplets are forgiven. Gran has her money, and Ember is done with the Horsemen."

Rio finished rifling through the duffle and tossed it behind us. "You came through."

Something akin to hope swelled in my chest.

"And our deal?" Royal pushed.

"The triplets are forgiven following a discussion about where their loyalties lie. Your grandmother will receive an unexpected check from the insurance company. And as for the lovely young Ember—"

My door unlocked with a soft click. Scrambling out of the car, I made to slam it with the full force of my contempt.

"—we're done for now."

I froze.

"For now?" Royal and I repeated.

Rio addressed him. "The note may not have been a message but the fact remains she knows Frank and Lenora Bancroft better than anyone. She is the best bet to finding them and I intend to." Rio twisted to give a smirk that curdled my insides. "You did not get what you deserved, Ember, but what is a Horseman if not the hand of retribution? One day we will deliver yours."

He peeled out with the money and my damn peace of mind in the backseat. Rio Cruz was never going to make it easy.

"Shit," Royal swore. "I knew he'd pull this. Twenty-five million is too much for him to ignore."

Royal encircled my wrist, drawing me in. I planted my feet but found myself skidding over the gravel and curled into his side. "He's not fucking with you again. That's the first and last meeting you'll have with Rio. Whatever shit he wants goes through me first.

"Today was too close. Rio likes to get rid of people who aren't useful anymore, and he doesn't give them the chance to prove otherwise."

I stared at him, watching his jaw work, and making little sense of what he was saying.

"If he truly believes you can't lead him to your parents, he might get it into his head you know too much. We can't let him get there." He looked down at me. "What? Why are you looking at me like that?"

"Your father," I burst out. "That man is your father!?"

"We've all got one," he replied, tone measured. "He just happens to be mine."

"And the money was for your grandmother. Is there a reason you couldn't have told me straight out?" I twisted out of his hold.

"Yes. There is a reason. You would have tried finding her and dealing with her one on one. Not a damn option since she would've refused to accept money from you and definitely would've lost her shit if she knew about the Horsemen's involvement."

I shoved him. "That's no excuse! I'm so fucking tired of your lies, Royal! I'm starting to think you'll keel over and die if you ever told the truth!"

"You want to pull that, princess?" he snapped. "How about you and the triplets lying about the payments and getting us into this mess in the first place!"

"Yeah, I want to pull that," I screamed, shoving him again. Stress, fear, rage, helplessness, and about twenty other emotions I didn't have a name for ravaged me into a mindless husk acting out of instinct. "Because my uncle did not give you a fucking cent! I don't know who that man was or where the money came from, but they did not pay the ransom."

I plastered myself to him willingly, fisting his white cotton shirt. "So, tell me, Royal, where did you get one hundred grand in less than a day?"

"They—"

"Do not open your mouth to lie to me again." I said once I'd never seen anyone snarl. Who knew weeks later I'd direct one of my own to the boy who put my world back on its axis?

Royal's lips peeled back, matching my ferocity. This spot for lovers warped in our charged atmosphere like a horizon bending in the haze of heat.

"My car is on the other side of the park," he said out of nowhere. "Let's get out of here."

Royal strode off. I stood there, steamed to hell, until he disappeared into the trees. The jerk wasn't about to piss me off *and* leave me stranded in the Estate.

I caught up to him just outside the tree line.

A convertible Camaro awaited us. I prepared myself for red or bright green, and instead got black. Like his hair. Like his drawings. Like his soul.

"Nice car." My tone didn't match the compliment. "Did you steal it?"

"Nope. Paid in cash."

"With money you got from stealing other cars," I shot back.

"Naturally." Royal slid into the front seat and unlocked my side.

I plopped down, slamming the door shut. "It'd be beautiful karma if this was jacked out from under you."

Royal dropped the keys swinging around. "Want to tell me what your problem is? You've been hissing and spitting at me like I set your cherry ass on fire."

"I want the truth, Royal. All of it. Right now."

His eyes burned in the dim light. "Or what?"

"Or this car will be jacked out from under you. You shouldn't have taught me how."

Royal barked a laugh. "You're going to steal my car?"

"I'm going to drive your car off a cliff and dance as it explodes into flames. Test me," I said. "I've had the worst day of my life. I was almost killed and he forced me to talk about Rory. I'm done playing around."

He had the decency to stop laughing at me. "I didn't want any of this," he said, looking me in the eyes. "You know that, right?"

My anger lessened a fraction. "I know." Sighing, my strength leeched out with my expelled breath. "Just tell me the truth, Royal. Not even for a second did I believe my aunt and uncle would pay the ransom. I'd have sooner believed that duffle bag was filled with condoms and candy wrappers because money was impossible."

"Answer me first." There was an odd note in his voice I couldn't identify. "Did your sister have the same birthmark?"

Every muscle in my body tensed. My story was pulled out of me. It didn't mean this topic was open for discussion. "Royal…" I warned.

"She did, didn't she? Identical down to the same birthmark and probably in the same place."

My chest heaved with my rapid breaths. "No," I whispered. "She was my mirror. Mine on the left. Hers on the right."

"Then I'm sorry," he replied. "I won't call you Cherry again."

Tears spilled over, clinging desperately to my lashes. "Thank you."

"And no, your uncle and aunt did not cough up the money. I didn't even speak to them. They have no idea you were ever in danger."

I jerked my head up. "What? But then how—"

Royal faced straight ahead. He was cloaked in darkness, but I didn't imagine I'd be able to read him in the light. "I called in a favor from a person who now owes me nothing. We're on our own from here."

"Me and you?" My hand shook as I reached for him. Still, he didn't look at me. Royal inched closer, turning his palm up and accepting mine.

We held hands in the dark, and the tendrils unfurled, spreading from my soul and seeking his. Wanting that connection we formed the night we met.

"Me, you, Cassius, Clay, and Hiro," he said. "Our crew. Rio's forgiveness means he won't kill them, but he doesn't take betrayal or disrespect lightly. It's going to cost them literally. Their minimum payments to the pot will go up. Knowing Rio, he'll come up with tests to prove their loyalty."

"What kind of tests?"

He let his lack of reply be the answer.

"All of this because the triplets wanted to free me from a debt that wasn't mine," I said. "You should have told me my parents stole from your grandmother."

He shook his head. "You don't understand."

"Then help me understand. You said she would've refused to take money from me. If you knew that, why'd you go against her wishes and threaten me anyway?"

Royal's head snapped around. "You think I had control over this? They might not have known it, but your parents stole from the mother of the Horsemen's leader. They took her for every last cent and forced her out of retirement. She cried for weeks watching the life and future she built crumble into nothing.

"It wasn't about what Gran wanted at that point. Rio wasn't going to let that stand. He's a bastard," Royal spat, "but no one fucks with his family. He was getting Gran's money out of you, and if I refused to handle it, he would've gotten someone else. And you saw today how Rio and his men take care of problems."

My grip on him tightened. Jay and Damien so easily beat two of their own guys. I didn't want to know what they would have done to me when I told them to fuck off.

"Rio was coming after you, Ember, and Gran wasn't going to find out about it."

"She's receiving a random insurance check," I said. "I'm supposed to believe she won't question where that money came from? Are you telling me she doesn't know Rio is in the gang? Or you?"

Clenching his teeth, his jaw ticced.

"Royal, please. I shared more about my family than I ever wanted to. You can tell me the truth."

"I just— Fuck!" Royal shoved out of the car, storming off.

I calmly got out and trailed him. My raven-haired Angel didn't express himself well off paper. That was okay. He could struggle to get this out as long as he did.

Royal broke through the trees. I listened to him snapping twigs and trying to put distance between this situation he couldn't control.

The grasping naked pines welcomed me inside. A pleasing mix of earth and fallen leaves tickled my nose, enveloping as the wind danced through the branches. Above us a cascade of stars showed off their beauty, as breathtaking as the diamonds they were so often compared to.

This was a place for lovers at night, and now it would be our place. The place I got Royal to do something even harder than love.

Jogging to his side, I clasped his arm to my chest and rested my head on his forearm. He was wound like a predator coiled to strike.

"Relax," I soothed. "If you do, we may even hook up again. I remember how you like your hand jobs."

That had the opposite effect of loosening up. "What the hell?" he sputtered. "I can't keep up with you, Bancroft. I never know what's going to come out of your mouth next."

"Well, I know what better come out of yours, if you want to put something in mine."

"You think that pussy has me under some kind of spell that ultimatums are going to work?"

"Yes," I teased. I went ahead of him, walking backward as I tugged him toward the gazebo. "But it's not an ultimatum. We can't move forward if you're not willing to talk to me. Be honest. Your secrets have hurt me one too many times, Royal. There's not going to be an 'our crew' if we don't cut the bullshit right now."

My foot hit the step of the gazebo. I brought him with me, plunging us in darkness.

The twinkle lights shut off with the closing of the park. The moon and the stars spread a teasing glow through the trees. Together we sat on the wooden bench. I felt him in the dark, seeking his heartbeat and pressing my ear over the arresting music.

"Tell me what happened to the sweet boy who took my virginity all those years ago."

"That boy wasn't sweet." Royal tangled his fingers in my hair. My eyes fluttered shut as they caressed my strands. "Rio just wasn't through destroying him."

I lay quiet, waiting for him to go at his own pace.

"My dad wasn't in the picture growing up," he began. "Gran raised me, telling me about the father who wasn't ready to be one and smiling as she said the best thing he did was give me to her, so she could give me more love than I could stand.

"That's Gran. She's good. A real angel if there could ever be one. Rio dumped a baby on her and took off and she never once resented him or me. Some days it fucks me up wondering how a woman like her could have a son like him. But I guess that's just a trick of nature. Your true self always wins out."

His heartbeat picked up speed, fueled by loathing.

"Life wasn't perfect. It's not for anyone who lives in the OB. But Gran and I were good. We didn't need anything. Or at least, I didn't think we did."

"What changed?" My hand trailed up and down his stomach, basking in the ability to touch him.

"Gran met a guy when I was in middle school. A nice guy. Surprised her with flowers. Said things on the phone that made her giggle and shoo me from the room. Eddie is one of the good ones. He married her, got us out of our shitty neighborhood, and moved us to a nice place on the Eastside. Everything was perfect until Rio came back."

"Back?" I repeated. "Where was he?"

"Off becoming the slick, arrogant criminal you met today. New York, Chicago, California, and then Europe when he got the money. Year after year building his reputation and contacts as a fence."

Goodness. Why in the world did he come back? It seemed like the people he left behind were doing just fine without him.

"Gran was a single mom. She had to work two jobs to raise him while he got messed up with drugs and all the wrong people who hang out in our neighborhoods. She didn't know what to do with him. Then he got a girl pregnant at eighteen, left her with the kid, and disappeared without a word.

"When he came back smiling and charming and singing a tale of rehab and rebuilding his life, she was so happy, Ember. Her only child had come back to her whole, healthy, and ready to make amends. She hugged him and cried in the kitchen, saying how much she loved him as I watched from the doorway."

A fist clamped around my heart. "It was a trick, wasn't it?"

"In his head, it probably wasn't. Rio did get clean. He taught himself business and economics, and then he revamped his entire image. From street thug to businessman dealing in the finer things. I'm sure he believed he was ready to be a father."

Tilting my head back, I kissed his throbbing jaw. "He came back for you."

"Yes," he said simply. "Rio couldn't just take me, of course. The guy fucked off and abandoned me. Gran had full custody. But he wanted in my life. Picking me up from school. Nights at his place. Long stays with him so Gran and Eddie could take vacations. He sold her the dream."

"She wanted you to have a father," I said, putting myself in his grandmother's shoes. "And she wanted to believe the best in her son. So, she said yes."

"I did too," he said so softly the wind almost snatched his words away. "I never truly hated him. Gran did not frame Rio as a person to be hated. He was the man who did the best he could in a situation he couldn't handle. He returned for a chance, so I gave him one."

"What happened?"

"At first, nothing. I was thirteen. You remember how it was five years ago?" he asked. "The Horsemen were always around, but back then, they were at their worst. That's when they started to consolidate power. As in when Rio came back, took over, and approached other gang leaders to unite under one name.

"Gran and I didn't know about any of this. He was just the cool guy who took me for ice cream after school, let me stay up past my bedtime, and bought me a car two years early when I got into the academy. He said it was incentive for me to come home and let him give me driving lessons."

"Oh no," I breathed. My stomach twisted realizing where this was going.

"It started small," Royal said. "One day he picked me up from the academy and said he'd teach me how to break into my car in case I ever locked the keys in. Another day, he taught me how to hack his car's internal computer—just for fun.

"That's what no one tells you, Ember. You don't just wake up one day and decide to throw everything you learned about good and wrong out the window. It's a bunch of little things you know you shouldn't do, that you rationalize away. 'If this was really wrong, Dad wouldn't ask me to do it.' Or 'they can afford to buy another one.'

"Those little things add up and then you don't know which way is right anymore. You're numb. Looking at the world behind glass, and nothing is real because nothing can touch you."

I squeezed his hand tight, too wretched to find the right words. How could Rio believe he had nothing to answer for? He came into a happy, innocent boy's life and dragged him to the depths.

"Rio had me stealing cars by fifteen. He let me keep most of the money too. I was his son. I didn't pay the pot. I did whatever I wanted... as long as I did what he wanted."

"When did you find out he was a leader of the Horsemen?"

"After he got me dancing to his tune, he didn't bother hiding it. He'd go on and on about the Raveners being happy to see the OB sink into hell. We had nothing to do with them and their"—he gestured at our tranquil haven—"perfect lives. The Horsemen would save the Outer Borough because they were the only ones who could."

"But you couldn't have bought that nonsense?" I sprung up, finding his chestnut eyes in the dark. "You must have seen him for the megalomaniac psychopath he was."

"I couldn't see that. By sixteen, he was keeping me in the dark about most of the stuff he was into. All I saw was exactly what he was spouting about—the Horsemen helping people. I hooked up with the triplets. Heard my dad was responsible for paying their way into the academy and preventing child services from splitting them up and sending them away. He was a hero to them.

"And I knew what I did with my money, helping out people from my old neighborhood. Dad even encouraged me. Said this was what the Horsemen were all about. I told you, Ember, by the time we met, Rio wasn't done with me yet."

I dropped kisses on his jaw. I sensed that he needed them. And maybe I needed them too if I was to hear the rest.

"What did he do to you, Royal?" I cupped his cheek with a hand that trembled.

"Technically, he did nothing." His voice reached me—low and toneless. "Rio intends for me to take over for him one day. It's why he showed up on my doorstep and wrecked my life. I'll be the next leader, but that doesn't happen if I get hurt. He keeps me out of the worst of it—off the front lines. I steal Ravener cars, and I help the doctor."

"The doctor?"

His chin moved against my palm. "You've heard that all gunshot wounds have to be reported to the police."

"Yes."

"The Horsemen can't have that. If one of the guys gets shot, they're sent to the doctor. He's a surgeon who lost his license after trying to cut someone open drunk. He left the city and crawled back to Raven River with his tail between his legs. Now he works for the leaders, stitching together their broken *toys*." Emotion leaked into his voice.

"Royal..."

"Half-dead. Bleeding out. Fucking guts held inside by blood-soaked bandanas." Royal grabbed my hips, crashing me to his body. "I had to hold them down as Doc dug bullets out of them. I lifted the feet and carried the bodies of guys I grew up with, tossing them in the back of his van!"

"Oh, Royal, no." My cry was piercing and tangible. Wetness soaked my face, and then it soaked his as I kissed his cheek, nose, forehead, and mouth. His pain was raw. Biting. All-consuming. And my affection was the single force beating it back, pushing in the memory of the boy who helped me off the ledge, and used to see the world in color.

"The life you've chosen. The art you've created. It's not too big of a leap to assume something bad happened to you after that night. Something that broke you."

I imagined a myriad of horrible, traumatic events that ate Royal from the inside out. A member of a violent gang, it wasn't hard for my mind to draw on every mafia movie I saw and guess from there. I prepared myself to hear he sold drugs. Knocked off gas stations. And though it pulverized my heart to dust, I readied myself for the awful confession his knife was stained with more blood than mine.

Those sins I was ready for, but this would never have crossed my mind because as I was harshly reminded, this wasn't a movie.

Rio forced his teenage son to kneel helpless before death. To watch people he knew die, listen to their screams for help, and forbade him from saving them. For a disgraced surgeon was nothing compared to doctors and nurses and thousands in medical equipment, and the limit of Doc's care was inevitably smaller than theirs.

In all likelihood, he lost boys that could have been saved, and those deaths bore down on Royal's conscience until it shattered.

This is what broke him. Peeling back his father's mask and meeting the monster beneath, and then crumbling under the realization he was no better.

"But you are," I forced out, clutching his neck so tight I throttled him. "You are better than your father, Royal. No part of you is like him."

"You can't say that," he barked. Royal pulled me off. "Especially not you."

"You're messed up. I'll be the first to say it. I'd put it to music, announce it to the media, and write it in the damn sky." I ripped out of his hold, throwing my arms around him, my cheek on his stubbly jaw. "But you're not Rio. Rio would have killed me. You saved me. You stood between me and your father. You traded a favor that must have been massive to pay for my life. And you still carry your time with the doctor while I assume your father doesn't spare a second thought to those boys."

I laid my palm over his chest. His heart thrashed wildly against its cage, pulsating with ever-present anger, rage, and adrenaline. Like a predator surrounded by beasts waiting for him to slip and make him their prey.

"There's no color in your world, Royal Cruz. It's why you draw one without." I kissed him. Not a frantic, wild thing. But a gift on his lips. "Living in that pain proves you feel. You'll truly be lost if your father takes that from you too."

Royal hung on to me. His grip dug into the soft flesh between my thumbs and forefingers. He ached to push me, my words, my truth away. The thing about pain is when it torments you long enough, you begin to cling to it. Suffering is preferable to the terrifying fear that without the pain you might be numb.

The need for redemption swirled in his moon-lit eyes. He breathed harder, faster, sucking the air from me.

"Don't run from this, Royal." Our foreheads. Noses. Chests. Souls came together as one. "Don't run from me again."

Royal clutched me closer still. The air was charged with heat, tension, and a touch of arousal. His erection poked my inner thigh. Royal said I was perfect like this—just as broken as him.

"I didn't run from you, princess. I sacrificed you. The beautifully sad girl who stepped onto the balcony wearing agony only I could see. I ate your pain because that's what I do. And then I left you because I'd give it back. That's what I do too.

"You don't want me, Ember. And matter of fact, you don't want Cassius or Clay either. Life has been shitting on you since before you learned to spell the word. Hooking up with us will drag you further down."

I rocked forward, a slight twitch of my hips, and positioned him on my sex. "It's too late now. We're a crew. The Angels."

"That name never did fit."

"You're *my* angels." I pressed down as his length flicked my clit, igniting sizzling electricity in my lower belly. "Guardian angels. I don't need protection, but I know you won't leave me without it. Will you?"

Royal guided my hips back and forth, up and down his length. "Nothing is going to happen to you while you live in this town."

"Then let's stop pretending we didn't trade 'you and me' for 'us' a long time ago."

Royal stopped, holding me firm though a moan escaped me trying to remold our bodies. He said nothing for so long the sprinklers kicked on, raining down on a deserted park.

"We should get out of here."

He put me on my feet and walked out of the gazebo, uncaring of the massive hard-on leading the way. Catching up to him, I linked our hands the same way we came in. I picked up on his anger—what else was new—but pushing me away didn't work when he said in the same breath he'd always be there to protect me.

"Where are we going?" I asked. "It's too late to go back to school."

"We're going to my place. I'll take you to school in the morning."

"Okay," I said easily. "Before we go, there's one more thing I want to ask you." I looked up at him and the steady way he avoided my gaze. "Why didn't you tell your grandmother the truth about Rio?"

"Because it would have destroyed her. She was so happy, Ember. Gran had everything she wanted in the world. I couldn't tell her it was all a lie."

I poked his side. "And that, Royal Cruz, is why you're nothing like your father."

We made it to his car, buckling in, before I asked the final question pressing on my mind. "Royal, what about your mom?"

The engine purred to life. "Don't know her."

I gave him peace as he peeled out of the parking lot.

Royal drove us out of the Estate, winding through the Outer Borough down unfamiliar streets and past ramshackle buildings. The OB at night was a lonely place. We passed a few cars on the road, but saw no people on the sidewalk or poking their heads out of their homes. Only trouble would be found on the streets at this time of night.

On the way, I tried calling Cassius and Clay. Both of their phones went to voicemail.

"Do you think the triplets are okay?" I asked. "Rio backed out on leaving me alone. What if he broke his promise about hurting the triplets? And what about Hiro? He went to the Horsemen's 'doctor' and not a real one, didn't he? Can we find out how he is? Can we get him to a real fucking doctor!?"

"Slow up, Em." Royal rolled to a stop before a red light. "We can't go busting in and take Hiro from the doctor. That shit will get back to Rio immediately and any good grace we've won tonight vanishes. Doc is sober now and he's good at what he does. He'll patch Hiro up.

"As for the triplets, I can tell you straight up Rio will let them go. The two of them bring in too much money. He needs them working for him."

"What does he need money for?" Bitterness made acid on my tongue. "Looks like he has plenty."

"The Horsemen are making big moves. It requires big cash."

I trailed a finger along his jaw. I loved touching him. I loved that he let me. "Any point in asking you what those moves are?"

"None."

I chuckled despite myself. "Thought so."

We lapsed in quiet for a spell, me drawing lazy circles on his stubble.

"Are we going to your grandmother's place?" I asked.

"No. It's my apartment. I got it as soon as I turned eighteen." He finished his sentence with a right turn, pulling into the drive of a nondescript two-story building flanked on both sides by more nondescript apartments.

Royal parked and I climbed out, following him around to the back staircase. I felt oddly nervous going up those stairs. Royal and I had sex. Our hands had been down each other's pants so recently I still felt him inside of me. All the same, every new step I took with him equal parts rattled and excited me. He opened up to me in the gazebo and invited me into his space. I had no doubt he'd been with a lot of girls at the academy, but I guessed he didn't bring them here.

He let me go inside ahead of him. Royal's home was everything I expected and nothing I pictured at the same time. His sketches covered the wall, grimmer in the wake of my understanding. A simple couch sat before a flat screen and armchair. The marbled tile was cool on my bare feet as I toed off my shoes. I padded to the middle of the rigidly tidy space.

My toes sank into a clean, vacuumed brown rug, and looking past the dining table I saw the kitchen was wiped down and clear of dirty dishes.

"How often are you here?" I asked.

Royal shrugged out of his jacket. "Most weekends."

"It's nice." I skimmed a finger over the coffee table. After being handed three thousand dollars from Caesar, I had an inkling Royal was well-funded. His apartment confirmed it.

It wasn't that his furniture was glaringly expensive like my uncle's. But leather couches, flat screens, and cars like his didn't come cheap to anybody.

"The bathroom is that one," he said, motioning to the door closest to the kitchen. "Grab the first shower. I'll get you some clothes."

"You can go first," I replied. "I'm going to text Eli. He should still be up and I need to reassure myself he's okay."

He nodded. Royal disappeared through the second door I assumed was his bedroom.

Getting comfy, I plopped in his armchair, putting my feet up as the shower turned on.

Me: Hey. Are you up?

Eli: Watching a movie with Tatum. Eating in front of the TV. Mrs. Wallis snuck us sundaes with dinner. When are you coming back?

Mrs. Wallis was one of the cafeteria workers. I was wholly unsurprised Eli burrowed under her skin and managed to get special treats out of her. Something about that cherub face melted the coldest hearts.

Me: Tomorrow. I miss you. You're my only family. It's you and me and I'll always be there for you.

Eli: I know that. Why are you being weird?

Me: Loving you isn't weird, jerk.

Eli: It is the way you do it.

Pinching my nose, my head fell back on the seat. Who invented fourteen-year-olds and why weren't they stopped?

Me: I'm going to trade you for a real handbag one of these days.

Eli: No, you won't.

The imp shot me half a dozen emojis sticking out their tongue.

Eli: Are you staying at the mansion?

Me: No, I'm at a friend's place. Want me to bring you back something from the real world?

Eli wasn't to know what happened that day. My brother had enough to deal with. Fearing the Horsemen would not be on that list.

Eli: No, I'm good. I gotta go. Love you.

Me: Love you too. Text me if you need anything.

Eli: K.

Eli was undoubtedly fine. I tried the triplets again to find out if they were. They didn't pick up.

"Ember." Royal leaned against the frame. Droplets traveled down his body, greedily clinging to skin, traversing the dips and ridges that was his perfect form. It wasn't an exaggeration to say a thousand talented artists given a thousand years could not draw a man more striking than the one in front of me.

Call it the surge of adrenaline that came with escaping death, my world was in sharp focus. His inky locks iridescent from his shower, appeared blacker than black. His eyes shone brighter than yesterday. Mingling scents of sandalwood, charcoal, and man overwhelmed my senses. And my skin tingled like it never had—sensing Royal in the air and responding outside of my control.

"The shower's all yours. Clothes and towel by the sink."

I brushed against him going inside. "Thanks."

There was another door in the bathroom that likely led to Royal's room. I tried the handle and found it locked. The other door I left unlocked and cracked open, hoping he'd take the hint.

I stripped off, surrendering to the steamy shower and washing the horrid day down the drain. My dorm shower was filled with fruity shampoos, moisturizing bodywashes, three kinds of conditioners, and kiwi bubble bath. Royal kept it simple with one brand of shampoo and one type of bodywash.

I used both, soaking Royal's citrusy flavor into my pores. I took my time but Royal didn't join me. Eventually I got out and donned the big t-shirt and drawstring shorts he left for me.

Royal was in the kitchen when I came out, unwrapping a microwave meal. I snaked my arms around his waist from behind.

"I smell like you now."

I felt his laugh like my own. "Did you want to?"

Wriggling around, I got between him and the counter. "Yep."

Royal bent, scraping his teeth over my nose and gently nipping the tip. My knees gave out like snapped twigs. "Lots of ways we can achieve that."

"Oooh. Tell me more." I fisted his shorts. By all the stars and good fortune, Royal forewent a shirt and unwittingly seduced me in his half-naked glory. I drew his pants down a little.

Forwent briefs too.

"I'm a 'show, not tell' kind of guy." Royal cupped my thighs and lifted, wrapping my legs around him. He carried me to the armchair and set me down. "I'm making you something to eat. You can watch TV while you wait. Or snoop in my room."

I sighed. My signals could not be more obvious. Why were we dancing around something we'd done already? I should be bent over in the shower screaming his name.

But snooping in his room does sound tempting.

I tiptoed inside before he changed his mind.

Royal's bedroom welcomed me with a queen-sized bed. I flung myself on the downy sheets and rolled back and forth, cocooning myself in them. He didn't have much in his room to arouse scandal. Another television on the dresser. Scattered reflections of his mind sketched and taped to the wall. Photos of a young boy and elderly woman.

Secure in his blanket, I got up for a closer look.

This woman was Royal's grandmother and Rio's mother whether she liked it or not. Same eyes. Same hair, though hers was streaked with gray. And the same striking features that age could not diminish. She hugged a little boy with missing teeth and a grin made for mischief.

"Making yourself at home."

"Maybe a little," I teased.

"Food's ready." Royal tugged the blanket—and me—out of the room. "It's not much. Haven't had a chance to go shopping."

"It's okay. After we eat, we'll go to bed." I shed the blanket, picking up my mac-n-cheese from the coffee table.

"Bed? It's barely eleven. I'm not tired."

I answered with no shame. "We won't be sleeping."

Royal laughed. "Where do you get that sense of absolute certainty from, princess?"

Curling my legs over the arm of the chair, I flashed a grin over my knees. "Why? Do you like it?"

"I don't hate it." Royal stretched out on the couch, taking up space with his size and his presence. He balanced his food on one knee and a notebook on the other. "Finish that. You'll need your strength if we're gonna not be sleeping."

He flashed me that grin made for mischief and loaded it with ten kinds of naughty promises that contracted my muscles with pleasure.

That's what I'm talking about.

I dug in, skipping over the chitchat. We could talk while I was telling him harder, faster, and deeper.

Out of the corner of my eye, I watched him leisurely eat his food. His attention was focused on the sketchbook. The boy must have hundreds between his dorm and apartment.

I spoke up. "Can I have that one?"

"You asking this time?"

"You lost the right for me to ask the first time."

Royal grunted, not half pleased. "If you want more of my art, you'll have to take them, princess. I'm not handing them over."

"Fair enough." I leaned back on the chair, looking up at the ceiling. "I kind of like my new nickname. You called me that the night we made love."

"Made love?" A tinge of derision laced his reply. "Is that what we did?"

"You know we did," I said calmly. "It doesn't have to scare you."

Royal said nothing. I didn't have to look at him to see the clenched jaw and maelstrom of desire and frustration in his eyes. His raging battle made me think of something.

My mother didn't give me much advice, or attention, growing up, but once after a fight with Dad, she told me I had to seek love with just a tiniest bit of hate mixed in.

"Find someone that challenges you. Pushes your buttons. Ignites your anger like no one else. Because in that frustration is passion. The artist doesn't paint because he wants to. He paints because he has to. Even when he despises his creation. Even when he doesn't have two pennies to rub together and art demands his last one. Even when the world

tells him he's no good. His passion for painting is obsession, and that's what love is at the end of the day. It has to be you and only you. Their passion. Their obsession."

I remember thinking that sounded murder-suicide crazy. My next thought after that was I didn't know two people more in love with each other than my mom and dad. My thoughts after they ran off with the money were the con was likely my mother's idea, and my dad was so out-of-his-mind crazy for her it didn't occur to him to say no.

Maybe their kind of love wasn't all it was cracked up to be.

I peeked at Royal.

Maybe.

Royal finished his food. The plate lay on the table and his hand returned to his natural task, transforming a blank page.

"Have you ever thought about doing something with your art?" I asked. "Going to college for it? Selling it?"

"No."

"Why not?"

"You can love sex and not need to get paid for it."

"Huh. That was actually really well put," I mused. "It's fine if sketching is enough for you. But you should know that if you want more, you can have it." My eyes swept over the art papering the walls. "Your work is incredible."

"Shh."

The telltale wrinkle marred his brow. Royal worried his lip, eyes flicking from me to the page.

I set my half-eaten food on the carpet. "Are you drawing me?"

"Yes. Hold still."

"No," I cried. I looked at my oversized red Arsenal shirt, clashing orange pants, and damp spots from my dripping hair. "Don't draw me looking like this."

His amusement saved me from being hushed. "You don't have a choice."

"That's not true." I trapped his gaze as I stood and wriggled out of my shorts. Kicking them in his direction, my panties went flying after. His flicker of surprise disappeared between fabric. I languidly drew the shirt over my head and then tossed it on the growing collection at his feet.

"Better," I purred, biting my lip. "So, how do you want me?"

His charcoal pencil nearly broke in his grip. "Twice on the couch and three times on your knees."

"We can make that happen." It's amazing how I went from staring death in the face to flying high on lust and happiness in one day. There was nowhere I wanted to be more than here with Royal.

I draped my legs over the arms of the chair, opening up to him. His hardening ridge had me damp before I slid a finger past my folds. "I'll let you keep this sketch."

"You would've had to pry it from my cold grip before they closed the casket," he growled. "And I still wouldn't have given it up."

I giggled. I was drunk on sex, arousal, and pulsing excitement running through my veins, awakening every corner of my body.

The true term for goose bumps was piloerection. The involuntary act of your body responding to heightened emotions. That was me with Royal always. Responding to him outside of my control. Sensing him before I step into a room. Hearing him before he speaks.

I went deeper, finding that spot. A moan slipped out of me. "You're not drawing," I whispered.

Royal jerked like he forgot the notepad was on his lap. He tore a page roughly flipping to a clean one. "Two fingers," he ordered.

I complied, melting into the cushion as I moved. My toes curled dangling off the chair. This was hardly the first time I played with myself but it was the first time doing it for an audience. Cassius didn't have time for my teasing. He was on me before I got my bra off. Doing this for Royal made it all the more sweeter.

I spread my fingers, opening up to him completely.

"Fuck," he breathed.

Royal couldn't take his eyes off me. His pencil glided over the page of its own accord. Usually you'd have to go as far as lighting him on fire to take his focus off a sketch. Not this time. For once, it was all about me.

Cupping my breast, I gently twisted and tweaked the hardened pebble, pulling out more breathy cries. I wanted to draw out every delicious moment of this but my orgasm was approaching fast.

"Three fingers."

I didn't hesitate. Three fingers and my eyes rolled in my head. "Oh, Royal."

"Do that again." Royal flung the notebook away. He stalked toward me, gripping both arms of the chair as he bore over me. "Say my name again."

"Royal," I cried. My fingers found my clit and flicked the poor thing mercilessly.

"Shit, Ember. You're a fucking work of art."

Royal freed himself. I used my foot to push his shorts all the way down. He was already weeping for me. I leaned forward, lips parted.

"Wait," he said, even though he didn't. Royal stroked his length as he tilted my head up. "What about you and Cassius?"

"You know about us?"

He nodded. "He said you two were hooking up."

Leaning back, I secured my legs around his waist, fingers still playing with my sex. "Hooking up barely covers it. Cassius pogoes on my G-spot every other night like it's an Olympic event."

Royal's cock jerked in his hand.

"The sex is fantastic," I continued, grinning. "But we're still figuring out what we are, and he doesn't mind sharing while we do."

"He said that?"

"Yep. So, if you thought some kind of Angel loyalty thing was going to hold you back tonight, you were wrong."

Royal took my wrist and pulled my fingers out. He locked eyes as he licked my arousal clean off my middle finger. I almost came on the spot.

"That's all I needed to know," he said.

Royal dropped to his knees. Gripping my calves, he propped my legs on the chair. He zeroed in on his target like a dying man did the well of life. I gripped my knees as his tongue slipped between my folds.

Bang! Bang! Bang!

"You've got to be kidding me!" I shouted.

The interrupter pounded on the door. "Royal? Royal! I know you're there, man. Your car's out front."

"Clay?"

I dropped my feet to the floor. Sexy time was over. The two of us scrambled into our clothes—flushed, hot, and struggling to shake off the power of our attraction.

Royal let them in.

"Royal, do you know where—" Clay saw me and the relief on his black-and-blue face punched me in the gut. "Fucking hell, Em."

"I called you," I said. "Both of you."

"Our phones died." Clay closed the distance and scooped me into a fierce hug. I lost myself in his embrace, breathing him in, and reassuring myself he was okay. Clay put me on my feet only for Cassius to do the same.

"We didn't know what to think when Rio came back without you," Clay explained.

Cassius sat us both down in the armchair, me on his lap. I burrowed into his chest. They hadn't been beaten again. The collection of cuts and bruises I tended were healing. I was so happy they were okay; I forgave the interruption. Glancing at Royal didn't tell me if he did. There was nothing to see as he watched me with Cassius.

But he knows that I want this and we have all the time to make it happen.

"What's going to happen now?" I asked.

"We got off easy," said Cassius. "Our minimum payments went up and now we're responsible for finding out who's dealing at the academy."

"We find the dealer?" Royal swore. "I said he'd pull this."

"But not you, Em," Clay said, sinking into the couch. "He says you're to focus on finding your parents."

My lips peeled back. "That's cute. Rio thinks he can hand out orders to me now."

"We're not letting him think differently," Royal warned. "The five of us are lying low at the academy for a while. Rio's got some big plans coming up to distract him, so he'll take a break from fucking with us."

"What about Hiro?" I asked. "Is he okay?"

Royal tossed his head. "I called the doc when you were in the shower. He didn't pick up. I'll call again in the morning."

"But—"

"Trust us, baby." Cassius kissed my crown. "Doc lets us all know when we lose a brother. Not hearing from him is a good thing."

I buried my face in his chest. All of a sudden, I was bone tired. "I want a pillow and a mattress. I need this day to be over."

"Cool if we stay, Royal?" Clay asked. "We're not trying to crash with our dad."

"The couch is all yours." Hands snaked under me and lifted me free of Cassius's hold. "Food in the freezer. Drinks in the cabinet. Em and I are heading out early tomorrow, so lock up when you leave."

Royal carried me unceremoniously to the bedroom. The triplets watched us go. The question in their eyes was the same in my head. Were we going to pick up where we left off with them ten feet away?

Laying me on the bed, he went out, rescued his comforter, and draped it over me. Royal stretched out by my side but very distinctly did not touch me.

"Are we...?"

"We're all wrecked and you're a screamer," Royal said. "None of us will get any sleep once I get you going."

Heat steamed my blood. "Shut up."

"Besides," he said, his chuckles filling the dark. "I was serious about getting up early. There's something we might have to do."

"See Hiro?"

"Maybe."

Rolling over, I tumbled across his bed and landed in the warm crook between his arm and body. "Good night."

His hand moved down to my waist, keeping me close.

Secure.

Safe.

"Night."

Chapter Two

A familiar sound burrowed under my unconsciousness and roused me more effectively than an alarm clock.

"Serious question," I gruffed, my eyes shut. "Will your fingers fall off if you don't sketch every second of every day?"

His laugh was warm and full. "Never stopped long enough to find out. But you'll like this one."

Peeling my eyes open, desire crushed the last traces of tiredness. Royal was truly gifted. He captured my impish smile. Puffy lips. Curled toes. And dampness on my fingers as I toyed with my sex. The exacting detail of *everything* was so perfect it transported me to last night and my devouring need for him.

"I love it," I said. "Never been a muse before."

"It's a full-time job. You'll have to pose for me often. Possibly every day."

I pressed my smile into his bicep. Snuggled in bed with Royal, the morning light streaming through the blinds and casting stripes on his wild hair but serene expression. Outside Clay and Cassius were safe and with me. There wasn't a word for how I felt, and it scared and thrilled me.

"I'm prepared to take on my duties."

A swat landed on my backside. "Time to go. Get dressed. We'll pick up something to eat on the way."

I twisted to look at the clock. It read seven in the morning.

"To Hiro," I confirmed. "Did you get on to the doctor?"

Climbing out of bed, Royal grabbed clothes out of the closet, stripping and dressing in front of me. "He texted me saying Hiro was okay, but he's not coming back to the academy with us today."

"When will he be back? It looked like his arm was broken and then getting shot on top of it. What will we tell Hart about him being out?"

Royal gripped my ankle under the sheets and drew me out of the covers. I happily let him take my clothes off and dress me.

"That's on Hiro," he said. "He'll tell Hart he broke his arm in some accident and come back with the cast to prove it. She's got us covered in bandages. No one is going to notice one more."

"So, we just go on like nothing happened?" I took hold of his chin as he bent to pull up my pants. "Rio gets away with it."

"What did you think we were going to do, Em?" His eyes were tsunamis of crashing waves. Rage. Resentment. Hate.

"Rio lets you in on his plans," I said. "His son. His successor. You also know the other three leaders and what they're planning. Tell me I'm wrong."

Royal said nothing.

"You could walk into a police station and topple the Horsemen like a house of cards. So, why don't you?" I stroked his cheek. "It's not out of loyalty to Rio. When he shot Hiro, it was written all over your face how you truly felt about him. Turn him in," I pleaded. "Then this can be over."

"It's not that simple."

"Why?"

"Rio's not a good guy, but what he's after isn't all wrong. The Horsemen help a lot of people in the OB. Especially after your parents took most of them for everything they've got. One of the leaders gives loans and he has kept folks from losing their homes.

"We track dealers and shut them down. Last year, the Horsemen found that pimp that was turning out fourteen-year-old girls and put an end to that shit quick. No one else is going to step up for my neighborhood the way the Horsemen do. There are consequences to us being around. But there are consequences without us too."

I chose my words carefully. "Royal, I know people in the OB are struggling. I also know that you've done good and seen good done by the Horsemen," I said, thinking of the triplets. "But when the consequence is people dying, the alternative is always the right choice."

He scoffed. "There's that absolute certainty. I've seen the cost, Em. I see it every single night when I close my eyes. But taking down the Horsemen won't turn the OB into a gang-free paradise. All the gangs we've put down will rise up and claim the free territory, and I promise you, they're not looking to help the OB."

"Why do you keep making excuses for them?!" I burst out.

"Because I'm no fucking saint!" Royal pulled my pants up and me with it. "I've done worse than most of the boys I'd be sending to jail. If I even got that far. I don't know as much as you think. The people Rio's got on the force, slipping him information about your parents' case. I don't know who they are. The contacts he moves his goods through. Can't name them. And the full list of people who'll hunt me down if I turn on the leaders, I don't have that. I'm taking over for him, Em. There's no changing that plan."

I splayed my fingers over his chest. Royal's heart was forever racing a mile a minute.

It's why he runs from me. A heart like this can't slow long enough to trust.

"We can change that plan," I said. "I'll find a way."

A harsh noise strangled his throat. "It's not your job to save me, princess."

I softly pecked his lips. "Someone has to."

I was first out of the room. Cassius and Clay were knocked out on the pullout bed. Low, breathy noises leaked through Clay's parted lips, proving he snored despite his denials to his sister. I couldn't resist that sound. I listened to it as I lay awake in Cassius's arms, spent and sated from our sex, and turned on from Clay watching.

His soft snores were cute. A word not often associated with a tattooed, bruise-knuckled gangbanger.

Trying not to wake him, my kiss gently swallowed his breath. I moved around and kissed Cassius too.

Royal came out and jerked his head toward the door. Time to go.

"Should we bring Hiro anything?" I asked as we climbed in his car. "Food. Change of clothes."

"We're not going to Hiro," he said. "I'll text the triplets to stock my place up. Doc is going to bring him here to ride it out until he can go back to the academy."

"We're not? Why? Where are we going? And why is he staying here?"

"Hiro's parents are dead. He's got nowhere else to go."

That shocked me so much we were ten minutes into our drive before I noticed he didn't answer my other questions.

"If we're not going to Hiro, where are we going, Royal?"

Royal eased into the next lane. "Your parents' note... Did you ever do it? Leave flowers for your sister?"

One question and memories crashed into me. The music box splintering. The squeal of brakes. My mother screaming.

I didn't notice I was crying until Royal wiped a tear from my cheek.

"No," I rasped. "I didn't."

"Do you want to?"

Ten seconds passed.

Then thirty.

Then a minute.

Then five.

I nodded.

"Then that's where we're going."

Royal stopped by the florist. He went inside to buy the bouquet of carnations and peonies because I couldn't get out of the car.

"Raven River Cemetery?" he asked as he placed the flowers on my lap.

"Yes."

"We'll be there in twenty minutes."

"Okay."

Royal fell silent. He wasn't pushing me to talk about Rory. Maybe that's why I did.

"There was nothing for me," I said so softly he might not have heard me. "In their final note. They wanted Rory and Eli to know they still loved them, but not me."

"They were bastards, Em. What happened to your sister was an accident. Terrible, tragic, and hard to live with. But still an accident. They were wrong to make you feel like you didn't deserve forgiveness."

"I don't." My voice. My heart. My soul was dead.

Royal laid his hand over my clenched fist. "You do."

His touch didn't reach me. "I wanted to visit before," I said. "My uncle wouldn't give me the car unless I told him where I was going and I... couldn't."

"It's okay, Ember. You're going now."

Raven River Cemetery was a pocket of land on the edge of town, bordering the forest. It was oppressively silent. No birds singing in the trees. No critters skittering over the forest floor. No bustling noise from the town. The sounds of life did not touch this place. As though man and creature alike knew to give the peace these people did not have in life.

Royal parked just as the workers opened the gate. Eight a.m. on the dot.

"I figured it'd be empty at this time," Royal explained. "You'll have privacy."

"Thank you." I made no move to leave the car.

"Do you want to do this by yourself?"

"No."

My feet stayed planted on the floor mat.

"Should I carry you inside? How literally are you taking this princess thing?"

I cracked a smile, and marveled that he made me do that. "You dress me, cook for me, chauffeur me around, and carry me to bed. A girl can get spoiled."

"I'm good to spoil you today."

Royal came to my side of the car. He reached a hand out to me, patiently waiting for me to take it. We walked into the cemetery fingers laced.

Fingers strangled more like. I held on to Royal so tightly it must have hurt, but he didn't say anything.

My sister's grave was at the back by the fence. Two evergreens were planted beside her, shading her from the sun. Only the best for a Bancroft. My grandfather bought this plot for all of us to rest together, and he lay ten feet away.

"She slept in my bed every night," I said as we closed the distance. "She had her own, but she'd crawl into mine after our parents put us to bed. When I die, I'll sleep next to her again."

Royal didn't reply. I couldn't blame him. Not many people would've known what to say to that.

Royal stopped a few feet away. I tugged him but he refused to move.

"Go," he said simply. "I'm right here."

I kept going. Kneeling down, the well swirling sorrow spilled over at the state of her grave. Dead flowers in her vase. Leaves covering the headstone. A wrapper stuck in the grass from some disrespectful piece of shit.

I flung it away with a scream. I should have come back sooner. I should be taking care of her. It's just the three of us now.

"Ember?"

On my knees, I bowed before the headstone, pinned by an invisible force.

"Don't look away from her," Mom hissed. *She clamped down on my neck. "You did this. Face her. Tell your sister you love her."*

The marble dug into my forehead. Tears dripped down the blades of grass, soaking the earth, seeking Rory.

"I love you."

"Ember? Ember, I'm sorry." There was something new in Royal's voice. "This was a mistake." He grabbed me under the arms. "I shouldn't have brought you here."

"No!" Clawing his hands, I ripped them off. "I have to face her!"

"Em, stop!"

"I did this!"

I collapsed on the grave. Royal picked me up and crushed me to his chest. I flailed as he dragged me to Grandpa's memorial bench.

"It's not your fault," he cried. "It was an accident. Don't do this to yourself anymore."

Wailing and screaming, I pummeled him. Royal grunted under my assault but didn't let go. Over and over he repeated forgiveness.

"You don't get to say that to me!" I shoved him. We tipped over crashing onto the grass. "You haven't forgiven yourself!"

"And I won't until you show me how!" Royal grabbed my wrists. He pinned them to the ground and covered me with his body. "You want to save me, princess? Start right now."

Violent sobs wracked me. I couldn't breathe for the pain and Royal on my chest. He touched our foreheads together, silently sharing what he couldn't find the words to say.

I couldn't move. Couldn't breathe. Couldn't get to Rory or leave her. But this wasn't Mom's unbreakable grip as she marched me to the grave. Rio cracked a seal that wasn't ready to break and passing through the gates crumbled it to dust. Thirteen years and I never said her name. Thirteen seconds in this place and I fell apart.

Royal held me down, but it was truer to say he held me together. My tears slowed under his soft murmuring, and my broken pieces reformed like a video of a smashed vase played in reverse.

My hands came up, clutching his back. "I'm sorry," I rasped. "Did I hurt you?"

"You clawed me to fucking ribbons." The cuts on his face told the truth. As did his grin. "But I've taken worse."

"I'm okay now." My voice was small. "I want to give Rory her flowers."

"We'll do it together this time."

Royal helped me to my feet. He held my hand as he picked up the flowers and guided me to her grave.

Holding them to my chest, I knelt, gazing at my reflection in the polished marble. She cried, but her tears fell gently, and her eyes were soft.

"I do love you," I whispered. "If I could go back, I'd give you a thousand music boxes. I pray you have forgiven me... because I'll never forgive myself."

Taking out the dead flowers, I picked up her vase.

Ting.

I frowned. *What was that noise?*

I shook the vase. Something rattled inside.

"Em, what's up?"

Tipping it over, a glint of refracted sunlight struck my eyes.

A key.

"Royal." My tears vanished under horrible understanding. "Royal, oh my gosh."

"What is it?"

"The note they left me." I showed him the small silver key. "It was a message."

"HOLY SHIT."

Royal put his key in the ignition some time ago but didn't try to go anywhere. We sat in his car as the rising sun brought more guests to the cemetery. This peaceful place did see life. It saw families and loved ones through the worst times in their story and, as I finally discovered, it also kept a secret.

The seal was reforming. The effect of my time with Rory and being violently forced to face her again clung to me like film. I wasn't fine, but as had been the case over the last thirteen years, other things crowded my mind to the point I was able to lock my tragedy away to deal. My eyes were red-rimmed but clear as I faced the new problems of the key.

"Holy shit," Royal repeated. "That's why they didn't flat-out write for you to go to the cemetery. If the cops got their hands on it, they wanted to make sure you were the only person to come here."

"It's the only explanation," I said, pieces clicking together. "Something like this wouldn't end up there by accident. No one else has a reason to go near that part of the cemetery. Grandpa bought that plot for the Bancrofts."

"Your parents left you a key."

I nodded slowly, gazing at the piece of cut metal that turned everything I knew upside down. "They left me a key."

"A key to what?"

"I have no idea."

"We have to get out of here." Royal started the car. "This changes everything, Em."

I tore my eyes away. "Changes everything? You're not— Royal, you can't tell your dad. You can't tell anyone!"

"He's Rio. Don't call him my dad." Royal screeched out of the parking lot, zooming onto the main road. "I'm not telling him shit. He believes that message meant nothing. He has to keep believing that."

"You promise me?"

Royal gave me a hard look. "Do you really need to ask?"

I searched his face. "No," I said. "I don't."

Inhaling deep, I held my breath till my lungs ached. It burst out of me as I made up my mind.

"Pull over."

"What? Why?" asked Royal.

"You know why."

The road to the cemetery was a lone dirt path surrounded by forest. Royal veered off the road and drove us through the tree line.

It was too much. Rio. Hiro. Cassius. Clay. Damien and the brutes. Rory. The key.

Forget crowding my pain out with more of a different kind. I wanted the brief relief to not feel pain at all.

We were on each other before he shut off the car. One hand tore at my zipper. The other yanked the key out. I drew back, throwing open the door, and my heart thumping like the bass at a rock concert. Royal's growl at my escape was an injection of lust straight to my core. I was an attractive girl and boys flashed me interest often. But it was nothing compared to the burning hunger in Cassius's eyes. The lingering desire in Clay's touch. Or the possession in Royal's actions. I wasn't used to being wanted the way these boys did me.

We met in the backseat, lips clashing in a shower of sparks. The first night we were together was incredible in every way, but there was something different about this kiss and what was to come. Royal and I weren't kids anymore. We were older. Sharper. Jaded. Smashed to pieces and then put back together not quite right. I was the girl he talked off the ledge. He was the boy still dangling on the edge.

"Don't be gentle," I gasped. "Fuck every bit of this awful weekend out of me."

Royal scraped my bottom lip between his teeth. "Whatever the princess wants today, she gets."

I couldn't get his pants off fast enough. Royal panted in my ear, biting my lobe as I shoved his jeans down. Our clothes came off in a flurry of grunts and filthy promises.

"I should've fucked you while the triplets listened outside the door." Royal licked a stripe between my breasts, collecting the sweat beading on my overheated skin. "Give my little screamer what she wants."

Grabbing my hips, Royal flipped me on my hands and knees. "From here on, I'm not showing that much restraint. When I want you, I'm taking you." His finger found the bundle of nerves between my legs. "Unless you have objections."

"No objections h-here," I breathed. Royal was squeezing and tormenting my clit between two rough, calloused fingers. He shoved two digits inside of me and my knees gave out. "You have two years to make up for."

Royal picked up speed and I clutched the door, moaning as I rocked back, matching his frantic pace. "Two years' worth of sex is a lot to make up for in two weeks."

"I didn't say you had to make it up in two weeks."

It was hot in the car. Sweat stuck my hair to my forehead and slicked the leather seats.

"I'm pretty sure that's what I heard."

Crooking his fingers, he found the spot. I kicked back, smacking him square on the ass as I gave him the screams he accused me of. "No," I cried. "It was... a week. Definitely one week!"

"Oh, baby, did I miss you."

Royal's erection was digging in my thigh. I wanted it inside of me now, and kicked him again to convey the hint. His chuckle filled the car.

"Easy, Em. I have my orders. One hard fuck coming up. But first, we're picking up where we left off."

Royal pulled out. Taking me by the neck, he drew me up, pressing my face to his. His breath cascaded over my lips. "Lick it clean," he ordered. "Just one. Save the other for me."

I swallowed his finger to the knuckle, sucking it like a lollipop.

"Mmmh." Royal licked my cheek. "See how sweet you taste, princess? Better than that cream stuff you love."

My sex was near enough weeping. I thought Cassius and I got up to some kinky fun but my dark prince was on another level.

"Bend over."

I dropped—ass in the air, chest on the seat. I was so ready for him, I couldn't stay still. Wiggling and rocking my hips back and forth. The sound of a wrapper broke through my fog.

"We don't need that," I said. "I'm on the pill."

"Sorry, Em. I was an eighteen-year-old's mistake. I always bag it up."

I smacked the door. "I'm not one of your random hookups! And nothing we do could be a mistake. I want to feel *you*, Royal! Just you. I get what I want today."

"You gotta be—! Fuck!"

The condom landed on the floor beside me. Royal melded our bodies in one single thrust. The thrill of my victory washed under stronger, primal emotions.

He started pumping and I arched off the seat, fingers curling around the handle.

"That's it, princess. Scream for me."

I did.

There was no holding back. I moaned so loudly it covered the sounds of our bodies.

Royal pounded that spot with a single-minded determination that would have earned him a medal if making me come was a sport. My head bumped the door on every thrust. Fireworks exploded in my mind as he drove me closer and closer.

I wasn't stupid or blind to the consequences of our bare romp. What I wanted from him was exactly what I said: Royal. The two of us had been separated by space, time, differing worlds, others' mistakes, and hate. I had my boy in the flowers back and nothing would separate us again.

Royal thrusted and I choked on my cry. I came hard, body shuddering so violently it closed my throat. Seconds later, Royal pulled out and exploded on my back.

We collapsed on the seat in a sweaty, sticky mess.

"Holy shit," I whispered, echoing him. "You held out on me the first time."

He pressed a kiss to the back of my neck. "Don't worry. I won't be doing that again."

I lay still and content as he got his shirt and cleaned me off.

"The ending was a surprise." Reaching over my head, I found his arm and moved it under me.

"Figured that's what you were going for ordering me not to use a condom."

I rolled over, curling into him. "I kinda liked it."

Royal bit my shoulder. "You know you're not a random hookup."

"I do now."

His lips skated along my skin up to my mouth. We kissed slow and deep—the opposite of our wild lovemaking.

Though he probably won't call it that.

I sighed happily into the kiss. It didn't matter what Royal called it. I knew what we were. What we had always been.

"I'm noticing a pattern with us," I mused. "We're always getting together after emotionally destroying stuff goes down. Think we'll ever have a relationship approaching normal?"

Squeezing my ass, Royal gazed up at the ceiling. "My father tried to kill you and you're sleeping with half of my friends. So... no."

I poked his ribs. "I'm sleeping with one-third of your friends actually. We can talk about it if you want."

"You want to be with both of them," he stated. "I saw the way you looked at Cas and Clay this morning."

"It's new with Clay," I said softly. "I still don't know what we are or where it'll go, but he just has this way of making me feel safe. And Cassius, he understands me. I can be myself with him. I know it's complicated, but yes, I want both of them." I propped my chin on his chest. "You and I have a lot of stuff to sort out together and on our own, but it doesn't change that I want you too. Can you do non-exclusive?"

"No."

My heart sank. "No?"

"No," he repeated. "Fuck non-exclusive. We are exclusive as a crew. I said it at the academy and I'll say it again. You're our girl. I'll share you with whoever you want as long as that guy has an angel on his arm. Anyone else touches you, they'll wake up with me at the foot of their bed."

"Oh?" I said, trying and failing not to show how happy I was. "Is that right?"

"Yep. You got something you want to say about that?"

I swung my leg over, straddling him. "Nope. We understand each other perfectly. But I do have another question?" I moved his hands to my breasts. "If we're cramming two years of sex into one week, how many blowjobs am I averaging a day?"

Those light eyes darkened to their true nature. "Pick a number and I'll tell you if you're close."

I hummed. "Two."

"Nope."

"Five."

"Not even close."

I was cracking up. "Six?"

"Wrong again." Royal bolted up and tackled me squealing to the seat. "We'll start with the first one and go from there."

ROYAL TURNED IT OVER in his palm. The two of us stretched out in the back of the car, sweat cooling on our bodies, and fog dissipating on the windows. I don't know how long we spent in our little pocket of forest, exploring each other's bodies, but eventually the real world demanded to be let in.

A key more unremarkable than this did not exist. The single distinguishing mark was the number twenty-two stamped on the face.

"It's small," he said. "Not a house or car key. It could open a locker. Locker number twenty-two."

"But what locker? Where? I'm wracking my brain but it's coming up blank," I admitted. "The feds searched everything. Our house, the lake house, the boat, the cars, Mom's real estate office. Everything connected to their name was found and ransacked. If there was something closed up with a tiny key like this, they'd have just busted in."

"They still could have missed something," he said. "What about a safe-deposit box?"

I shook my head. "If the police didn't find something like that, it would mean they hid it under another name—which could be anything. Assuming my parents left this for me to find them or the money, they'd have to believe this key was enough to get me there. A safe-deposit box that not even the federal government could find? Impossible."

"All right. That's true." Royal crossed one arm behind his head, resting on the door handle. "Did your parents have gym memberships?"

"We had a home gym."

"That could be it, Em. Who is going to think someone with a home gym had a membership somewhere else?" He tapped my arm as a thought came to him. "What about the Estate Country Club? They have numbered lockers."

"It's been months. Wouldn't an unused locker have been cleaned out by now?"

"We won't know until we check it out. If that's what you want."

"I... I honestly don't know what I want." I buried my face in his neck, allowing his soap, sweat, and a scent that was exclusively Royal to calm me. "This town tortured me because they believed my parents left me a message. Now it turns out to be true. This morning I was innocent. Blameless. I was the true victim whether anyone believed it or not.

"Everything has changed. If I announce this and hand it over to the police, I may be sending my own parents to federal prison. If I ignore it, Eli and I live the rest of our lives without closure. Wondering where they are. Why they left us. If we'll ever see them again. And if I follow where this key leads— Well, that's the hardest option of all, because it might take me to them."

"I won't tell you what to do, princess. It's selfish as fuck, but Gran has her money. It's over for me, so if you toss the key in the forest right now, I won't say a word about it."

I shook my head. "I have to think. Let's go back to school, okay? I need some time."

We dressed in the tight space and then got back on the road. Raven River Academy was on the opposite end of town from the cemetery. We had a long drive back. Royal didn't push me to speak, allowing me the time to think that I asked for.

Driving over the bridge to the academy felt surreal. So much had happened since the last time I crossed this bridge. Hiro was shot. The triplets were in deeper with the gang. Royal made a deal for my soul with an unknown person and for an unknown cost. And I found that key.

My life turned on its head, but Raven River Academy was the same. The towers swept the sky, imposing in design, weathered in age. My feelings were in a tangle over being back. I had too many enemies to name within these gates. Eli's attackers were on the loose. The Raveners were out for my blood.

All that said, I was a lot safer in here than I was out there with Rio Cruz.

Royal pulled into the parking lot. "So, princess."

"Yes."

"Want to fill that thinking time with sex? I've got a free Sunday and an empty room."

My body responded before I did, legs clenching thinking of Royal between them. "I'll take you up on that. Just give me twenty minutes. I'm going to check on Eli."

Royal went on ahead of me. I trailed him at a slower pace.

Do I tell Eli about the key?

I was as open and honest with my brother as I could be, but of course, I did not tell him everything. There were some things you did not put on a fourteen-year-old's shoulders.

This was different. They were his parents too.

Tatum answered the door. "Hey, Ember. Eli just went in the bathroom."

I stepped inside to wait for him. Eli and Tatum's room was on the right side of messy. Hamper overflowing. Backpacks tossed anywhere. Beds unmade. But I could see the floor and the room smelled of forest from the windows they left open.

Eli came out of the bathroom and favored me with a hug. A sign he missed me even if he didn't admit it.

"What happened to your head?"

I almost forgot my latest blow to the skull.

"I tripped. It's no big deal. Can we talk outside?" I signed. *"It's important."*

He nodded. Shoving his shoes on, Eli walked with me outside and on through the grounds. My destination was the tennis courts. The court was out in the open, but people couldn't sneak up on us.

"What's up?" he asked. *"Something happen?"*

"Yes."

I swung my leg over, straddling the bleacher. Eli did the same.

"I went to the cemetery today."

Worry swept under a blanket of grief. For two sisters, not one.

"Are you okay?" he signed and then took my hands.

Eli was a baby when Rory died. He didn't remember his oldest sister. Her death was infinitely more tragic in that way because Eli never got to see the family we were when she was alive. He knew my parents as they became after the accident. And he knew the person her death made of me.

I kissed his forehead. "No," I said honestly. "I'm not okay. After all this time, I've accepted that I'll never be okay."

Eli's face crumpled.

"Hey, don't do that," I crooned. "Your sister is a big fat mess. You know that better than anyone." I squeezed his fingers. "You also know that I'm tough. I have to be for us, so I am."

He tugged free. *"You don't have to be tough for me."*

"I do," I replied. *"Because I found something at the grave that might make life very difficult for us."*

"What?"

I showed him the key. *"This was in the flower vase. I believe Mom and Dad put this there for me to find. It's why they left the note."*

"Surrender an offering to the goddess." If Eli said it aloud, his voice would've shaken. He was stricken. Eyes wide and staring at the key like our parents' location was written on it.

Eli and I shared the true meaning of the note from the very beginning. He was there as my father knelt before the headstone, laying flowers for our goddess. In Eli's case, the police believed him when he told them he didn't know.

He leveled huge eyes on me. *"It was a message for us the entire time. They didn't leave us, Em."*

"No, they did leave us," I returned. "They took off with half the town's money and dumped us on Uncle Harrison and Aunt Violet's lap. Because of them, we've lost our home, friends, and our life. I'm harassed every day and you were attacked."

Eli flinched.

"This key doesn't change what they put us through for the last couple of months," I told him. "It doesn't change that they're criminals."

"They're not criminals. They're our mom and dad." He set his jaw.

"Oh, Eli," I sighed. "This is why I thought about throwing the key in the forest and forgetting I ever saw it. Finding this doesn't mean the four of us are heading toward a happy reunion. Do you realize what this means?"

"It means we have to find out what this opens."

"And what happens if we do?" I pressed. "What if this is for a safe-deposit box and there's twenty-five million dollars inside? We'd have to turn it in to the police. Or what if inside there's an address to where they're hiding? Then we have the awful choice of turning *our parents* over to the cops."

"We don't have to tell anyone." His reply was angry and jerky. *"If we find them and the money, no one has to know."*

"Eli Francis Bancroft, is that really an option for you?"

My brother shoved away, face tight. He glowered at the green synthetic court. It came slow, but he shook his head.

"*No. Okay? No, that's not an option.*" He pinned me with a look. "*But you're wrong too. Those aren't the only two choices. We could find Mom and Dad and make them do the right thing.*"

"They're looking at prison cells if they do."

"*No, they're looking at being without us if they don't.*" He tapped my palm. "*If they were fine with that, they wouldn't have given you the key. I told you they wouldn't just leave us. I told you.*"

I dropped my head in my hands, rubbing my temples. Why shouldn't this be impossible? Everything else in my life was.

A light touch grazed my cheek. "*I miss them, Em.*"

I'd never been able to say no to my brother when he looked at me like refusal would rip him apart.

"*Please.*"

This time was no different.

"Okay," I said, feeling myself rip apart instead. "I'll do whatever it takes to figure this out."

"*I'll help you.*"

"No, what you'll do is be a fourteen-year-old kid and let your biggest problems be studying for midterms and getting that cute girl in Spanish class that you think I don't know about to notice you. I'm your big sister. I will take care of the rest."

We hugged tight, cried sloppily, and tilted on the edge of the irrevocable consequences facing us. Our parents and the town's future were out there. Time to bring them home.

Chapter Three

"The kid has you wrapped."

"Ugh. Don't rub it in."

Royal grinned up at me. I rode him straddle-style, sitting on his lap while I considered the key. My human seat was looking pretty pleased with himself, and why wouldn't he? I dropped Eli at his dorm, cleaned up, and then slid into his room for hours of mattress acrobatics. I was told eighteen-year-old boys couldn't find a G-spot with a magnifying glass, and conked out before a woman got close. Cassius and Royal dropped those stereotypes on their heads.

"Eli tells you to find them and that's it."

I flicked his nose. "We've established that there's a hold on my judgment shaped like Eli's fist. Move on."

"Hmm. All right." He hooked me around the waist and dragged me down. I squealed as he licked my breast.

"Not to that." I laughed. "I meant move on to helping me. We've ruled out car or house. What else could this key open?"

Royal bit my nipple. Rippling pain and pleasure made my thoroughly fucked pussy sit up and beg for more.

"You're no help," I breathed. My common sense was heading south fast. I grabbed the last shred of it and pushed him onto the pillows. "Focus. Key first, then sex. What else could this open?"

Folding his arms behind his head, he actually seemed to be considering it. "We got the gym and country club lockers. You said no to a safe-deposit box. It could open one of the lockers at the bus station. Or a storage unit."

I gripped his forearms. "The bus station. Mom and Dad took off in her car. The cops know they drove, so they had no reason to check the bus station. It's the perfect place to lead me."

"Easy enough to find out."

A knock sounded on the door.

"Who is that?" I asked.

"Triplets."

"How do you know?"

"Hiro's not here and no one else in this school has got business with me. Or wants some."

"We can hear you, man." Cassius's dry statement came through the wood. "Open up."

"Let them in," I said, climbing off him. "But don't say anything about the key. I know how you feel about Rio, but Cassius and Clay speak about him with gratitude. Rio can't find out about this."

"Those guys went against him for you, Em."

I clutched the blanket to my chest. "I know. I'm not saying I don't trust them. This is a tough spot to put them in and the fewer people that know the better. Who knows? I may not find what this goes to and it won't matter anyway."

Instead of arguing he tossed me his shirt. I pulled it on and left the rest of my clothes on the floor. All of these guys had seen me naked multiple times. Too late to get shy.

"Hey," said Clay.

The two of them took in the scene.

"Came to tell you how Hiro was doing, but it doesn't look like you two are missing him much." The term devilish smirk was invented because of Cassius Walker.

"Asshole," I said. "Of course I want to know how he is. Does your doctor really have him at Royal's place by himself?"

"He'll be fine there," said Clay. "Doc'll keep him till he's on his feet."

"Got room for me?" Cassius dove on the bed. He burrowed into my chest, making himself comfortable. "I got my ass beat this weekend," he said. "I was kinda hoping you'd slide in my bed and make me feel better."

I grasped his smooth jaw and kissed that smirking mouth. "That's exactly what I was planning to do."

"Y'all should do that now," Clay said. "Royal, we've got to talk about this dealer. Rio wants him found and he isn't giving us much time to do it."

"Whoa," Cassius said. "Why should I go? You think you're leaving me out?"

"I'm not leaving you out of shit." His eyes flicked to me.

"You're trying to get Cassius to lure me out of the room with his dick," I stated. "You can call that plan a bust. If you're looking for the drug dealer, I'm helping. This is the one and only thing the Horsemen and I agree on. This piece of crap is peddling their poison to freshmen. My brother's already gotten caught up in it."

Royal propped up on the wall. He folded his arms over a bare chest, unbothered with wearing boxers and nothing else. "This isn't your punishment, it's ours. It also happens to be of particular interest to me." His lips curled. "I don't like this shit showing up on our turf out of nowhere. And I don't like the trouble I smell coming for the OB kids. If the dealer is one of us, the Raveners will make us all pay for it."

I knew he meant the grown Raveners sitting in the Estate cursing Headmistress Hart for changing the rules.

"I'm going to find this guy, Em," Royal said. "And you're not going to like what I do to him."

His tone took me aback. "Why do you have to do anything to him? We can just turn them over to Hart or the police."

"That's not how it works," said Clay.

Royal nodded. "We lay down rules and the kids in this school follow them. We said day one there's no dealing on campus."

"Whatever people want to sneak and snort on their own is their problem and their risk," Cassius added. "But selling it and catching up girls like Melina who have everything to lose? That's got to be handled before other people get it into their heads to go against the Angels."

I opened my mouth. "But you—"

"No buts," Royal pushed through clenched teeth. "Your hesitation is why you won't be involved."

"My hesitation is why I should be involved," I snapped. "I'll keep things from going too far."

"You don't keep me in check, princess."

"Don't call me that like it's a fucking insult!" We glared daggers, air thick with anger when only a while ago it was thick with fevered promises and sex. "Make up your damn mind. If we're a crew, we decide stuff like this together."

Royal laughed. "I see. You think this is a democracy. My boys here will be happy to tell you who's in charge."

Clay and Cassius met my eyes. There wasn't a trace of mocking or irony as they said, "Royal."

Scooting out from under Cassius, I strode up to Royal. He tracked my approach, eyes narrowed, like I was packing a switchblade somewhere interesting and waiting for my chance to pull it on him.

Holding his gaze, my lips quirked up in time with my leg, skating up his thigh and then curling around his hip. My borrowed shirt rode up, exposing my bare ass as the other leg followed. My hands found his hair, twining his strands through my fingers as those crackling chestnut eyes swallowed me.

"You've made yourself clear. You're in charge of the Angels. Now I'll make something clear," I purred. "You three are going to stop treating me like I'm nothing more than a shared fuck. You protected me, looked after Eli, and saved my life. I can't just walk away after everything we've been through. I *will* help you find this dealer for your reasons and mine, and when we do find him, we're turning him in. Not hurting him." I pressed my mouth to his lips. "The Angels are about to become a democracy or this pussy closes up shop."

A low, dangerous growl rumbled against my lips. Royal did not like that one bit, but if the last twenty-four hours revealed anything, it's that my body most certainly had him under a spell and ultimatums worked like a charm.

I kissed him—soft and sweet. "Don't be angry, baby. We both know I'm worth it."

Cassius chuckled. "Rio said she'd make a fine Horsewoman."

"So," I pushed. "What do you say, Royal?"

The stiff jaw and lined brows vanished. "I say the princess gets what she wants."

The words were right. The blank expression was harmless. Still, suspicion tightened my hold. Royal Cruz stood between his father and a gun. This was not a guy who gave in without a fight.

Royal deposited me on the bed. His motive for agreeing to my demands eluded me, but knowing him, I'd find out soon enough. Until then, I'd be the steadying hand behind this whether he liked it or not.

I crawled up to Cassius, tucking myself under his arm. The incorrigible man tucked his erection between my cheeks.

"Where do we start with finding this guy?" Clay jumped on Hiro's bed, reclining on the headboard. "From what I hear, the Raveners are repeat customers but they won't give them up easily. We shut down the dealer and there goes their party favors."

Royal lifted his shoulders. "We don't need them all to talk. Just one."

"None of them are fans of yours," I piped up.

"Don't know if Destiny Hamilton would agree. She seems to like me just fine."

The smile wiped off my face. "Destiny Hamilton? You slept with Destiny?"

"The lady likes a cuddle too," Royal went on. "She tells me all about her problems. I'm sure I can get her to spill on the dealer."

I shot up, knocking Cassius off. "How the hell are you planning to do that?" Biting, spitting jealousy rose the temperature in the room a thousand degrees. I was no dummy. Royal didn't take a vow of celibacy while we were apart and I accepted he had a past. But finding out one of the girls who tortured me tangled up in *these* sheets with the first guy I had real feelings for was not welcome news.

"You're not sleeping with her."

Royal's brows climbed up his forehead, pissing me the hell off.

"You don't want to test me, Cruz. The same rules apply to you. We're exclusive, which means you don't get with anyone who doesn't have an angel on their arm. Unless you, Cassius, Clay, or Hiro want to cross swords—in which case I'd like to watch—you're not sleeping with anyone other than me."

"I feel like we're missing something, Cas," Clay said mildly.

To my surprise, Royal burst out laughing. "Relax, princess. Sleeping with her was never on the table. Don't need to go that far to ask a simple question." Royal cut to the triplets. "Ember's not hooking up with anyone outside of the Angels. She was making that clear."

"I was making clear *you're* not hooking up outside of the Angels." I reclaimed my spot under Cassius. "The reverse is true too," I murmured to the triplets.

"I'm cool with that," said Clay.

Nuzzling my neck, Cassius squeezed my knee. "You give me the best gifts, baby."

"This means you can only sleep with me, Cas. Still on board?"

His hand crept north. "All-access pass."

"Cassius," I warned. My giggle took away the heat.

"Pretty sure that's what we agreed to."

"Don't recall that." I was laughing.

"Should I remind you?"

He snuck under Royal's shirt and cupped my sex. I wriggled, ineffectively knocking him off and not trying harder.

"We do what we want to do when we want to do it," I said. "But the whole crossing swords thing. I wouldn't mind—"

"Behave." Cassius rolled on top of me and squished me laughing into the sheets. "No one is crossing swords even though I *feel* how much you like the idea." Cassius slipped past my lower lips, unheeding of the boys watching.

I escaped him and ran to Clay, jumping on his lap. "Clay," I cried. "Save me from your brother."

"With pleasure." Clay grasped my arms and caressed down to my wrists as he draped them around his shoulders. "You know, I was beat to shit too."

The cuts, bandages, and bruises on his still-perfect face backed him up.

He brushed his nose against mine. "I could use some cheering up."

"Oooh. What do you have in mind?" It was entirely possible I was high on sex. It was also entirely possible being near Clay was kicking my pulse into overdrive.

I touched a palm to my chest and the organ fluttering wildly in its cage. Yes to both.

"I could... bring you breakfast in bed?" I teased.

"Not what I was thinking."

"Want to cuddle up and watch movies?"

He shook his head, eyes lasered on mine. "Before or after, sure."

"After what exactly?" I whispered.

My lips hovered millimeters above his. Our breaths mingled. Our fingers entwined. Need grew in his eyes and between my legs. We'd been dancing around our feelings for reasons I was sure had nothing to do with Cassius and me. The night in his bathroom said it all. He believed what I truly wanted was to be free of the Angels, and in my darkest, quietest moments, I recognized a lot of terrible things wouldn't have happened if they hadn't forced their way into my life.

But that moment would pass under the acceptance that a lot of wonderful things wouldn't have happened either. The Angels made the school back off taunting me. They got Fiona to delete the video of me in the shower. They comforted me after Eli was attacked. And they stood between me and the true person intent on destroying—even taking—my life.

"Come back to my room and I'll show you," Clay said.

"Not today," said Royal. "Cas, off."

The next thing I knew I was lifted off Clay and placed on Royal's bed.

"Ember and I have plans today. Tomorrow, I'll talk to Destiny and we'll figure out the rest from there. The minimum payments," Royal said, stopping them as they got up to leave. "Can you cover them?"

Clay and Cassius shared a look. "We'll have to take on more. Up some of our prices. But yeah, we can cover it."

"If it's looking like you'll come up short, I'll spot you."

Cassius scoffed. "Because Rio didn't just tell us what he thinks of that?"

"My money isn't marked. He will never know the difference. I warned you guys we have to lie low and coming up short for the pot is exactly what will get us his full attention."

"We won't come up short," Clay clipped.

The triplets filed out, leaving us to our afternoon activities. Royal stretched out on top of me.

"He's stubborn." I cradled his neck and brought our foreheads together. "Clay believes he has to take care of everyone on his own."

"We do have to take care of everything on our own. In our world, no one comes to save us."

We shared a kiss that awakened more than just desire in me.

I'm going to save you.

ELI WAS OUTSIDE MY door the next morning.

"I'm guessing you're not here to indulge my wish to walk you to class every morning?"

His pinched lips answered that question. *"I don't need to be walked to class. And I want to know about the key. Did you figure out what it opens?"*

I peered over my shoulder. Camila was in the bathroom getting ready for breakfast. We wouldn't have to worry about her picking up our conversation.

"Come inside." I shut and locked the door behind him. *"I will tell you as soon as I know something, Eli. I promise. Don't stress about this."*

"But I can help you."

"You can't," I said and signed it, getting my point across. *"There are a lot of people willing to hurt me to get their hands on this key. You are not getting caught up in that. As soon as I find out what it leads to, I'll tell you. Until then, trust me."*

Eli planted his feet when I tried to steer him toward the door. *"Did you think about the bus station, gym, or the bank?"*

"Yes. Now go to breakfast."

He danced around my grasping hand. *"And the lake house? The key doesn't have to open something in town. Remember Dad had that shed that he kept padlocked."*

"The police would have busted in there already."

"Doesn't mean Mom and Dad didn't hide something there that they missed. You have to check the lake house."

The lake house was a five-hour drive up the coast. The feds, and a thick layer of undisturbed dust, confirmed my parents hadn't stopped by the lake house on their way to the airport. But...

"I will go to the lake house and check it out."

"I'm coming with you," Eli replied.

"No."

"Yes."

"How's that going to happen, Eli? I can sign myself out, but you need permission from Aunt or Uncle. What are we going to tell them about a five-hour trip?"

"We could say—"

"Oh, hey, guys." Camila broke into our argument. "Were you waiting for me? I'll be ready in a few minutes."

"We could say we want to be somewhere that feels like home," Eli plowed on. *"I could cry to sell it."*

"This kid," I muttered. *"It's not happening, so drop it. I have to keep you safe whether it pisses you off or not."*

"Who asked you to?!"

Eli slammed out the door.

I sighed. Is this karma for all the trouble I caused my parents as a teenager?

Camila came out of the bathroom. "Ready. Where did Eli go?"

"He left to meet up with his friends." I eyed her as she donned her backpack and grabbed lip gloss off the dresser. "Have you talked to your brothers yet?"

"No. Why?"

I shut my mouth. Her carefree attitude made sense if she hadn't seen what was done to the boys. I didn't know how much Camila knew or how her brothers wanted to explain this.

"Just asking," I said simply.

Camila's sunny morning ended on the bottom floor. We exited the dorm just as Royal, Cassius, and Clay rounded the building.

"Oh my god!" Her backpack crashed on the concrete. "What happened to you two?!"

"We're fine, Cam," Clay tried. "Don't—"

She burst into tears.

The boys gathered her up, carrying her inside and away from prying eyes. I thought Royal would wait for me, but he loped off, disappearing through the back door into the main building.

I went to breakfast by myself. Camila was in a state. Eli was steamed at me. Royal was off being Royal. That left just the two of us.

"Hey, Em— What happened to your head?" Brandon's touch was gentle on my forehead. "Are you okay?"

"I'm fine when I'm not clumsy. I got banged up tripping over my own feet." *Into the butt of a gun.*

We stepped up to the food line, grabbing trays, cups, and forks as we went. "How was your weekend?"

He shrugged. "Hung out. Did homework. Played video games with my roommate. The usual."

Our table waited for us at the back of the senior loft. It wasn't empty. Gabriel Lighthouse sat there speaking to the last person I expected to see.

Pomona stood over him, arms crossed, and body angled away so we couldn't see her expression. She pointed over her shoulder—couldn't be certain at what—and then shook her head. Gabriel leaned forward, eyes, posture, and frown pleading insistence. She handed him something, turned her back, and walked away.

Pomona brushed past me. "Bitch."

"Fuck you."

Good to see some things never changed.

"What was that about?" Brandon asked as we dropped our trays and joined him.

"Nothing." Gabriel shoved his hand in his pocket. "Mona was driving the point home that I'm out. Mrs. Bancroft and the society mothers are throwing a Thanksgiving party for us when we all come home. I'm not allowed to show up."

"It turns my stomach that they're mad at you and not Leo," I spat. "What more does Leo have to do? Who else does he have to hurt before they see him for what he is?"

"They don't believe he hurt anyone, Ember. They won't take your word over his." Gabriel dropped his head. "Can we change the subject?"

Gabriel was a handsome guy, even cloaked in misery. His coarse brown hair was shaved on the sides and the tips of his ears pointed to an almost elven effect. Those were his unique features. Every other bit of him was classic good looks from the charming smile on his full lips, the strong jaw, and up to those light brown eyes.

It might have been a consequence of growing up in the Estate that he didn't realize the world was much bigger than the Raveners and what they thought of him. Once he set out of this town, he'd find the world opens up for smart, handsome rich boys who respect women.

"Good idea," said Brandon. "Camila's coming and she looks upset."

I followed his line of sight to the triplet ascending the stairs. From across the space I saw her splotchy cheeks and red eyes. Cassius and Clay came behind her.

A low whistle sounded to my right. "Damn," said Brandon. "What happened to them?"

Camila sat down across from me. "Hi, guys." She was the picture of anguish, and I couldn't blame her. I didn't fare much better when I came face to face with what those guys did to them.

Gabriel's and Brandon's questioning of if she was okay faded in the background. Now they were in my orbit, I could look nowhere else but at Cassius and Clay. Broken and bandaged from head to toe, it didn't hinder their status as the most gorgeous men in the room.

With the biggest hearts. They took that beating for me, and I know they stay in the gang to get Camila out of Raven River and away from this life.

Clay caught my eye and sent me a smile that made my stomach bubble and my core clench at the same time—for his smiles were always tinged with naughty.

He glanced down at his lap. Seconds later, my phone buzzed.

Clay: What are you doing tonight?

Me: Spending time with you.

Clay: Correct answer. I've got my and other people's home-work to finish, but I'll be done by nine. Too late?

My grin split my cheeks so wide it hurt.

Me: Not too late. Nine is perfect.

Clay: Good. Wear something warm.

"Let's talk happy things," I spoke up, putting away my phone. "Like getting far away from this town. Where are you guys going to university?"

"I got accepted to Dartmouth early admission," said Gabriel. He scraped the strawberries off his pancakes onto a separate plate and passed it to Camila without her asking. Apparently, he noticed she often helped herself to more fruit.

Further proof the Raveners can act like decent human beings when they're removed from the cult and deprogrammed.

"I want to be somewhere warm," Camila said. "I applied to a bunch of schools in the South. The University of Florida is my top choice."

"Going the opposite direction," Brandon said. "New York. I'm biting my nails waiting to hear from Columbia and NYU. What about you, B?"

I shook my head. "I applied to a bunch of places last year but things are different now. I'm not leaving Eli here on his own. After he graduates, I'm looking at schools in the cities. I'm over this small-town life."

"Hit me up in New York when that happens, B," said Brandon. "We can share a..." Brandon trailed off. His face went slack. "You can't be serious."

Brandon was looking at something over Gabriel's and Camila's heads, and when I saw what, my good mood deflated like a wheezing, screaming balloon. A roaring deafened my ears, blocking everything out as Leonardo Tremaine climbed the stairs.

Leo climbed the stairs holding a breakfast tray.

He climbed the stairs with his breakfast and in full uniform.

He climbed the stairs with his breakfast, uniform neat and pressed, and backpack hanging off his shoulders.

He climbed the stairs, ready for his first day back to school, looked me right in the eyes, and winked.

Leonardo Tremaine climbed the stairs of the senior loft and two things happened at once.

Camila clapped her hands over her mouth, tears springing to her red eyes. And Cassius and Clay launched over their table, tackling him just as the smirk wiped off his face and his tray hit the floor.

Chapter Four

The loft devolved into complete pandemonium. Seniors were screaming, shouting, and either trying to get near the fight or get away from it.

Leonardo and his disgusting wink disappeared in a sea of bodies. His Ravener friends ran to help him. A few OB kids ran to pull Cassius and Clay off, and others just ran.

Camila sprang up, cheeks soaked, and pushed through the throng to reach her brothers. I was right on her heels.

We shoved Fiona and Remington aside and broke through the circle. Beau, Wilder, Nolan, and Julian pulled the guys apart. Beau and Wilder struggled to hold on to the triplets. It took four more guys to stop them launching at Leo. The same number of officers that had to hold them back as they arrested Leo.

The filthy winking piece of garbage probably wished those officers were here to protect him. His blazer was torn at the shoulder. Blood dripped from his nose and lip, collecting in a growing stain on his bleached white shirt.

Roaring, Clay threw off three guys. "You don't fucking eat here!" Clay snatched his pancake off the floor and smashed it in Leo's face before the guys grabbed him again. "Get out! You're not anywhere my sister is, you rapist fuck!"

"I didn't touch her!" Leo screamed. "Bancroft lied! The bitch fucking lied!"

Cassius got free. He dove for Leo who almost knocked his friends on their asses scrambling away. Camila shot in front of him, halting Cassius in his tracks better than anyone else could. She threw her arms around him, sobbing into his chest.

"They were stupid not to lock your ass up, but not as stupid as you for coming back here," Cassius snarled. "From now on, you don't eat in this cafeteria. You don't walk in the same hall as Cam. You don't sit in the same class! Am I fucking clear?!"

Julian bared his teeth. "Fuck off. No one is scared—"

"What was that?" Clay knocked one of his captors down launching at Julian. They were red-faced and grunting holding him back. "What the fuck did you say, Hart? Did someone tell you to open your mouth?!"

I was stuck to the spot. Kids jostled me and the crowd only grew as underclassmen ran up the stairs. The Cassius and Clay before me were men I'd never met before.

Clay got his hand free and pointed at Julian. "You've got a lesson in respect coming your way, bitch, and you'll get it after we've taken care of that shit *and* Ives!"

Nolan jumped, eyes bulging, and whipping his head around like he couldn't understand why he was included.

"Say something else!" Clay dared.

Julian looked like he wouldn't say anything else for the rest of his life. He flushed so pale his silver hair appeared white, but contempt chilled his icy blues and roused me to move.

"Clay, please." I reached through his shield and cupped his cheek. "Camila needs you right now."

Camila's cries only backed me up.

Julian bit off a curse and grabbed hold of Leo. He and Nolan took him downstairs.

"You're a ghost, Tremaine," Cassius barked. "A fucking ghost!"

"What is going on?!" a teacher shouted way too late. "Break it up. All of you get to class now!"

Clay growled at the guys with their hands on him. "If you don't fuck off—"

They released him before he finished his threat. I held my breath as he bore down on me. Raw power charged the air and automatically set off my base instincts of fight, flight, or freeze. I went with freeze. I wasn't frightened—more like I was so turned on, I was worried if I moved, my clenched thighs would betray me and I'd fall flat on my face.

Taking hold of my chin, Clay pulled me in for a kiss that set fire to the last of my self-control. It was hot and brutal and perfect just like Clay Walker.

We broke apart, me gasping in dazed delight.

"I've got to take care of Cam," he said, "but I'll see you tonight."

Clay and Cassius led their sister down moments before Mr. Geske forced his way up, looking for the culprits.

GESKE NEVER DID GET answers to his questions.

Brandon and I slid past him like nothing happened.

"I can't believe they let him go," Brandon raged. "What does it say to every girl in this school? That if they've got a little bit of money, an attempted rapist can run free on campus. Fuck your safety."

I might have said something but Brandon was covering it pretty well for the both of us. Disgust turned my stomach and shot bile in my throat. He wasn't even gone that long. It took no time at all for the system to say screw you to the OB girl and toss the rich Ravener back on the street.

"Headmistress Hart has to do something about this," I said. "We've got a dealer on campus slinging out drugs and roofies on demand, and the Raveners buy his stuff. At their next party, Leo could try again to take advantage of a vulnerable girl."

"I'd like to think even though the Raveners are defending him, in the back of their minds they're looking at Leo twice. They won't let him walk any drunk girls back to their rooms ever again."

"It's not enough."

"I know, B." He drew me to his side. "I know."

Brandon and I climbed the stairs to the third floor. We topped the landing and the question of where Royal Cruz was during the breakfast showdown was answered in an instant.

Royal propped his arm on the locker, boxing in a Destiny Hamilton who looked extremely pleased at the proximity. She grinned flirtatiously at him, lip between her teeth, upturned nose wrinkled cutely, and cleavage pushed out as far as it would go. Destiny rested her foot on the locker, letting her knee brush his inner thigh, and a vivid picture flashed through my head of those knees sinking into his mattress while he pounded her from behind and ordered her to scream.

Royal must have sensed me drilling a hole in his head because he suddenly looked up and saw me standing there. Royal captured my gaze... and winked.

If one more asshole winks at me today, I swear.

I streamed past, flipping him off, and was treated to his laughter all the way down the hall.

"What was that about?" Brandon asked.

"It's another one of those secret national holidays for men to be as infuriating as possible."

Brandon slid in front of my locker. "But not me, right?" He fluttered his lashes, widening those green eyes. "You love me."

"You wish I did," I said with a laugh.

He heaved a sigh. "It's true, I do. But the de-quillification process is a long one."

I tossed him out of the way, giggling. I read nothing into his wish that I'd love him. In the time we've hung out, Brandon didn't give the slightest signal that he was interested in me as more than a friend. I might not have been his type, or maybe he wasn't interested in dating a girl with more baggage than an airport. Either way, it was nice to have one uncomplicated relationship in my life.

"You get points for bucking the holiday and not being irritating," I said as I spun the dial. "I was thinking maybe the three of us, or four if Gabriel's down, should hang in our room this weekend and binge on movies with Camila. I want her to know she has support through all of this."

"For sure, B. You don't have to ask. I'll even stomach some rom-coms if it'll make her smile."

I flashed a grin his way. "Oh? How sweet. I'll make sure Camila knows how much you care about her smile."

I was teasing, but Brandon ducked his head, mumbling something, and turned his back on me to open his locker. I threw open mine to an unwelcome, but unsurprising present. A single folded note delivered the horrible, crushing visions of Eli battered and bleeding on a cot.

Silently, I unfolded it in the locker, careful not to let Brandon see.

No magazine cut-outs this time. This note was longer and typed in simple, small black letters.

You were lying about not having any money. Too bad you made us resort to that to get you to cut the bullshit. Now that we understand each other, one thousand dollars in locker 487 by next Monday. You know what will happen if it's not there.

I crumpled the note and flung it behind my textbooks.

No, I didn't know what would happen because they sure as hell weren't touching Eli again. Mr. Johnston was ten times more vigilant and Eli was rarely alone between me, his classmates, and his roommate.

Maybe they mean they'll attack me next. If that's the case, I'm tempted not to pay. I want those fuckers to come to me. I'll snap every finger that touched Eli.

I marched off to homeroom. Royal sat in his usual seat, taking up the back row alone. The triplets weren't here and I didn't expect them anytime soon. I hoped they were in Hart's office finding out what she planned to do about Leo.

Royal's head was in a sketch. I sat down and leaned back in my seat. Arms surrounded me, pressing me into the chest on my back. Royal rested his chin on my shoulder and placed the notebook on my desk.

"What do you think of my latest?"

He lazily flipped through drawings of me, me, and me in various positions and in all of them naked. Me with my ass in the air and my face stuck to a leather seat. Me riding him like a mechanical bull. Me wet and laughing in the shower while he cupped my breasts from the back. And a particularly detailed sketch of me on my back in his bed, legs spread and finger crooked begging for more.

I shifted in my seat, panties damp and the day just started.

"Nice," I said casually. "Glad you were able to fit drawing these beauties in between flirting with Destiny."

Royal's laugh was the real drug. I'd cut myself open if it'd make him do it again.

"Jealousy looks good on you." He licked my neck. "Tastes good too."

"Is that what you were trying to do?" I asked. "Make me jealous? Because when you've got me where you want me..." I traced the outline of my drawn curves. "Doesn't seem like a smart move to get on my nerves."

"Very true. So, take this as a peace offering." Royal flipped the page. "I drew it for you."

I stilled. It was me, but I wasn't naked or begging for Royal through the page. I knelt before Rory's headstone, holding a bouquet of brilliant reds, golds, purples, and pinks.

Royal drew in color.

From the crystal-clear sky to the vibrant green grass, his sketch was alive with beauty, expression, and meaning only I would under- stand.

"Too far?" he asked, voice soft. "I know this topic is off-limits, but I thought you'd want to have this. You're always with her, Em, even when you can't be there."

Tears prickled behind my eyes. It wasn't fair that he kept doing this. Drive me insane one minute and then the next do something above and beyond. My heart expanded taking in the drawing of Roy- al's that would forever be my favorite.

"No," I whispered. "Not too far. I love it."

"Good." He pressed a kiss under my ear. "Want to know what I found out from Destiny?"

Nodding, I took the notebook and held it to my chest. "I'm lis- tening."

"She doesn't buy the stuff direct. Destiny gives the money to her friend Vera who texts a number asking for what they want and how much. The person on the other end texts back a different unassigned locker each time and they stick the money in one day and drugs ap- pear in the locker the next. This guy is smarter than we thought, Em. Destiny swears they never met the guy. They can't even say if they are a guy."

"Unassigned locker number," I repeated. "Eli's attackers pulled the same trick. Do you think they...?"

"Could be," he said, picking up where I trailed off. "We don't have anything to go on for either of them, so there's no reason to think they're not the same person."

"They sent me another note."

"When?" His anger was unmistakable. "What did it say?"

"They want one thousand dollars by next week. He's not buying that I don't have money after the last drop, so he's testing his limits. The note came with the standard 'or else.'"

He swore. "We can't talk about this here. My room after class."

I agreed. Fishing out my homework, I busied myself with English to take my mind off the impending disasters.

Leo. Camila. Eli. The dealer. The attackers. The key. All of it spun in my head demanding my attention.

By some miracle, I made it through the day. I stopped in my room on the way to Royal's. Camila was curled up in her bed, music playing on low.

"Hey," I said. "I'm not staying. You can have your space."

I went to my nightstand and tucked the drawing Royal gave me into the music box.

"Don't leave because of me." Camila sat up, wiping her face on her comforter. "I'm glad you're here. You won't believe it, Ember."

I sank onto my mattress. If Camila wanted to talk, I was here to listen. "What's going on?"

"We went to Hart after the cafeteria and she called Officer Ramadi so we'd hear it from her. There isn't enough evidence to make a charge stick. Leo wasn't on the video spiking my drink or pouring alcohol down my throat."

She sniffed. I passed her the box of tissues before she reached for it. "What happened after I can't remember, so it's your word against Leo's," she continued. "He told the police he brought me in the room, laid me down, and I started going on about getting into my pajamas. I began taking my own clothes off, too out of it to wait until he left, and then you busted in and got the wrong idea."

"Bullshit," I cried. "My screaming brought other girls out of their rooms. A few of them saw him scrambling to put his dick away. How does he explain that?"

"According to him, he wasn't wearing a belt and his pants were sagging. They came down when he tripped. You catching him pulling them up was completely innocent."

I scoffed. "You're right, I can't believe this. They swallowed that heap of lawyer-fed garbage and sent him right back here."

"There's no physical evidence." It sounded like Ramadi's words, not hers. "You saving me in time made the case difficult to prosecute, and I'm not sorry for that."

I moved over to her bed. She let me take her hands. "I am sorry, Camila. I wish there was something I could do."

She gave a smile that trembled. "Weren't you listening? You've already done everything, Ember. I couldn't be more grateful to you if you went back in time and stopped me from ever going to that damn party or dating Nolan Ives."

I bumped her shoulder. "You are doing and you have done everything right, Camila. It's those guys who've done wrong and them who will pay the consequences for it. One way or another, they are not getting away with it."

Camila held my arm to her chest, tugging me close to put her head on my shoulder. "I know they won't."

She said that with such confidence unease trickled in. Does she know they won't because her brothers are taking over?

"What happens now?" I asked.

"Cassius and Clay told Hart to transfer Leo out of my classes and install cameras in the dorm. Turns out she was going to do both of those things anyway. Leo is now on probation and she's kicking him out if he so much as talks back in class."

"What do Cassius and Clay think about it?"

"We're relieved Hart is taking this seriously. It'd be even worse if she believed his garbage too." She looked up at me. "Hey, are you busy? I thought maybe we can watch a movie or something."

"I'm swinging by Royal's," I said. "We might be closer to figuring out who attacked Eli."

"Oh, that's good. I can't wait to see those bastards expelled."

"Me too. When I come back, we'll watch the movie."

I waved bye to Camila and crossed two locked doors to knock on Royal's.

He opened the door in his usual state of undress—boxers only. He started in on the click of the lock.

"One thousand in a week," he said. Royal returned to his bed. "They're upping their game. Might ask for more the next time. Do you still have money from the Porsche?"

I nodded. "I've saved it for this, but if they are going to ask for more each time, I'm going to be out quick."

"We can do another job, but not from the student parking lot. The Raveners have that Thanksgiving party coming up. That's the best time. If it comes to it, I'll cover you until then."

I didn't say anything at first. Instead, I rested my head in the crook of his neck. He was ready with the solution like this situation was our problem and not mine.

"You don't need to cover me," I said. "You've got an apartment, rent, bills, gas, and an endless supply of notebooks to buy. You have enough responsibilities. Draining your bank account for this blackmailing trash isn't one of them."

"I'm not draining anything. This won't hurt me, but it might hurt you. Eli's harder to get to now. He's not going anywhere alone. You, on the other hand, have a lot of people willing to look the other way if masked guys run up on you. That's not fucking happening while I run this school."

I guided him flat on the mattress and sat on his lap, grinning as he immediately grasped my waist and rocked me on his middle.

"Thank you," I said. "If it comes to that, I will pay you back."

This wasn't the time for pride. Eli was harder to get to but that didn't mean the bastards wouldn't try. Mr. Johnston didn't follow my brother into the bathroom or locker room. And if they busted into his dorm, Tatum was as much protection as a short, thin, fourteen-year-old boy could be. While there was even the slightest chance that they could hurt my brother, I wasn't turning down offers of help.

"The Thanksgiving dinner," I ventured. "Why does it have to be then?"

"Those parties are Christmas for a car thief, princess. On a normal day, their cars are locked up behind gates, security systems, guards, and garages. It's a whole different skill set breaking onto property. A different crime too.

"Nah, I want them driving those cars off the driveway themselves, parking them in a darkened lot watched over by one bored valet, and then leaving it alone for hours while they get wasted."

"Huh." Hearing him say it, his reasons made perfect sense. So perfect I had to think it'd cross a few other minds to sling their shot as well.

Royal hardened under me. I wasn't sure if he was turned on from the car-stealing talk or his practically screwing me through my clothes. Possibly both.

"I see what you're saying, but if you do this regularly, why haven't they noticed their cars go missing during these parties."

"I mix it up for that reason. I'll hit a party maybe once or twice a year." He tapped my chin. "That's why it took so long for us to meet."

"Lucky for me you picked that party."

He grinned. "Lucky for me too."

I rolled my eyes, but in a way that was so damned fond I should've skipped to kissing him.

"They have upped security," he admitted. "But I've got ways around it. So, you in? Same deal as before. You do most of the work, you get the pay."

A noticeably harder thrust pushed a moan from my lips. Royal was waiting for my yes, so we could move on to the other part of the evening.

Am I honestly doing this? Is this who I am now? A car thief?

You're protecting Eli, another voice countered. *You don't do this because you want to. You haven't touched the money from Caesar other than paying the blackmailer. This is about nothing more than surviving an impossible situation.*

Sighing, I squeezed my eyes shut, holding my breath. There were real people involved. People who'd leave the party and suddenly find themselves the victims of what I'd done.

"I can't do this for weeks, months, years," I said. "I have to find the person or people coming after me and shut them down."

"We will. They're going to slip up, make a mistake, and the Angels will be there when they do."

Royal got under my blazer and got it off in one smooth move.

"I'm supposed to hang with Camila this afternoon," I said while undoing my buttons. "And then I'm with Clay tonight. I can't stay."

"We got plans this week, princess. Don't think I'll make it easy for you to get out of this bed."

"Roy— Ah!"

He flipped me on my back and set to work.

The guy most certainly did not make it easy. He flung his clock across the room, literally tied me to the bed, and said I couldn't leave until I asked nicely. I was very much not nice through multiple orgasms. When I finally stumbled to my room, I was surprised to see it was pushing seven o'clock.

"Sorry it took so long," I said to Camila. She was sitting up in bed with dinner on her lap and a computer resting on her calves. I guessed she got through a few movies already. "I'll hop in the shower and then I'm all yours."

"Okay. Are you feeling Matthew McConaughey or Adam Sandler?" she called after me.

I cracked the bathroom door, speaking to her as I undressed. "Adam Sandler? Which movie?"

"*50 First Dates.* It's my go-to feeling-crappy movie. Don't judge me."

I laughed. "How can I when it's mine too? Queue that bad boy up."

Camila clapped. "Yay."

We weren't insta-friends after Leo and her moving in here. Camila was growing on me, though, and if anything I could do would make her feel better, I was happy to do it.

"Did you eat dinner?" she asked. "I can ask Cassius to bring it up for you."

"No, that's what my brother is for. The kid is vexed with me anyway, so it's my chance to force him up here and love him into submission."

"You're hilarious, Em."

My eyebrows shot up. Nicknames? Maybe we were friends.

I shot Eli a text and then hopped in the shower. My afternoon with Royal sluiced down the drain, but I'd be back again the next day to indulge the heady perfume of citrus, sweat, and sex we made together.

Eli showed up with a tray soon after I got dressed. His face was pinched like it got when he was ticked at me and was planning to hold on to that grudge until one of us died. Proving I was hilarious *and* honest, I took the tray off his hands, picked him up, and tossed him on the bed. Eli flailed as I jumped on him, peppering him with kisses, and tickled the breath from his lungs.

He eventually got away from me. Red-faced, Eli threw all the pillows on my bed at me as was my standard punishment.

"Please understand, Eli." I got serious. *"You can't come with me on this. It's too dangerous."*

"If it's dangerous for me, it's dangerous for you. Who is going to have your back?"

"Royal is helping me."

Surprise overcame his features. *"He is?"*

"Yes. I won't be on my own. Eli, you can't do this with me, but I will tell you everything. I promise. No holding back or keeping you in the dark. If I find out where our parents are, you will be the first one I tell."

He dropped his shoulders, anger and tension seeping out. After a minute, he nodded.

I held out my arms. "I'll take my hug now."

Eli pinked, cutting eyes to Camila, but in the end, he squeezed me tight.

"Want to stay for the movie?" I asked him.

He nodded yes. The three of us scrunched up on Camila's bed, laughing at jokes we laughed at before, while I snuck glances at the clock. Clay was picking me up at nine for our... date?

Was it a date? Or were we skipping to bed like I did with Cassius and Royal?

He told me to wrap up warm. We have to be going outside.

Doesn't mean there won't be sex involved, added the sex-drunk vixen that was my new alter ego. *It's good I put on my sexiest underwear just in case.*

The movie wrapped up a little before nine. I walked Eli out in time for Clay to come out of the boys' side.

"Hey, Ember. You ready?"

Clay was so perfectly perfect a goofy smile fought my lips. His hair was damp from a shower. A warm sweater and loose jeans clung to his frame—much like I planned to.

"I'm ready. Walk Eli to his dorm with me and then we can go."

"Sounds good." As though it was natural, Clay laced his fingers through mine and kissed my hand.

Shivers traveled up my arm and turned my goofy smile up to maximum. We stood there grinning at each other until I noticed Eli openly staring at me.

"*Are you guys going on a date?*"

I couldn't fault him. He got his bluntness from growing up around me.

"*Yeah. First one.*"

He crooked a brow. "*What happened to 'stay away from the Angels, Eli'?*"

If anyone could inject wry smugness into sign language, it was my brother.

"*Things change. They're watching out for us now. The Angels told the school you're not to be touched.*"

"*Really? That's cool of them.*" He cocked his head. "*Does this mean I can ask Royal to design my future tattoo?*"

"*You two can design plans to drive me crazy. You're both the experts.*"

Laughing, he stepped on the elevator.

"Why does it seem like I witnessed a battle you lost?" asked Clay.

"Because that's my every day with this imp." I hooked Eli around the shoulder and dropped a kiss on his crown. "He's particularly amused by my going on a date with a guy I warned him to stay away from a few weeks ago."

"A date, huh?"

I peeked at him through lowered lashes. "Did I use the wrong word?"

Clay stroked my thumb. "No."

We said bye to Eli on the first floor. I waited till he was in his dorm and then turned to Clay. "So, why did I have to dress warm? Are we going outside?"

"We are."

"Hmm. What's a date with Clay Walker like?"

I left the dorm tucked under his arm.

"Haven't been on enough to form a pattern," he said, chuckling. "I don't really date. I stick to hooking up."

"Why?"

"You see our lives. Cas and I don't have time between doing our schoolwork and everyone else's. We've got the poker game. We've got the SATs. We've got Rio. Few women are willing to put up with it, and they shouldn't have to. They— *You* deserve a guy who will be there for you one hundred percent."

It was my turn to kiss his hand. Clay was so damn sweet sometimes; I'd forget he was the same guy who burned my underwear.

I like my new ones much better anyway. I held his hand between my breasts and the black lace bra he'd be seeing shortly.

"I've got three of you," I said. "If you think about it, each of you only has to be there for me thirty-three percent and I'm covered."

I wasn't sure how my joke would go over, so for Clay to throw his head back howling was a win. "You're going to get a lot more than thirty-three percent out of me."

Happiness flooded me and curled my toes. I could get three percent of Clay and feel like I won the lottery. Life was busy, chaotic, messy, and short. My parents taught me the hard lesson of cherishing the moments you had because too soon, they would be gone.

Together Clay and I ambled past the tennis courts. Looming near the millennium garden stood the pavilion. A shaded area for students to sit outside and enjoy their studying with a side of fresh air. I slowed down, assuming this was our stop, but Clay tugged me on.

"Not here."

We kept walking and walking. Past the basketball court. Past the soccer field. Past the open area where Coach Sutton liked to have her obstacle courses.

Clay led me to the edge of the academy's property where a single fence separated us from endless forest. This part of the grounds was cloaked in shadows. I barely made out Clay as he moved to the fence.

"Do you have your phone?" His voice reached me through the darkness. "The flashlight is enough." Clay's flicked on at the end of his sentence. "There's a break in the fence here. I've been sneaking through it since I was a freshman."

"Wow." Clay held it open for me to pass. "Does everyone know about this? Is this how Hiro gets product in?"

"No. Hiro's secret is actually much simpler than that. You'd be surprised."

"You could end my curiosity right now."

Ducking through, Clay pecked between my brows. "You'd have to get him to tell you. Good luck," he joked.

"Nice."

"As for this way out, I bet other people know, but I've never seen anyone else out here."

"This is your place to get away. Chill. Think." My light beam swept the undulating branches and the soft earthen blanket of dirt, flowers, and fallen leaves. "A beautiful place."

"Wait until we get there," Clay said, reclaiming my hand. "You'll see beautiful."

Clay was sure-footed, ushering me over felled trees and sneaky roots without a break in his step.

"How are you?" I asked. "This morning in the cafeteria was… bad."

In the dim light, the line of his shoulders went taut. "We're not stupid. The cops say there isn't enough evidence, but if an OB kid was accused of the same thing, they'd be expelled. Hart says she is doing everything she can. It's not enough."

"Are you going to do more? I thought you guys decided to handle things peacefully when you didn't go after Nolan."

"Ives is still breathing because Cas and I will be the first ones they look at when he goes down. My sister has gone through enough without throwing the two of us getting kicked out of school on top. We'll get him when the time is right."

"Will you hurt him?" I said Eli got his bluntness from me.

"Should I?" His reply was light and easy. "What does a man deserve for leaving a girl stranded in the forest for not sleeping with him and laughing while drunk shits drug his girlfriend?"

I swallowed hard. "Deserves worse than whatever you're planning, I'd say."

Clay twisted, meeting my eyes in the dark. Something passed between us that we did not voice and I didn't consciously understand.

"It's just through there," he said.

Clay guided me over a small mound. The forest opened up beneath us.

"Wow," I breathed. "You can say a lot about our craphole town, but nothing against its namesake."

Raven River was a stretch of clear rushing water. It teemed with life that zipped away from kicking feet and splashing fists. I learned to swim in the river, held by my dad as I stuck my head in the water searching for fish. I carried only happy memories of lying on the bank, toes lapped by the waves and soaking the sun beating through the trees. Clay brought me here to make another one.

A blanket was laid out on the bank. Lamplights covered the corners and the river reached for it, lapping at the earth like it once did my wrinkled feet.

I kicked off my shoes, dropping down on the blanket with Clay. We stretched out, me on top of him, propping my chin on his chest and my hips on his.

"This is incredible, Clay."

He pointed to the tree nearest us. The roots rose high out of the ground. "That's where I sit. Just come out and do homework. Read. Dry off after a swim. It's a different kind of quiet out here. Know what I mean?"

A different kind of quiet.

The forest was far from quiet. The river babbled its retreat to the oceans. Fish splashed leaping in and out of the water. Birds cheeped in the trees. Raccoons chittered. Squirrels scurried. Foxes slipped through the bush. Those sounds melded together to sing a soothing symphony of life and grant you the peace you'd never achieve among honking horns and loud neighbors. It was—

"A different kind of quiet," I said softly. "I know exactly what you mean."

"Someone honestly would clean up building a resort in this place," Clay reflected. "There's something about it."

"There's something about it being untouched. You can find little spots like this and claim it for your own. We won't have that anymore if tourists discover this place. I was swimming along the bank the first time I saw a baby fox. He didn't know to be scared. Didn't know there were parts of the forest he had to steer clear of."

"Camila freaked out the first time she saw a fox. Screamed and pushed Dad off the dock."

"What?" I laughed. "Did she blame him?"

His chuckles shook my body. "The last part was an accident. She ran, jumped on him, and knocked him off balance. They both went down and Mom snapped that bug-eyed surprise just before they hit water."

"Your mom?" I scooted up, pressing my nose on his. "You never talk about your mom."

"You never talk about yours."

I clicked my tongue. "You triplets are forever catching me out."

Clay dropped little kisses on my pouting lips. "Absent moms are a tough topic for anyone. No one can mess us up quite like they can."

"Therapists bank second homes and yachts just on mommy issues."

We cracked up on what had to be the least funny issue ever. All the same we couldn't stop.

"My school counselor walked away with complexes of her own after dealing with me," I said. "I get the added gift of looking just like Mom. I start every day seeing her in the mirror, wondering where she is and if she spares a second of her day thinking about me."

"She does," Clay said, assured like he spoke to her himself. "You're not the kind of girl that can be forgotten."

I kissed him longer, slower, deeper.

We weren't doing anything above a PG rating. Clay folded his hands behind his head, mine were above the waist, and our clothes were neat and buttoned. Somehow, here with Clay in his tucked-away spot, was one of the most intimate moments of my life. I felt myself growing closer to him.

"Your mom thinks of you too."

"I know she does," he replied. "She tells Cas all the time she wishes our lives were different."

"Tells Cas?" I lifted my head. "What do you mean?"

Clay gazed high above the trees. "He can't resist seeing her when he goes to the clinic."

"You mean you—"

"Know where she is," he finished. "Yep. She left home but couldn't get far out of town without money. We didn't know how to find her when we were little, but by now we know her favorite shelters and the friends that let her crash on their couch. Cas checks on her, gives her money, and talks her into coming home sometimes. She doesn't stay long but Dad is always happy to see her."

I smoothed out the stiff lines around his eyes. Clay put on a matter-of-fact show, but he was tensing underneath me. "I can't imagine how hard it is for you guys."

"It is what it is. Mom goes off her meds, gets confused, and slips away. We can't force the meds down her throat. We can't lock her in the house. And we can't stop the old man from drinking. Life is about accepting the crap you can't change and focusing on what you can."

I hummed. "I would say that's cynical if life hadn't kicked the same lesson into my head."

"You know what I can do right now?"

"Whaaat?" I drew out as I spotted the smirk.

"Get you out of those clothes and in that water."

Just like that, giddiness returned in a flash. "I don't think you can, Clay Walker. The water is freezing!"

"I'll sweeten the deal for you." Clay flipped me over and stood. "I'll ask you questions. Anything I want. For every honest answer, I'll strip something off."

"I'm liking this game so far."

He chuckled, grabbing the hem of his sweater. "The catch is I step closer to the river for each question, then my naked ass is jumping in, and if you want to get your hands on it, you have to jump in too."

Holy crap. This player is about to get me in that chilly river.

I swung my legs back and forth, rocking on my hips. "I accept your terms," I purred.

"Sweet. First question: Bottom or top."

"Don't you know the answer to that?" I laughed.

"Just 'cause you end up on the bottom, doesn't mean it's where you prefer to be."

I loved that there was no weirdness about this. I was sleeping with his friend and brother—often in front of him—but Clay and I were just us. Mature and secure in wherever our relationship was heading.

"Bottom."

Clay dropped his sweater at my feet. "Next," he said, backing up a couple of steps. "If you get out of this craphole, where will you go?"

"Ooh. Somewhere with lots of life, people, foods, and noises. I've had this dream about New York since I was little."

"You ever been?"

"Two questions means the shirt and the pants," I teased.

"Sounds fair."

"No, I've never been. Mom and Dad didn't like cities. We vacationed on islands or lake retreats."

"Not a bad trade-off." Clay stripped out of his shirt and jeans as promised. He backed up and moonlight embraced his sculpted inked body. He was so beautiful. Dark and tortured, but reformed in a righteous battle for those he loved. A true angel.

I rose up, shrugging out of my clothes. Clay feasted on me in my lace bra and panties that left nothing to the imagination. My toes imprinted the soft earth as I swallowed the distance between us and stepped into Clay's waiting arms.

"Next question," I whispered.

"Do you want to be with me, Ember?"

My reply was instant. "I want to be with you more than I want Nerds, cream soda, and world peace." I tugged his boxers down. "Ask a hard one this time."

Clay chuckled as he removed my bra and helped me out of my panties. Together we stepped back, sinking knee-deep in the water.

"Do you know how I feel about you?" he asked, lips brushing mine in a kiss that wasn't but should be.

"That's the thing about you, Clay. You're smart, strong, fearless, and feared, but you wear your heart on your sleeve. I don't know anyone who loves harder than you do. Who has sacrificed more. I know how you feel about me, and it makes me happier than I can put into words that I'm someone you... care for."

It wasn't right to name his feelings anything else. Not before he did.

"Care for?" he repeated. "You say you can't find the words but those are still too small."

I kissed him. "What words would you use?" Then kissed him again.

"I wouldn't use words at all."

We sank into the rushing water, mouths clashing heat, fire, lust, and more. The water was bitterly frigid. I clung to him tighter. My source of heat.

Protection.

Safety.

Clay held my hands as he told me he'd free me from the Horsemen. He held me as I sat in that terrible office, waiting to die. And he held me then. In the water desperate to carry us away, Clay was my lifeline.

It wasn't right to name his feelings, but I could name mine as Raven River embraced us, reminding that this was the one place where we didn't have to be scared.

"TELL ME A SECRET."

Clay glided on the surface, relaxed on his back, and hands lazily slicing the water. I was wrapped around his waist, satisfied to let him carry me.

"I don't have secrets," he replied.

"Liar."

Clay barked a laugh. "Fine. I don't have interesting secrets. Not ones that you don't already know about."

"Tell me an uninteresting one." A firefly drifted close to my face, joined quickly by a mate. The two flew off together, hopefully to live uncomplicated lives.

"I've been to New York."

"You have? When?"

"Two years ago, Rio sent Dad on a job and he took me. I think Rio made him bring me along to ensure it got done. But whatever the reason, I got to leave this town. Turns out there is a whole world out there. The globes they've got in class aren't a prank after all."

I bopped his nose. "How'd you like it on the outside?"

"New York is everything you want, Em. You'll get there one day."

Tilting my head to the moon, a smile graced my lips as I pictured. "Eli will have a room that's half library. All of the books he wants. Every morning, I'll eat muffins on the couch while the sun streams in. At night, I'll sit on my balcony and listen to the city. In the summer, Eli and I will walk on melting sidewalks through the boroughs, and in the winter, we'll ice-skate and drink every kind of hot cocoa until spring comes back."

"There is one guy in this future. Do you have room for any more?"

"Maybe one, two, or three," I teased. "You never know."

"Kids?"

"Yes."

"Pets?"

I swept out my arms. "A menagerie. I want so many pets the neighbors call animal control on us. Pets were the one thing we couldn't have growing up. Mom was allergic."

"You're going to have everything you want, Em." The river made his touch cool on my cheek. "I know you will."

"You'll have everything you want too, Clay. Even the things you won't let yourself wish for."

"Life doesn't work that way. Not for me."

I heard a splinter eerily similar to my heart breaking. Clay truly believed his life wouldn't change.

Clay swam to the bank. "Your turn. Tell me a secret. Make it a good one."

"How good?"

"Something you've never told anyone. Not Royal. Not Eli. A secret you barely admit to yourself."

"Okay."

Clay secured my legs around his waist and lifted me out.

"I try to kill myself almost every day."

He slipped, falling hard on his backside. "What?! Holy shit, Ember!"

"Relax," I soothed. "Let me explain."

"How can you explain that?"

Threading my fingers behind his neck, I brought our foreheads together. "There are lots of ways to kill yourself, but the simplest method of all, is the only way it can't be done.

"Holding your breath. You can't hold your breath until you die. If you try. If you strongly fight the urge to breathe for as long as you can, you'll eventually pass out, and while unconscious, your body will make you take a breath. It'll force you to live.

"Sometimes when it's all too much, I hold my breath till it feels like my lungs will burst and at that last second my body will force me to let go. There's a part of me that wants to keep going. No matter how bad it gets or how hard I resist, I have to take a breath."

I lifted my shoulders, smiling at him. "It's weird, but it helps me. We've all got unique ways to deal."

"That's true," he murmured. "But if you're looking for another part of you that wants you to keep going…" Clay clasped my hand over his heart. "Here's one."

"Clay." A grin split my face. "That was *unbearably* cheesy."

"It was, wasn't it?"

We fell out, collapsing on the bank.

"You'll have to kiss me to make up for it," I said, rolling on top of him.

"Oh, yeah?" He captured me in a deep, passionate kiss that banished the chill from my bones. "Did that do it?" he gruffed. "Or should I try again?"

"I'll tell you when."

It felt like hours before we returned to the school. I would've stayed out by that river with Clay forever. We left for the same reason we decided not to have sex. It was cold as hell and we were freezing our na-nas off. Shaking and chattering teeth were far from sexy. An intense make-out session followed our dip in the river, then we scurried into our sweaters and jackets and cuddled up on the blanket, talking about everything and anything.

"Want to know another secret?" I spoke up.

Our clasped hands swayed between us.

"Sure."

"That was my first real date."

He blinked. "It was?"

"Yep. I don't count Nolan and his sickening bet. After we broke up, I was off dating and Julian's hounding didn't help. Then there was Royal, but I don't think taking my virginity and disappearing after I fell asleep counts as a date. So, you're my first."

"How'd I do?"

"Got me out of my clothes on the first one, so you did pretty good."

Laughing, he tugged me in, kissing my temple. "Wait till you see what I have planned for the next one."

Clay walked me to the dorm and didn't let go on the fourth floor. He said nothing as he tapped in the code for the boys' side. Cassius was fast asleep. A rising and falling mound that didn't stir from our chuckles and hushed whispers.

We shed our clothes and tucked beneath his sheets. I fell asleep listening to his soft, breathy sighs.

Chapter Five

There was something about being one of the Angels. And there was something about being on their arms. Mouths shut and eyes widened as I strolled through the halls holding Clay's hand, kissing Cassius, or talking to the infamously uncommunicative Royal Cruz.

In the two weeks since we returned to school, I didn't hear a word about my parents or the money. Everyone was too afraid I'd report their disrespect to the boys. Their fear made me uncomfortable, but their silence lowered my shields. For brief spells, I convinced myself I was a normal teenager. Those spells were broken when I delivered the second payment of a thousand dollars and got the note the next day demanding another thousand in two weeks.

"I wish I had the full list of who my parents cheated."

Royal and I lazed on his bed. Monday morning brought an end to our weekend. Breakfast and a full day of classes beckoned.

"I could narrow down the blackmailers," I continued. "It's still about half the school, but I'd know the right half."

"Rio got his hands on the note. It's possible he could get the cops in his pocket to give up the list."

I shot up. "Could he really do that?"

"I'll ask. He wants you searching for them. If I say it'll help you find them, he'll do what he has to."

I tossed my head. "I never thought I'd be hoping for a gang leader and a dirty cop to succeed."

"You're doing this to find the trash that attacked the little man. Don't worry about anything else."

"I know," I whispered. "Still, I can't help but wonder how we ended up here. Eli wouldn't be in danger if my parents hadn't defrauded the town. I've looked at it every single way. Gone over every moment of my life, and I can't understand it. They raised us to be honest. Never steal. Never lie. Wait your turn. Hold doors open for the elderly. All of that. How could those people do what they did?"

"There was never a sign they weren't the best people?"

I looked away. "To everyone but me, they were great."

"That's not what counts, princess. It's who you are off the stage that says what kind of person you are. Anyone can put on an act."

"Not you." I popped a kiss on his nose. "You are so wonderfully messed up on and off the stage."

He chuckled. "You posed for me all weekend, so I'll let you get away with that."

My cheeks warmed. Hiro was coming back to school and Royal got it in his head that we should spend his last weekend alone in his room sketching and having sex. He now had twelve drawings to add to his growing collection of naked Embers.

"You should draw some for me," I said. "I'd love my own collection of you in various compromising positions."

"Sorry, princess," he said with a smirk. "I warned you I don't draw for anyone." Royal got off the bed.

"That's not fair."

He pulled me up. "I return the favor in dick and orgasms. It's plenty fair."

"You saying you only sleep with me to feed your muse?"

Royal kissed my grinning lips. "I sleep with you because I can only go about two days before the withdrawal kills me. That spell your pussy has me under is strong."

"That'd make a nice greeting card."

I stole another kiss and then grabbed my stuff. I threw open the door and nearly ran into Julian. He put me back on my feet.

"Ember."

"Julian."

Leo dropped his eyes and picked up the pace, leaving ahead of his friends. Clay and Cassius's order that he remain a ghost was enforced stricter than traffic laws. The week before he tried testing their rule on staying out of the cafeteria, and all three of the guys hauled him bellowing out of the seat, dragged him down the stairs, and threw him out.

One of the cafeteria ladies reported it to Hart, and the result was the boys received detention and Leo had to take his meals either in an empty classroom or his dorm. Hart said it was to minimize disruptions.

Julian glanced over my head. "Royal." That name was chipped out of the block of ice reflecting in those blue-gray pools. Julian normally came off as an affable guy. It was an act, but one he kept to as the headmistress's son.

Royal called my poisoning the Angels and putting them in the hospital emotional castration. Looking at Julian then, his easy smile gone, and a storm brewing in his eyes, I couldn't help but think Cassius and Clay gave him the same treatment that day in the cafeteria.

And the self-named king of the Raveners wasn't happy about it.

Julian looked me up and down. "You and Royal. And Cassius. And Clay. You guys make a nice... whatever you are."

I reached behind, silently holding Royal back.

"Thank you," I said brightly. "So early in the morning for compliments, but I'll take them."

His smile didn't reach his eyes. "It makes sense now why I wasn't enough for you."

"Don't try it, Julian. I told you what to do if you wanted to be with me and you blew me off and ran back to your girlfriend. The truth is I wasn't enough for you to give up your throne."

"It wasn't like that," he gritted out. "I couldn't just leave Pomona."

"That's sweet. I hope you are very happy together."

My blank reply reddened his cheeks. "Look, I know I messed up after the party."

"Messed up?" Nolan asked. "Dude, what did you do?"

Julian went on like he hadn't spoken. "I ditched you and then that shit went down with your brother and the shower video. But seriously, Em, you don't need *them* to protect you."

"I don't need anyone to protect me," I corrected. "You and I grew up on separate sides, Julian. It's where we're meant to stay—especially while you side with Leo." I curled my lip at the boy next to him. "And him."

"We've been friends since we were four," Julian snapped. "Leo says he didn't do it and I believe him."

"Then you and I have nothing more to say to each other."

"You heard the lady." Royal snaked an arm around my waist. "Move."

Proving they had more balls than sense, Julian and Nolan came in closer.

"And if I don't?" Julian taunted. "You think you run this place—"

"I do."

"*I* run this place! This is my school! Built by Raveners, for Raveners! Do you know how easy it would be to get my mom to change the admissions back to Raveners only?"

I felt Royal's shrug. "I'm betting that change won't happen till long after I've graduated, so why should I give a fuck? In the meantime"—Royal shifted me out of the way, bearing down on Julian—"you watch yourself and how you speak to our girl. My boys say you've been getting mouthy. Three years and we haven't had a problem, Hart. Don't get stupid now."

"I'm not afraid of you," he said through clenched teeth.

Is he trying to convince Royal or himself? Either way, I have to put a stop to this.

"Guys, we don't have to do this. Like Royal said, you got along for three years. We can make it through another semester and a half. As for Leo"—I grabbed Julian's chin and made him look at me—"ask your best friend what he did to me Casino Night. He'll tell you a load of bullshit, and then I'll tell you the truth."

I shocked Julian enough that he let me through. I kept a firm hold on Royal's forearm just in case. When we were in the elevator, I blew out a rough breath. "Julian's got this look like he's itching for a fight. Cassius and Clay basically pantsed him in front of everyone. Plus, he's twitching about this *lesson* they're going to teach him."

Royal put his back to the wall, shutting his eyes like he'd drift asleep. "It's not my fault he's acting up. The Angels can't show weakness, princess. You know that better than anyone. They smell blood in the water and you're torn apart."

"We can't have blood. Especially not Julian's blood. He's the headmistress's son. If you guys get into it with him, she'll side with her kid and you three will be expelled in your senior year. I'm serious, Royal. Don't let this get out of hand."

He opened one eye. "Who's in charge? Me or you?"

"Hmm." I tapped my chin. "Let's see. You're in charge of the Angels, but I'm in charge of your sex life, so if you think of it like that—"

I shrieked as he snapped me to his chest. "Careful." Royal bit my lip, nipping just enough to straddle both sides of pain and pleasure. "That ass doesn't have me whipped yet."

"Give it time."

Royal smirked. He loved our banter though he never said it. A guy like him needed someone to fight him and push back. That's what a true partner does. They give you what you need—even if it hurts.

"When does Hiro get back?" Visions of scattered clothes and twisted sheets danced through my mind.

"He's in the cafeteria right now."

"That's good," I said, meaning it. The series of events that led to Hiro getting shot began with me and my family. I was glad he was recovered and back at school.

If Hiro felt the same about being back at the academy, it was hard to tell. His patented scowl and narrowed eyes surveyed the students passing by. Then he landed on me. Hiro's face shuttered closed.

Far from encouraging, but I won't let it stop me.

I marched up to the Angel table a step behind Royal.

"Hiro."

"Bancroft," he said slowly. His arm was in a cast, but otherwise he looked okay.

"I wanted to thank you," I said, "and apologize. The triplets said you were hurt defending me. I appreciate it and I'm sorry it came to this. Let me know if there's anything I can do."

"We need to talk," he replied without a pause. "After school."

What about didn't show on his face. Hesitating a beat, I soon nodded yes. "After school."

I turned to go.

"Where you going, baby?" Cassius piped up. "The Angel table isn't off-limits to you. Why do you keep sitting with that kid when you could be next to me getting fingered under the table?"

I promptly flung my muffin at his head. Cassius caught it one-handed, tearing off a bite as he winked.

"He's got a point," said Royal. "Why are you always hanging with Lacroix?"

"He is what we call a friend on this planet."

"Just a friend... right?"

I made a strangled noise. "How are you asking me that? Of course he's just a friend."

"And Lighthouse too," added Clay. "He was feeling you up the other day."

"You mean when he pulled a leaf out of my hair?"

"He took his sweet time with that damn leaf."

"I'm leaving now."

I turned my back on them, shaking my head. Clay and I were officially dating while Cassius and Royal maintained hookup status. This didn't prevent either one of them from acting like overprotective boyfriends when the mood struck them.

"Morning, B." Brandon was his usual cheery self. "I see Hiro's back. What happened to his arm?"

I repeated the agreed-upon story. "He broke it flying off a motorcycle."

"Ouch."

Camila caught my eye. She knew there wasn't an accident. Her brothers told her he was beaten, but she didn't know the full extent of what went on in the gang. The boys refused to put her in the dangerous spot of knowing too much.

"Did you guys hear about the party?"

I groaned. "Haven't we had enough parties?"

Brandon threw his arm around me. I peeked to see if the boys were watching.

They were.

"For sure we have and I'd understand if you guys didn't come, but my roommate is throwing this one," said Brandon. "He's a cool guy and it'll be chill. Just music and hanging out."

"Maybe," said Camila. "I'll see if I'm up for it."

"Craig is cool," I said. Brandon's roommate waved and kept it friendly the times I ran into him. When the rest of the school was calling me a bitch and jumping me in the locker room, indifference was welcome. "I could go for an hour or two."

"Sweet." Brandon got to his feet. "Time to sneak in some tennis practice. See you guys in class."

We lingered over our breakfast, talking classes and plans for the future. The bell rang and sent us scattering through the main building.

My academy classes were challenging. Teachers piled on the homework and took sadistic pleasure in dropping pop quizzes on us. The only class I had approaching fun was Coach Sutton's.

The seniors headed into the locker room to change. My butt stayed on the bleachers. I tugged my uniform shirt over my head and shimmied out of my skirt. Three days a week I wore my gym clothes on under my uniform and rushed to the dorm to shower after PE. Students were publicly nice to me due to the boys. Sneaking blackmailers, on the other hand, would jump at another chance to snap me with no clothes on.

Sutton said nothing about my public changing room. She didn't know about Fiona and Remington filming me in the shower, but she did know my brother was beaten and students hissed and snapped at me during PE. She let me be.

"What are we doing today, Coach?" I asked as I stuffed my clothes in my backpack.

"Basketball mini golf."

I shot up. "Are you serious? But that's—"

"A Coach Kiki classic," she said. "Your old coach and I caught up for dinner last weekend and she said this was a favorite. Thought I'd try it out with my students. Did it with the freshmen and juniors already and they are begging for more."

"Coach Kiki also taught us backwards soccer. Can we do that too?"

She laughed. "Let's not put too much on an old traditional girl like me. It's been a tough semester, so we're doing something fun today. Next class, you kids are on the tennis court and I'm back in my element."

The other students trickled out of the locker room, filling up the bleachers. Camila was the last out. She dropped next to me.

"Afternoon, seniors. You're in for a treat today." Coach motioned with her clipboard. "We're playing basketball mini golf. As you can see, I set up nine 'tees' from where you'll shoot the ball. The challenge for each tee gets harder as you go. Tee one, you just shoot. Tee two, you shoot wearing sunglasses. Tee three, you shoot on one leg. Tee four, you shoot with one hand. And then on and on until you reach the last tee where you must shoot blindfolded.

"If you make the shot on the first try, or get a hole in one, you receive ten points. If you miss the shot, you try again from where you caught the rebound. You only have to do the challenge for the first shot. Making the shot without the challenge is four points. After five tries and you haven't sunk the ball, move on to the next and take a zero for that tee. Any questions?"

Remington raised her hand. "Are we doing teams?"

"No teams. This is an individual game. You'll line up and go through the tees one by one." She held up a stack of papers. "Use this to keep score."

"This sounds like fun," Camila said.

"All right, everybody up," Coach called. "Line up at the first tee."

We bounded off the bleachers and shuffled, pushed, and traded spaces to form our line. It wasn't an unfortunate trick of fate that Brynn and Pomona ended up next to me. Pomona smirked as she sidled up.

"Hey, Ember."

"Go away."

She tsked. "Don't be like that. I just want to chat."

I fixed my attention on the first boy to tee up. "You and I have nothing to say to each other unless you've got a few years' worth of apologies you want to catch up on."

"Me apologize to you?" The sickly sweet fled in the wake of disbelief. "For what?"

"Want to start with pushing me in a pond?"

"Ugh. That was forever ago. Move on."

"Take your own advice and move your ass on. Like I said, we have nothing to say to each other."

Brynn jumped in. "This is why you have no friends. You're not very nice."

"Oh, she has friends." Pomona stepped into my line of sight. "She and the Angels seem *very* close."

Brynn nudged my arm. "How does that work exactly? Do they pass you around? A different bed every night?"

"Do they tag team you? One dick in your mouth. One in your ass. And the other in your pussy?"

These two were really enjoying this.

"Let me see," I began, grin playing on my lips. "Different bed every night? Pretty much. Do they tag team me? No, but you're painting a tempting picture."

Their nasty smirks twitched.

"Is that the price of protection?" Brynn asked. "Were we so horrible you had to become the Angels' *girl*?"

"You're pathetic," Pomona spat. "You went down on those flea-infested thugs for nothing because they won't be scaring people for much longer. Pretty soon, the Angels will be back in their OB slum where they be—"

Camila lunged.

Pomona screamed, jerking back as Camila swiped the spot her head had just been in. I grabbed the triplet around the middle, struggling to hold her back.

"Watch your fucking mouth, Winchester!" Camila roared.

Coach's whistle cut through the air. "What on earth is going on?!"

"It's them, Coach," I grunted. Camila was tiny, but damn was she strong. "They said that Eli's battered face was the funniest thing they've ever seen and that Leo should have finished the job."

Whistle falling out of her mouth, Sutton's eyes bulged. "They said— How dare you! Both of you, locker room now! Let's see how funny you think assault is when you're scrubbing the grout with a toothbrush!"

"But, Coach, we didn't!"

"We never said that!"

Sutton marched the pleading girls off the court, bellowing the whole way.

Camila goggled at me. "Wow, Em."

Smirking, I made a show of dusting off my sleeves. "See? There are better ways to handle those girls that won't land you in Hart's office."

"You're good."

We tapped knuckles. As we stepped up to the first tee, I knew without a doubt, we were friends.

MY LAST CLASS OF THE day was precalc. I caught Hiro looking at me a few times and my mind flashed to what he planned to talk to me about.

What doesn't he want to talk to me about? That day in Caesar's garage was a nightmare that almost ended permanently for Hiro—be-

cause of me. He was right to want to stay far away from Bancrofts. We've brought nothing but pain into his life.

A steady chime interrupted Mrs. Turner's explanation of the homework.

"Okay, class," she announced. "Complete the practice problems at the end of the chapter. If you need help, I'll be in the tutoring room today and tomorrow."

A chorus of zippers, scraped tile, and chatter about afternoon plans filled the room. I bent over, shoving my notes and textbook in my bag.

"Bancroft." A pair of sneakers planted themselves next to me. "You ready?"

"Um, yeah."

I threw the last pencil in and stood. Hiro swung around before I got a read on his face. I had no choice but to follow him into the hall, down the stairs, and past where I'd turn for my locker. He didn't speak the whole way.

"Hiro?" I asked. "What's up? Where are we going?"

"Outside."

I waited for more. Got nothing.

I'll find out soon enough.

Hiro took me out to the pavilion. He climbed the steps and stopped, not allowing me past.

"Bancroft."

"Yes?"

Hiro faced forward, his back to me. "I'm sorry."

I blinked.

"No." He turned and looked me in the eye. "I'm sorry."

"You're... sorry?" Saying it out loud didn't help me understand either.

He dropped his head, looking to where he gripped his bad arm. "For that day in your room. Grabbing you and almost breaking your box. You didn't know where your parents were and it wasn't right even if you did. So... I'm sorry."

I was quiet for a long time. "What happened to real men don't apologize?"

He shook his head, still not looking at me. "Real men don't believe seven letters can make up for their mistakes. And it doesn't. I'm sorry isn't good enough, but I'll give it to you anyway if it helps at all to make us good."

Hiro backed into the pavilion. Slowly I trailed him, taking a seat on the wooden bench opposite.

"I was worse than a dick to you," he said, "and I was ready to pay for it when Rio pulled his gun. What you told him about your sister—"

My jaw clenched.

"Right there." He gestured to me. "That look in your eye. I know that look. I know what it took to give up your secret."

"You know? How?"

Hiro's voice was steady and clear. "I know because I'm the reason my parents are dead."

"You..."

And then I saw it. In his eyes, burning so clear it's a wonder I didn't see it before. That look. The one I saw every morning. The one that said nothing would ever be all right again.

"I'm sorry, Hiro," I rasped. I wouldn't ask for details. I knew better than that.

He nodded. "You saved my life, Bancroft. I was wrong about you. I understand if we can't be cool like you are with Clay, Cas, and Royal, but as for me, you and I are good." He stood up. "Let me know if there's anything I can do."

"Hiro."

He halted on the steps.

My lips quirked up in a smile. "I could use more cream soda."

"It's free for you."

"Oooh. Oh, yeah. This will be the start of a beautiful friendship."

He barked a laugh. Hiro turned to me and I saw for the first time—

His smile.

"CAMILA SAID YOU GOT Brynn and Pomona a week's detention." Clay's nose caressed my cheek in motion with the shivers running up my spine. "Impressive."

The two of us were in his bed. Me sitting between his legs and feeling plenty happy about it. It wasn't just us. Cassius propped up on his headboard while Hiro and Royal sat in their desk chairs.

"Thank you," I replied. "Although, they did have some interesting tips to spice up my sex life that we should talk about."

"Later," said Royal. "Now that Hiro's back, we can step it up on finding this dealer." He looked to Hiro. "Your method for getting product in. Is there a chance the dealer is getting their stuff in the same way?"

"It's possible." Hiro was back to the half-pissed, half-bored, all-annoyed guy he was. That gut-punching, knock-you-on-your-ass smile was nowhere to be seen.

How do I get it back? I thought there was no man more beautiful than Hiro Saito. Then he smiled and blew Angry Boy out of the water.

I traced his face as he spoke. *There's not a lot to smile about after causing the death of your parents. What could you possibly have done, Hiro?*

I wanted to know, but I'd never ask. It was for him to decide if and when he wanted to speak about it.

"I'll look into it," Hiro continued, "but I'm wondering if it's even simpler than that. The police questioned the Raveners and searched their rooms after what happened to Camila, but the rest of the dorm hasn't had a surprise room or locker search all semester. The guy might just be walking the shit through the gates in his backpack."

"A senior could get in and out whenever he runs low," I said. "We sign ourselves off campus."

"Or the guy pays a senior to bring in the drugs," Clay added. "Either way, Hiro's right. He might be keeping it simple."

"How do we find them if they are?" I asked. "Tip off Hart to do a search?"

"Nah," said Hiro. "You know how many times my room's been searched and they never found a thing? If the guy is smart—and he obviously is—a room search isn't going to do him in."

"Then what do we do?"

Crossing his arms, Royal leaned back in the seat, eyes falling closed. "We force him to make a move."

Clay sat up, draping his arms over his knees. "What are you thinking?"

"We run him dry. We ask for more drugs than he could have on hand and we say we need it by a certain time or he doesn't get his money. He'll have to leave campus or send someone to get more. We find out who all of a sudden took a quick trip to see Mommy, and we'll be closer to finding him."

"I like it," said Clay. "Only issue is this can't be connected to us. We can't ask for the drugs and we can't get anyone else involved."

"Let me take care of that," said Royal. "Em, come with me. We need to talk."

Royal left without waiting to see if I'd follow. I twisted around to kiss Clay and then hopped off the bed. Royal ducked into his room and held the door open.

"What is it?" I asked.

"I talked to Rio about the list. You'll have it by next week."

"That's it? Just like that?"

"I doubt it's 'just like that' but he didn't give me the details. All that matters is you'll have the full list of the people your parents defrauded."

"What did you say to convince him?"

"Something about your parents using their victims' lost assets to hide out. Those summer homes a few of the Raveners said bye to is a good place to lie low."

"The way that mind works is incredibly hot, Royal Cruz."

Backing up, he said, "You know I'm a 'show, don't tell' kind of guy." He cocked his head at the bathroom and that was it. We were naked and in the shower in two minutes flat.

The next morning, Brandon and I bumped into each other on the way to the elevator.

"B, you still on for the party this weekend? Hiro says he's back in business, so we'll have decent food. You've turned me on to that cream soda stuff."

"I start trends, Brandon. I step into people's lives and make them better with my ways."

He rolled his eyes. "I start drinking one soda and the lady thinks I can't be without her."

"You can't."

Brandon and I fell into normal conversation as we made for breakfast.

"How are your sisters? Still loving Wesley Middle?"

"They do actually," he replied. "Chloe and Layla want to move up to Wesley High with their friends but Mom made it clear they're going to the academy if they get in." He glanced around the wide expanse of wealth and privilege. "I don't get a vote, but they should go to high school with their friends. At least they'll have them watching their backs. My sisters shouldn't have to put up with the crap OB kids deal with here."

"They shouldn't," I agreed. "The way things are around here proves how busted this town is. It's insane the way we treat each other, and for what? I was thinking the other day how little this Ravener/OB stuff will matter once we're free of this place."

"New York is calling me, B. I'll be just as broke and struggling as most of the people there and it'll be glorious."

I cracked a smile. "Exactly."

Brandon and I joined the breakfast line and walked away with chocolate hazelnut crepes, bacon, a side of fruit, and vanilla pudding.

"The food is so good here," I said. We headed up to the senior loft. "That's one thing I don't miss about Wesley High. We…" I trailed off.

Brandon didn't ask why. Our gaze fell on the same boggling sight.

Julian, Pomona, Nolan, Brynn, and Destiny were sitting and eating like it was no big deal—at the Angels' table.

"What the hell?" Brandon hissed. "What are they doing?"

Julian zeroed in on me like he'd been waiting for me to arrive. The smugness in his grin turned my stomach. He was looking forward to the shit he was about to cause.

"This is what I'm talking about," Brandon growled. "These guys stir up crap for no damn reason. We can't get one day off."

I had to agree. I knew a power play when I saw one. Clay and Cassius shut him up in front of everyone and Julian was bouncing back to show he was still in charge and the Angels couldn't do a thing about it.

I stomped up to them. "What are you trying to prove, Julian?" I shot off. "That testosterone really is poison? No one is interested in the fight you're trying to start."

"Look at this. Backwater Slut is rushing to her owners' defense," Pomona taunted.

"Sit down, bitch," Brynn snapped. "Sutton made us clean the entire gym because of you."

"You were so busy lying on us, you didn't give us a chance to warn you this was coming," said Pomona. "We're sick of gangbanger trash making us feel unsafe in our own school."

"Sit down, Em." Julian didn't pause in cutting his crepe. The guy was the picture of calm. "We're just sitting here eating our breakfast. If the Angels start a fight over that, it's them with the problem, not us."

Brandon took hold of my arm. "Let's go, B," he said under his breath. "You're not getting them up. They want the Angels' attention, let them have it."

He had a point. They weren't going to get up because I told them to.

I let Brandon lead me away. Camila and Gabriel were at our table, fixed on the same group as the rest of the seniors.

"I tried to get them up too," said Gabriel. "You can see how well that worked."

"Forget it." I took my seat next to Camila, facing the Raveners. "Half of them are on probation. They can't afford to get into a fight and they know it."

"But they're fine with my brothers starting a fight and taking the blame." Camila glared a hole in Nolan's head. "You know Hart isn't about to expel all of them. Especially not Julian."

"Yeah, I know," I replied.

I no sooner finished speaking than Royal's raven crown crested the stairs. On his wings were Cassius, Clay, and Hiro.

"I kinda like this table," Julian said loudly. "Nice view out of the window. Right under the vent. The Raveners sit here now."

A hush fell over the loft. All eyes pinned on the Angels.

Neither Royal, Cassius, Clay, nor Hiro slowed their stride. The boys strode past them without throwing their table a single glance.

Dozens of heads swiveled watching them walk right up to our table. Cassius, Clay, and Hiro sat in the remaining free seats. Royal put down his tray, scooped me up, and plopped me in his lap. The boys carried on eating.

I flicked from the Angels to Julian's darkening face. They didn't touch him. Look at him. Or breathe his air. Yet the Angels showed him up all the same. The Raveners looked like petty children provoking a fight over a table, while the Angels gave a tantrum all the attention it deserved—none.

"Eat, princess," Royal said lightly. "Crepes are your favorite."

"How do you know that?"

He popped a slice in my mouth.

"You like all things sweet."

I stroked the soft strands at the nape of his neck. "Are you going to be sweet?"

His grin was wicked. "Always. Unless I'm given a reason not to be."

"This spot is nice, Julian," Nolan spoke up. "Matter of fact, this whole loft is too nice for the OB trash."

Raveners and OB kids traded looks.

"I have to agree with you. I think we're all done with them." Julian pushed back his seat. "Guys, how fucking sick are you of having to share your school with these OB charity cases? Everything has gone downhill since the academy stopped being Raveners only. There are drugs all over campus. A freshman was attacked and beaten. Fucking *gangbangers* sit behind us in class."

He threw a hand at our table. "They don't even deny it! The Horsemen are killers and they wear that angel tattoo like it's an honor instead of a fucking insult to everyone in this town that's been hurt by them."

Royal's grip constricted on my waist.

"We don't want them here but everyone from the janitors to the teachers are afraid of what the Horsemen will do to them. Raveners built this school to get away from the violence. Get away from the *trash*! And I want my school back!"

Julian turned on us—that beautiful face twisted into something horrific. "OB kids, get out. You don't eat up here with us anymore."

"That's right!"

"Leave!"

"Get the fuck out of our school!"

Most of the shouting came from Julian's little posse. Although, more than a few Raveners nodded their heads during his speech, and they were getting to their feet.

I squeezed Royal in a near strangling grip. I trusted he could hold his own in a fight, but twenty against one or even four was not a fight. That was a trip to the hospital with the ambulance booked and the OR prepped and waiting for you.

"Guys, this isn't good," Gabriel whispered.

"And you know what else, this eating in an empty classroom garbage is over. The police cleared him. The thugs are out and Leo is coming back." He threw out his hands, chest puffed out. "How is that for a lesson in respect?!"

It happened too quickly for me to react. Cassius shot up, tipping his chair crashing to the floor. He snatched his pudding cup and flung it at Julian's contorted face. Sticky white goo exploded all over his chin, neck, and clothes. Julian didn't get out the first shout before Clay nailed him with a second one. Then he stole mine off my plate and hit him with that too.

Julian practically leaped over Pomona rushing at the triplets. Royal stood and dropped me on the seat so fast the room blurred. My vision cleared on him seizing Julian and spinning him around. He got him under the arms and locked his fingers behind Julian's head. The boy thrashed and hollered but he wasn't going anywhere.

"Your little speech was cute," Clay said over his noise. "But you took a wrong turn at the end. The rapist fuck stays where he is."

"Did you like his speech?" Royal asked Clay conversationally. "I didn't like it. Hart here said a lot of mean shit. Almost hurt my feelings. Why don't we ask everyone else?" Royal hauled him around. "You guys from the Outer Borough, what did you think of Julian's speech? Of him and his friends calling you trash? Of them yelling at you in the halls, blaming everything that goes wrong in this place on you, and acting like they own this town and everyone in it?"

"Get off!" Julian bellowed.

"Go on, OB," Royal said. "Tell us if the Angels have ever put their hands on you? Have we ever called you trash?"

"No!"

The force of the shout blew me away. It wasn't just the Raveners on their feet now.

"Have we filmed your naked asses in the shower?"

"No!"

"Did we drug you and laugh while we sent you off with our wannabe rapist friends?"

"No!"

"Fuck the Raveners!"

"This is our school too!" This one came from Brandon. "You make this place a nightmare for no fucking reason!"

"They do, don't they, Lacroix?" Royal hissed in Julian's ear. "Don't you?"

"So, what do you say, OB?" Cassius called. "Who should leave the loft?"

"The Raveners!"

Royal shoved Julian away. The boy stumbled into the middle of the space.

"Why don't you help them get their shit and go?"

That was the cue they were waiting for. Pudding cups went fly-ing, pelting Julian, Pomona, Nolan, and Brynn. They took off run-ning, screaming abuse at the Angels.

They skidded to a halt before the stairs. The running, shouting, throwing—everything came to a stop.

Stepping around her son, Headmistress Hart surveyed the mess we made of the loft.

"Seniors." Her stern but even voice carried better than a shout. "My office. Now."

Chapter Six

"We're not going to get in trouble for this, are we?" Brandon fidgeted in the chair. His leg was shaking so much it's amazing it didn't rattle out of its socket and run away. "We didn't do anything."

The entire senior class crowded the administration office. One by one, we were called in to speak to Hart.

"Like you said, we didn't do anything," I replied. "If anyone should get in trouble, it's Julian for starting shit. He was trying to whip up a full-blown riot."

Julian had been in to see his mother already. He blew out of her office ten minutes later, red-faced and covered in pudding. He ignored Pomona when she tried to talk to him.

The receptionist cleared her throat. "Miss Bancroft, the headmistress will see you now."

Hart's nose was stuck in a file when I came in. *My file most likely.*

"Ember, please have a seat."

She set the file on her desk as I sat down. Looking at her up close, I read the strain in the lines around her eyes and displeasure in her pursed lips.

"Tell me what happened at breakfast this morning," she said.

"It didn't start this morning, Headmistress. This Ravener/OB thing has gone on for a long time and it finally set off at breakfast. Kids screaming at each other to get off *their* loft and get out of *their* school. It's too much and it's too stupid. Something's got to happen or it won't be pudding cups thrown next time. It'll be punches."

"Ember."

I lifted my chin, readying for the displeasure to unleash.

"You're right."

"I am?"

"Yes." Sighing, Hart pulled off her glasses and rubbed her tired eyes. "I see what you see. I've seen it long before you were born. There's an ugliness in the way the people of Raven River treat each other. Dare I say, a hatred. And it's one that's being passed down. I thought by opening up the school to the entire community, we could bridge that gap. Instead I've opened up those poor children from the OB to harassment, and brought a vindictiveness out of the Estate children that concerns me.

"These are the children I'm sending out into the world. Bitter. Resentful. Cruel. This is my legacy as headmistress."

A niggle of sympathy worked its way in. I forgot for a moment that she was truly kind at heart. She didn't want this any more than we did.

"It doesn't have to be," I said softly. "People don't just get along because they're thrown in a school together. It's something you have to choose. Work for. The academy can still be a place where the kids of this town aren't constantly reminded of their differences. And if anyone can make it happen, it'll be someone that cares… like you."

I might've imagined the brightness in her eyes. She blinked and shoved her glasses back on too quickly for me to be sure.

"Thank you, Ember. You've helped me make up my mind."

"I did?"

She pushed away from her desk. "Follow me. We're going to the gym."

I scurried after her.

Hart swept through her office, relaying the same order to the kids waiting. Twenty minutes later, the entire senior class sat on the bleachers while Hart and Sutton spoke with their backs turned.

"What's up, baby?" Cassius asked. "What did you do?"

The Angels, Camila, Brandon, Gabriel, and I took up our own space toward the bottom-end of the bleachers. Clay sat in front of me, head resting on my knees. I absentmindedly ran my fingers through his hair.

"Why does it have to be my fault?"

"Isn't it?"

I shoved his shoulder.

"Seniors, quiet, please."

Hart's order brought the murmuring to an end.

"The incident in the cafeteria this morning was unacceptable. I called you all in my office with half a mind to hand down suspensions and expulsions."

Students jerked at the e-word.

"It soon occurred to me that those measures would not solve the underlying problems of how you all relate to each other. I've been a strong proponent of open communication and it being the best way to bridge gaps. Well, now it's time to put those methods to use."

Whispers broke out. I hoped they weren't asking what she meant because it seemed pretty clear to me.

"Your morning classes are canceled," she announced. "That time will be spent here in a communication and bridging divides workshop. Afterward, you all will have lunch together in the senior loft with new outlooks and ways of relating to each other. If not, we'll continue these workshops every day after school until you do."

Cassius gave me a look. "Baby, if you are responsible for this, it's no sex for a week."

A flush crept up my neck. "You guys forget who went two years without. My willpower is a lot stronger than yours."

"True. Very true." Cassius put his head on my pillowy breasts. "I'd just be punishing myself."

"What am I going to do with you?" Damned if I didn't sound fond.

"We're going to jump right in here," said Hart. She pulled my attention away from the triplets. "This feud between the Outer Borough and the Estate is nonsense. Nonsense that's existed long before you. Nonsense that you were taught. But nonsense all the same." She held her hands out to us. "This is your home. All of you share this town together, and together you can make it a better place to live. The sins of my generation and the generations before me are not your burden to bear. Make a commitment today to change the way you see yourselves and each other.

"To light that match, we'll begin by spreading positivity to our classmates. I want one so-called Ravener and one so-called OB kid to stand up here and name something they like or admire about the other person. If you decide not to take this seriously, remember I am committed to working with you every day until you can."

Her threat came through loud and clear.

"First pair," she began. "Ember Bancroft and... Pomona Winchester."

Seriously, lady? I thought we had our own breakthrough. Why am I being punished?

Pomona and I faced each other on the polished maple floors. Pudding gooped in her hair, clothes, and a speck caught on her ear. She glared at me like it was my fault.

"Ember, you start. Share one thing that you admire about Pomona."

Believe it or not, it wasn't hard for me to come up with something. "Pomona's changed a lot in the last two years and I'm sure it wasn't easy. She was beautiful before, but there's another kind of beauty in being happy with what you see in the mirror. I think she feels that now."

And it's turned her into a smug, self-entitled asshat. And I mean no disrespect to asshats everywhere.

"That was lovely, Ember," Hart gushed.

Pomona's eyes narrowed to slits like she heard my mental addition to the compliment.

"Everyone, give her a hand."

The class gave me a smattering of applause.

"Pomona," Hart prompted. "What would you like to say to Ember?"

She looked from me to Hart as though she was weighing her hatred of me against Hart's threat to steal her afternoons.

"Ember is..."

Hart beamed. "Yes?"

"Ember is clever." Pomona looked at me head-on. "And she isn't someone to be underestimated."

My mirthless grin reflected in her eyes. I got her mental addition loud and clear too.

"Excellent, ladies. This is exactly what I want to see. Now, let's have Julian and..."

I knew before she called his name.

"Royal."

Royal passed me on the steps. The boys closing the distance between each other reminded me eerily of gladiators charging onto the arena. The expressions on their faces better suited men readying to fight to the death.

Royal and Julian.

Both boys different in every way. Royal, the dark prince of raven hair, bleeding ink, and eyes that held the torment he'd witnessed. Julian, the self-crowned king of silver hair, untouched beauty, and anger straining to get out.

"Royal, you start."

Royal jerked his chin. "Like your hair, man. It's the soul of an artist that expresses itself off canvas."

Smiling, Hart grasped Royal's shoulder. "Very nice." She glanced at Julian expectantly.

"I like your ink. They say a lot about you."

"Julian." Her smile fell away with her hand.

"What, Mom? I meant it in a good way." He was all charm, and it was all fake. "Soul of an artist, right?"

"Of course." Hart gestured behind her. "Everyone, form two rows. Students from the Estate on one side and students from the Outer Borough on the other. I want you to share something you admire about your partner, and then change up until everyone from both sides has had a chance to speak to each other. Understood?"

"Yes, Headmistress."

We tromped off the bleachers to do as ordered. Hart and Sutton circled us, ensuring people did the exercise.

I technically wasn't a Ravener or an OB kid, so I took advantage of my backwater status and joined the Ravener line. I only had a problem with Raveners who had a problem with me. Let the actual kids who couldn't think past the stupid Estate gate deal with this.

Brandon and I grinned at each other. "I love that you secretly love me," he said.

"I love that you don't let anything get you down."

Brandon's smile slipped. He was expecting me to whip out another smartass quip.

"Thanks, B," he said softly.

"All right, class. Switch."

I stepped to the side and came face to face with Hiro. He gripped his bad arm as our eyes met. I wondered if he was conscious of the act.

"Go on."

I jumped. Sutton appeared at my shoulder.

"What do you admire about Mr. Saito?"

"You— You're—" Sutton's watchful eye made sweat prickle the back of my neck. Hiro Saito was half pissed, half bored, and all annoyed. What did I say to the angry boy who broke all of his rules... for me?

"Your smile," I said. "It's beautiful."

Hiro opened his mouth and said the worst thing he possibly could.

"Yours is too."

I FELT STRANGE FOR the rest of the day—or I should say the rest of the week.

"Yours is too."

What the hell did that mean? Did he say that because Sutton was right there and it was the easiest thing to say? When was Hiro noticing my smile? Did he mean it? Was I a loon for stressing about three words thrown at me in a feelings workshop?

The questions spun around and around in my head. It didn't help that the Angels declared my table as their new one.

Things had been quiet, but tense, since Hart declared the new school order. Her promise to make fighting students resolve their issues after school was enforced to the letter. If a teacher so much as heard the word trash, that kid was sent to her. The result was lips sealed and glares intensified. The Raveners weren't pleased, and a nagging feeling that they were gearing up to do something about it gripped me.

Saturday night, I was actually looking forward to hanging out with Brandon and my friends in his room. He promised the party would be low-key. Just some food, games, and a chill vibe.

"We won't even have beer," he told us at breakfast. "Soda only. Craig and I don't need the trouble if it gets out alcohol got into the dorm again. Plus"—he glanced at Camila—"we want everyone to feel comfortable."

That night, Camila messed around on her laptop while I searched my closet for an outfit.

"Are you coming tonight?" I asked.

"Maybe for a little while. There's something I need to do first."

"Can I ask you something? What do you think of Brandon?"

The tip-tapping ceased. "Why? Did he say something?"

"No. Just asking."

"I think he's—" The tip-tapping started up again and faster. "Well, he's nice. He's my friend."

"What about Gabriel?" I asked. "It's sweet how he always passes you his fruit."

Splotchy patches reddened her cheeks. She was blushing like I saw Gabriel bend her over a desk instead of giving her his extra peaches.

"He's a friend too," she said firmly. "A friend going to college in New Hampshire while I'll be at the University of Florida."

"Oh my gosh, Cam. Did you get your acceptance?"

"Yes!" She hopped off the bed and ran into my hug. We jumped up and down, squealing and carrying on because the news warranted it.

"Congratulations!" I said. "You're going to fry like an egg down in Florida but something tells me you tan well."

"I do," she said, grinning. "My brothers and I are celebrating next week when we leave for Thanksgiving break. We're taking Dad's car out to the coast. Enjoying the sand and waves that will be my new life."

"That's amazing, Cam. I'm so happy for you."

"Don't be too happy." She went back to her bed, picking up her laptop. "They gave me a scholarship for twenty thousand a year, but tuition is thirty. I need more to bring down what Clay and Cas have to pay."

It didn't shock me that she said her brothers and not her dad. He was a figure often spoken about, but not relied on.

"I get you. Is that what you're working on?"

"Oh, uh— No. It's something else." Camila's grin abruptly disappeared. "It's about Leo."

My hand stilled on a hanger. "Leo?"

"Yes. Leo," she said. "I spoke to my brothers. They're angry and terrified of what might have happened. Everything they've done since he's come back is to make sure neither Leo nor anyone else tries to hurt me. I love them for that, but I've thought a lot about this since the police let him go, and dealing with Leo is something I have to do on my own. He took advantage of me. He tried to assault me. I'm going to see that he pays for it, and Cassius and Clay have to respect that and support me."

"Okay." I took a seat on the edge of her bed. "Is there anything I can do to help?"

"No, but thank you."

I patted her leg through the sheet. "I've thought it before—thought it while you were socking me in the eye—that you're tough, Camila Walker."

She chuckled. "So are you. Your return hit snapped my head off my shoulders. I see what my brothers like about you."

"Is it weird for you that I'm with both of them?" I asked.

"Nah. Cassius and Clay are like two halves of one person. It used to make me feel like the odd triplet out, but they were never that way on purpose. They think the same. Act the same way. Want the same things. They've shared girlfriends before, but like I told you, you're the first one I've liked."

"I'm glad. It'd be cool if we could be friends for real."

Despite whatever she was doing on that laptop, she raised her head to let me see her smile. "I thought we already were."

I hugged her tight, then I hurried to get dressed before I did anything sappier.

Brandon and Craig's room was the last one at the end of the boys' hall. They wedged a sneaker in the door to keep it open and a thumping stream of hip-hop poured through the crack.

"I've arrived," I announced.

"Ember." Brandon peeled himself off the wall where he was talking to a girl from our homeroom. A quick look around confirmed the party was Ravener-free. It was also Angel-free. No surprise since the boys shamelessly told me they come to these to scope out a hookup for the night. They had that covered now. Except for Hiro, who said he was taking his chance to find out if the dealer was using his method to slip product into the school.

I counted about twenty kids—seniors and a few juniors. Brandon was right about it being chill. People mostly talked, danced, and played pong on the makeshift table they made out of Craig's and Brandon's desks.

"Glad you came." He peered over my shoulder. "Is Camila with you?"

"She's finishing up something. She'll come by later."

"Cool. Gabriel was just here. He left with Nicole for a walk." He waggled his eyebrows. "If you know what I mean."

I laughed. "The entire party knows what you mean."

"You know you've thrown a good party if everyone's getting laid."

"You go work on that with that pretty girl you were talking to."

"Nah," he said easily. "I invited you. What kind of jerk would I be if I ditched you? Come on. Let's get you a drink."

Brandon opened a cooler full of soda and presented one with a "Ta-da!"

I took my creamy drink with a laugh. Brandon was a goofball but a girl needed a guy like that in her life.

"Hey, do you know those guys?" He pointed them out. "They went to Wesley Middle too."

"I do."

Two guys with short hair and short pants talked in the corner between Brandon's bed and the wall. They were a year below me in middle school. I recognized them when I came to the academy, but we never spoke to each other, so there wasn't a reason to mention the connection.

"Sweet. It's a reunion."

Brandon tugged me over. I sensed that he was pushing my socializing, so I wouldn't get bored and leave the party. I'd play along.

"Jorge. Mark."

"Brandon," one of the guys said. "Fun party, man. All it needs is beer."

"For real," said the other. "What happened? Saito's back. He would've hooked you up."

"Saito charges a lot for his services and his deliveries don't come with an expulsion-proof guarantee," Brandon replied. "Let the Raveners pull that shit. They can get away with it."

"Damn if you ain't right." He thumped his friend's chest. "Jorge and I were just talking about this communication workshop. Hart came into our class today and said we're using a PE class next week to 'bridge the gap' between the OB and the Estate. Can you believe that?

"We don't have the problem. The Raveners do whatever they want. Break all the rules. Treat us like shit. Then we have to waste an hour and a half talking about issues they started in the first place."

"Mark, my friend," said Brandon. "You. Preacher. Us. Choir."

"She has to do something," I found myself saying. "And the something she was planning to do was kick people out of school. A feelings workshop isn't so bad in comparison."

"The lady has a point," Jorge mumbled.

Mark squinted at me. "Hey, aren't you—"

"From your middle school."

"—Ember Bancroft," he finished. "That girl with the con artist parents."

"That's me." I gave him my back. "See you around."

"Whoa." Brandon pulled me up short. "Mark didn't mean anything by that. Did you?" A hard edge laced his question.

"No, honest. Your parents are legends."

That made me turn around. "Legends?"

"Uh, yeah." Excitement lit up his hazel eyes. "They scored twenty-five million freaking dollars and got away clean. It's sad the people who were ripped off and stuff, but you gotta be slick to pull off what they did."

"That's one word to describe them," I muttered. "People usually choose unflattering adjectives."

He put up his hands. "No doubt what they did was messed up. Taking the money and leaving their own kids. I just think it's cool that the Raveners were the worst hit. They got twenty million off them alone." An emotion I understood crept into his voice. Anger. "Now they know what it feels like."

Jorge simmered on the same rage. "Mark's dad used to work for Brynn Redgrave's father in his accounting firm in the Estate. Jobs in there are hard for someone in the OB to get but he worked for that bastard for eight years without a problem."

"One day something goes wrong." Mark picked up the thread. "Files were accidentally wiped from the drive and Dad was blamed on the spot. They fired him *before* they got IT to check it out. It was caused by a glitch and they were able to get back all the files. But Dad was still fired. They don't give a shit about us," Mark ground out. "So, yeah, your parents are fucking Robin Hoods."

Would this communication activity change Raven River and the way the townspeople felt about each other? Maybe not. But something needed to be done. The bitterness, resentment, and vindictiveness Hart spoke about salted the air whenever one group spoke about the other.

"My parents hurt people from the OB too," I reminded. "But I'm sorry about your dad. After eight years, Gus Redgrave could've stumped up some trust."

"Exactly," he agreed, skating over my comment on the OB. "I wish Dad sued—"

"Get that out of here!"

Our conversation came to a quick stop. Every conversation came to a stop.

Craig faced down two guys from my sociology class, and him facing people down had a different meaning. Brandon's roommate was over six feet and captain of the lacrosse team.

He hauled Major and Harley across the room.

"Chill, Craig," protested Major. He yanked free of his hold. "It's only weed."

"I don't care. I told you straight up not to bring that stuff in my room, and you smoke it in my shower. You wanted to piss me off; it worked. Get out."

"You said not to bring drugs," said Harley. "It's not like we rolled in here with E and oxy like the Raveners. Weed doesn't count as a drug."

Brandon stepped up. "It'll count when we're all thrown out of school. Stop arguing and leave."

"Whatever." The two stormed out.

"Brandon, I'll be right back," I tossed at him. "I forgot something in my room."

I caught up with the guys on the back stairs. "Hey."

They paused, giving me a funny look. "What?"

Major and Harley never said anything about my parents. They also had nothing to say when everyone was bitching me out. This could go either way, but I had to try.

Smiling, I propped my hip against the railing. "You guys hate me too much to let me smoke with you?"

Wide eyes looked me up and down, soaking in my tight jeans and bare midriff.

"Life's too short for hate, beautiful," Harley said. "Join us."

The three of us descended the stairs and looped around the building. We found a piece of wall the same as the rest of the wall and I leaned against it.

It was pitch dark. Harley used his phone's flashlight to help his friend roll up.

"That was harsh in there," I started. "I mean it's like you said. Raveners do it all the time. Why can't we?"

"For real!" Major nudged my arm and took his time pulling back. "And it's just weed. We're not doing the hard shit like they do every freaking weekend. This stuff is going to be legal soon anyway."

"It'd be legal already but the government's still figuring out how to make money off of it."

Harley threw up his hands. "That's what I keep saying!"

Of course he did. He told Mr. Jennings as much during our class discussion on youth in our society. He made an impassioned speech about us being informed like never before.

"Who'd you get it from?" I was no actress, but I hoped I was doing a good job keeping my tone light. "I heard there's a hookup on campus, but everyone hates me." I laughed. "No one will tell me who it is."

Major dropped his voice. "No one knows who it is. It's like covert ops texting this random number and getting our stuff from a different locker every time."

"But you don't have to worry." Harley draped his arm around my shoulder. "We're happy to share."

I forced a smile. This guy was all over me like we were down here for a threesome.

"But you might not need us." Major took a long drag. "You're in the best position to settle a bet."

"A bet?" I repeated. "What are you talking about?"

"The dealers." He shrugged. "It's gotta be the Angels. Who else could it be?"

"What?" I slipped out from under Harley's arm. "Why would you think that?"

"Because they came in here and said dealing wasn't allowed on this campus." Major passed the blunt to Harley. "That's what gangs do. They take over territory and drive out the competition."

"Plus, Hiro is the only one who can get stuff like that through the gates," Harley added.

"Ask them. I bet they'll tell you now that you're their girl."

Wow, that information was getting around.

"I've got fifty bucks on it being Hiro," said Harley. "Major thinks it's Cassius."

"Because he leaves campus every month," Major explained. "He must be doing something shady."

Visiting his mentally ill mother and going to a clinic to check on his health.

Harley held it out for me. "Ask them and I bet they'll give it up."

I ignored his outstretched hand. "I can't because it's not them. You can spread that around to anyone else who has it twisted."

They shared confused looks.

"Bye, guys," I said, backing away. "The party is missing me."

"What?" Harley cried. "But I thought we were—"

"You thought wrong, friend."

And so did I. These guys don't know a thing, and if I asked the dealer's other customers, neither will they.

This guy has everyone texting an unknown number and rooting through empty lockers. He was too clever and it irritated me. I told the Angels I had my own reasons for wanting this guy shut down. There wasn't a doubt in my mind that Leo, Brynn, and their buddies got the roofies they used on Camila from him.

Brandon asked how students on this campus could feel safe after they let Leo go. The answer was they couldn't. Not with him or anyone else with dark intent running around with a direct line to roofies whenever they wanted them.

Camila was at the party when I returned. Relief washed over her face and she waved me over to her, Brandon, and Craig.

"I'm so glad you're here. Brandon and Craig are challenging my movie knowledge for twenty bucks and no one has seen more movies than you."

"Incorrect," said Brandon. "*I* have seen more movies. Boys against girls, Walker. Let's do this."

"Just don't cry when we beat you."

I relaxed, settling into a fun, simple time with my friends. Hopefully Hiro turned up more than I did.

"NOTHING."

Royal and I walked to his dorm after classes Monday evening. We took the long way around, strolling through the soccer field.

"Hiro is sure the dealer isn't getting drugs in the same way," Royal finished.

"Am I ever going to find out what this secret delivery method is?"

"Ask him yourself."

"I got a big 'fuck you' the last time I did."

"It's different now. He doesn't feel that way about you."

I looked up at him. "How does he feel?"

"You can ask him that too."

"Fine," I sighed. "We'll see who is right about the response I have coming my way."

Royal chuckled. "I got you this." He shrugged off his bag and fished out a sheaf of papers. "Damien slipped it through the fence between third and fourth period. Full list of the victims."

"This couldn't come quick enough." I immediately began flipping through. Full names, addresses, and the amounts stolen from the victims inked on stark white paper. I recognized a few names on the first scan. "I dropped another payment in the locker today. I'm down to five hundred dollars. I won't have enough to pay him next time, but I'm tired of there being a next time. I'm finding this guy."

"Be easier if they told you the exact amount your parents stole," Royal said. "Which is why he didn't. He's smart."

"This list will narrow him down. It's a start."

"And this week we'll get you more cash to hold him off."

I tucked the list into my backpack. "The triplets are sunning it up at the beach over the break while we're stealing a car. Happy turkey day to me."

The long-awaited Thanksgiving break was almost here. We had two days of classes and then Wednesday the academy emptied out for students to celebrate with their families. The school never closed for the fact that busy Ravener parents couldn't always make the time for pesky things like holidays. It was better to have their children attended to on school grounds than getting up to unsupervised mischief in the Estate.

Eli would be one of those students this year. I wasn't bringing my little brother along while I committed a felony. On top of that, Aunt

Violet called the school *and* me to repeat that they were not coming to get us. They had travel plans that wouldn't be broken.

"I'm the worst sister there ever was. Leaving Eli alone on Thanksgiving when this will be his first one since our parents left."

"Was it a big deal in your house?"

"Yeah," I admitted. "We'd go to the lake house. Mom and Dad were friends with some of the families in the area, and they'd invite them to join us. Eli and I roasted marshmallows in the backyard and he'd sneak his peas onto my plate when Mom wasn't looking."

My gaze grew unfocused. The looming forest softened in a green haze. "It's not just them being gone, Royal. It's everything they took with them. Eli and I will never roast marshmallows over the fire while listening to Mom play Christmas music a month early."

"No," he said. "Instead you two will roast them over your stove in your New York loft. They didn't take everything, Ember. You've still got the person who made that memory special."

Tears welled in my eyes. The kind of tears that weren't quite sad or quite happy. "And you pretend like you don't know what to say." I threaded my fingers through his. "You're right. I still have Eli."

"It won't be that bad," he continued. "I stayed here one Thanksgiving when Gran and Eddie celebrated with his family. They cook up a feast in the cafeteria and have lots of stuff for the students to do. Eli will understand if you tell him we're using the chance to track down every locker in Raven River."

I wiped my damp cheeks with the back of my hand. "I'm glad you said that because I was thinking the same thing. We have five days off. This is the perfect time."

"We'll leave Wednesday morning and get to however many we can. The country club can wait till we're there on Thursday."

"Shouldn't we talk about Thursday? What will I have to do?"

"It's simple. Don't worry about it until later. Just hang with Eli."

I took that advice.

Monday and Tuesday night, Eli and I hunted down and watched all the best Thanksgiving movies. We quickly tapped out at two and accepted there weren't any good Thanksgiving movies. Our old favorites infiltrated the queue in their place.

It was just Eli and me that Tuesday night. Camila left the second classes ended for her beach celebration with her brothers. She said it was cool for Eli to sleep in her bed while she was gone, so we pushed them into one and piled snacks and candy between us. *Back to the Future* played in all its improbable glory.

"Will you be okay by yourself? I feel bad leaving you here alone."

"Don't feel bad," Eli replied. *"It's way more important that you figure out Mom and Dad's message. Will you go to the lake house too?"*

"It will take a while to hunt down everything this key could open in town. If we don't make it up there this weekend, we'll go another weekend. That's if we don't find what we're looking for."

"You promise you'll tell me everything?"

"Everything."

He nodded, satisfied.

The next morning, I woke Eli up, kissed him goodbye, and walked him to his room. My bags were packed and ready to go on my desk. I grabbed them and went straight to Royal.

Hiro let me in. "He's not here. He had to take care of something but he'll be back soon."

"Okay."

My eyes rolled in their sockets trailing him to his chair. I learned early on Hiro was comfortable in his nakedness. He strode around in black boxers that were more form-fitting than boxers tended to be.

He bent over to plug in his laptop cord and the cloth traveled all the way up to where tattoo stopped covering flesh.

My heart thumped against my rib cage so loud it could give me away. I averted my eyes, asking myself if my wandering eyes and racing palms counted as cheating. Then I asked myself where the hell that thought came from.

"So," I began, clearing my throat. "Royal said the dealer isn't getting their drugs in the way you get your stuff."

"That's right."

I spoke to Hiro's back as he messed with stuff on his desk.

"How can you be sure? What is this super secure method?"

"You asking because you need to know, or because you want to?"

"Want to," I said, blunt as a spoon. "You can't blame me for being curious about how you get everything from Nerds to gin past the gates." I threw myself on Royal's bed. "Tell me. I can keep a secret."

"I'm sure you can." Amusement laced his reply.

"So..."

Heaving a sigh, Hiro straightened, looking at me seriously. "You don't want to know, Bancroft."

"My name is Ember. And I do."

He considered me and I looked back unflinchingly.

"It's simple," Hiro said. "Packages have to go through the front office but Hart doesn't go through those herself. The receptionist, Mallory, does."

"You're saying—"

"Everything I order goes right into her hands and she passes it on to me. And when there's a surprise room search, she tips me off."

"Mallory? The quiet lady with the tweed sweaters? Why would she do that for you? Does she get a cut?"

"I told you, Ember. It's much simpler than that."

I stared at him, face screwed up, as it finally dawned on me. "Is she your girlfriend?" I rasped.

"That's not the word I'd use."

"How old is she?"

"Twenty-six."

My jaw worked. "And how long have you two been...?"

Hiro didn't fill in the gap. "See? You didn't want to know."

Slowly, I slipped off the bed and swallowed the distance between us. Hiro tracked my approach warily—the same way Royal often did. It killed me that closeness made them cautious, not safe.

"I'm not judging you, Hiro." I gently touched his forearm. He stiffened like it was a slap. "You're doing this to make your payments. It crushes me that Rio put you in this position and then Mallory took advantage."

"I wasn't taken advantage of. It didn't start until I was eighteen and, trust me, I'm willing. She gets what she wants and I get what I want. Everybody's happy."

"Okay." I wouldn't challenge him.

I understood why the boys insisted Hiro had to tell me this himself. This was bigger than my curiosity. And if Hiro wasn't honest about when it started, it was bigger than all of us.

"I'm called out for being judgmental, so I don't want this to come across that way. I understand you now, Hiro. Why you're so angry. When your choices are taken away from you, all you have left is how you feel about it. And rage feels just right. I know what that's like."

My hand moved down, curling around his fingers. "Now your minimum payments have gone up because of me. I'm so sorry, Hiro."

"It's not your fault."

"We both know this started with my family."

"No. It started with mine."

The door swung open. Hiro dropped my hand.

"Ready, Em?" Royal asked. If he noticed us holding hands, his face gave no sign.

"I'm ready."

Royal and I didn't say much on the way to the office. Mallory handed me the sign-out sheet, smiling away.

"You two enjoy your Thanksgiving."

I said nothing as I signed my name, pen stabbing the paper harder than necessary. This woman bought alcohol for minors in exchange for sex with a teenager. I was strongly tempted to smash a clipboard in her face.

Royal tugged it out of my hand. Hooking his finger through my belt loop, he got me out of there.

"Where do you want to go first?" Royal asked as we slid into his car. "Bus station. Gym."

I fished the list out of my backpack. "I need to tell Eli we exhausted all of our options. There are five gyms, one bus station, and two storage unit facilities between the OB, Estate, and on the outskirts. Do you think we can get to all of them today?"

He scanned my list, nodding. "Yeah. The bus station is twenty minutes from here. The OB storage facility is farther out but they don't close until six. And the gyms will be quick. You check the women's locker room, I check the men's, and then we're out. We'll do the country club tomorrow when we have a reason to be there."

"Let's do it."

I reclined my seat, shifting to stare out of the window. *What were we going to find today? Was I ready to face whatever it was?*

Twelve hours later, Royal and I pushed into his apartment loaded down with groceries and not much else.

What did our search of Raven River turn up? Nothing.

A couple of gyms didn't have lockers numbered less than a hundred, so we walked right out. The bus station had a twenty-two locker but the key didn't fit. Same result at the storage units and the remaining gyms. The only thing we accomplished that day was buying a prepaid phone.

"So, this phone is all we need to take down the dealer?"

Royal took the milk, bread, and eggs off my hands and carried them into the kitchen. I stretched out on the couch, resting my chin on the arm, and watching Royal over the countertop.

"I had Clay lift Vera's phone during PE. He got the number for the dealer and Monday I'll ask for a mess of coke, E, weed, and whatever else I can think of for an insane amount of money. I'll give him a week to get the stuff and pray we get lucky and he goes off campus. Mallory will let Hiro know who leaves and we'll narrow it down."

"We can't be sure the dealer will be one of the people who leaves campus."

"We can't be sure of anything," Royal said. "Right now we've got less than nothing and I'm hearing it from Rio. He wants results yesterday. Drugs are leaking into our territory. It makes it look like the Horsemen aren't in control."

"I'm with you on the having less than nothing. We hit all of those places today and the key didn't open a single lock. Could we have missed something?" I asked.

"Maybe. There are other places we didn't think of. We passed by a post office coming back from the store. I should've thought of it before. You'd be surprised how easy it is to set up a PO box that's not connected to your name."

I snapped my fingers. "A PO box, of course. Why didn't I think of that either? It'll be closed tomorrow, so we'll have to go on Friday."

"If it's not a PO box, how likely is it that there's something at your lake house?"

"Not very," I admitted. "The feds did the whole search and seizure thing and I doubt they missed anything. What Eli is relying on is Dad's knack for hiding things. He hid his tools and projects to keep me and Eli out of them. And our Christmas presents? Forget it. He'd bet me every year I could open them up early *if* I found where he hid them. I never did.

"There is a chance—a tiny one—that my parents hid something up there that the feds weren't able to find. I promised Eli I'd check, so I will."

"Projects?" Royal's voice floated out of the kitchen. "What kind of projects did your dad do?"

"He messed around in his shed building stuff," I said. "We lived off my dad's trust fund, but Grandpa put restrictions on it. He couldn't get it until he married or turned twenty-five. Until then, he was expected to go to university and graduate with a fancy degree. Dad went with mechanical and computer engineering.

"He loved it, but after meeting Mom his junior year, marrying her two days after graduation, and getting his trust fund with two 'I dos,' he never bothered getting a job in it. He was happy building stuff for himself." A smile spread on my lips. "He built Eli a mobile after he was born. It spun and lit up in all of these colors. Eli loved it. As much as you can tell if a baby loves something," I added.

"Mechanical and computer engineering," Royal said, picking out a part of my speech. "Difficult majors. Eli may be right, Em. Your parents weren't empty-headed trust fund babies. They were smart enough to pull off one of the biggest cons under everyone's noses. They're smart enough to hide something from the feds."

"That's true," I agreed. "All right. The lake house. I'll search every inch of it. Any chance you could give me a ride?"

"There's a chance."

I chuckled. "Thanks for today. It helps not doing this alone."

Royal emerged carrying two sandwiches and a couple of water bottles. "I said I'd help."

Flipping over, I lifted my legs for Royal to sit under me. We got comfortable. Him eating off the plate on my legs and me resting my food on my stomach. Suddenly, a vision of our future flashed in my head. Royal and me on the couch. Cassius and Clay on the carpet, leaning their heads against my thigh as we watched one of the two decent Thanksgiving movies that existed. And Hiro was in the kitchen—

I cut the daydream off. Why did I add Hiro to my happy family scene? The guy said he liked my smile. It didn't mean he was hopping on a plane to live a New York fantasy with me.

"Soup is heating on the stove," Royal said. "In case you're still hungry."

"Royal Cruz." I poked him with my toe. "I love this whole domesticated thing you've got going on. You'd make a great house husband."

Royal threw his head back laughing. "Think I'll fit in with the moms in baby yoga class?"

A rather rough snort burst out of me. Just picturing the tattooed, muscled Royal doing downward facing dog with a chubby-cheeked baby was too much for me to handle.

"You'd be fighting them off."

He smirked. "Now that's true."

I poked him again. "Keyword is fighting. You'll throw them all off and then come home to me."

"Is that right?" Royal grasped my nudging foot. Warm fingers encircled my ankle, tracing soft patterns that popped goose bumps on my legs. "You're going to domesticate me, Ember Bancroft?"

"A life making love to me in a city loft is much better than being stuck in this town jacking cars for Rio."

Royal pressed a kiss on my calf. "No argument here."

I held my breath, heart singing at his agreement. That even a part of him saw a life with me was more than I hoped.

"What do you want, Royal? If there was no Rio and no Horsemen. What would you do? Where would you go?"

He leaned back, looking up to the ceiling. "Tattoos. I've designed all of mine and a few for Cas, Clay, and Hiro. I'd get my own shop."

"That'd be perfect for you."

"But it won't happen." Royal moved his plate and set my feet on the floor. "We need to talk about tomorrow. We're not after a specific car."

Royal flipped the script so fast my head spun. The conversation about our futures was over.

"I'll scope out the parking lot and choose the best one. Older cars are ideal. Don't have to hack a computer, and if it's old enough, the parts are worth more."

"And the party? My aunt throws these events with her country club friends. I'm sure she and my uncle will be there."

"It's about timing, princess. We arrive when the party starts. Seven o'clock. We nod to the valet, say hi to the guys holding the door, and make sure security sees us go inside the party. Then we walk out onto the terrace and keep out of sight. The ballroom will fill up with people, and when it's crowded, we'll randomly go in and out, so when the police are called, witnesses will swear they saw us inside.

"The trick is to be seen, but not to draw attention. It'd be trouble if someone did notice how long we were out of the room. I've been doing this for years and that's never happened. The Raveners are too wrapped up in themselves to care who or where I am.

"As for your aunt and uncle, they might notice you, but you have every right to be there. These parties are open to everyone in the Estate and their guests."

I bobbed my head. "Okay, okay. Makes sense. Establishing an alibi when you don't have one. Smart. What do we do after we take the car?"

"We return to the party. You're ridiculously slow even for a new carjacker."

I shoved his shoulder.

"But the car I'm going to pick out for you should only take five or ten minutes to get inside," he said with a laugh. "Getting it to start will be on me, so fifteen minutes to get out of the parking lot and ten minutes to Donny. We'll be back acting like nothing happened in less than an hour. After the party is over and the cops have been called, we walk out under security's watch. They'll let me go like they have before. No one expects a car thief to hang around."

"Wow." I rubbed sweaty palms on my jeans. "We're really doing this."

"Are you up for this?"

"It's for Eli. I'm up for it. It's just... Taking Leo's car felt like justice. I can't say the same for this. It feels like—"

"A crime," Royal finished. "Because that's what it is. And if you don't want to do this, you don't have to. Stay here, Ember. I'll go alone and I'll pay the blackmailer until you find him."

"Royal, no. You stealing cars for me and paying off a problem my parents created isn't any better than Rio making you do this. I won't be another person who destroys you. I can't." I cupped his cheek. "Not when I'm supposed to be saving you. I'll play my part in this, Royal, and I'll find a way to make it up to the person whose car we steal. As soon as this is all over."

Royal's expression was unreadable. What he thought of my wish to save him or my hope to make up for what we were going to do—his color-changing enigmatic eyes didn't share with me.

"Come on." Royal picked me up, carrying me to his room. "You and I have another sketch to make."

I smiled into his neck. "How many poses are there left for me to twist myself into?"

"We're just getting started, princess. I haven't gotten creative yet."

Chapter Seven

Clay: I was made for the beach. Girls are secretly snapping pics of me to get through sex with their guys later. I'll send you shots of me in my trunks.

Me: Love that you guys are having fun. Take Cam out for a big dinner and order her a dessert off the menu from me. I'll pay you back.

Clay: I will and forget paying me back.

Me: I miss you. Happy Thanksgiving.

Clay: Miss you too.

Clay sent me pictures, but they were not of him in his trunks. My guy wore nothing but the tattoos on his skin. It wasn't hard to see why beach girls were snapping creepshots.

"Names?"

I tucked away my phone. Clay and I would continue flirting later. The gates of the Estate welcomed me.

"Royal Cruz and Ember Bancroft."

The guard ducked into his station to check his records. Soon after the gate rumbled open.

"He lets you in without questions."

"Sounds like you have a question," Royal said.

"Will I ever know the mystery person who put you on the list?"

"It's not important, Ember."

"You and your secrets." I eyed him. "Like how amazing you look in a suit. It's making more sense now how you ensnared me in your trap the night we met."

"You ensnared me," he returned. "You seduced me."

I gawped at him. "I did what?"

"You were unzipping that dress and grinning at me with that you're-not-going-anywhere grin before I knew what was happening."

"Absolutely not true," I cried. "I seem to recall you placing me on the carpet and pulling said zipper down with your teeth."

"You can remember it how you want, and I'll remember it how it actually happened."

"You're impossible."

Royal laughed himself sick. The boy took unnatural pleasure in messing with me.

The Estate Country Club rose in the distance, bringing our jokes to an end. We were about to steal a car out from under guards, cameras, and a party full of rich people unafraid to prosecute. Time to get serious.

We rolled up to the valet. Handing off the keys, Royal rounded the car, opened my door, and held out his hand like the perfect gentleman. My sunset ombré dress spilled out of the car. Aunt Violet's back-to-school shopping spree served me well. Stepping out in the backless flowy gown with diamonds sparkling on my lobes and hair teased into a bun earned me an appreciative look from the doorman before he caught himself.

One thing I could say. If guests noticed I was out of place, it wouldn't be due to my clothes. I looked like a Ravener from the top of my head to my orange toes.

The doorman bowed to us on the way in. We glided past security, coat check, and guests mingling in the foyer. The people who needed to see us, gave us a quick once-over and resumed what they were doing.

We arrived as the party started. Most of the seats were empty. The dance floor was bare. None of this diminished the spectacular transformation of this bland white room into a festive Thanksgiving scene. Carved pumpkins sharing a holiday greeting took the place of centerpieces. Fall leaves decorated the tablecloths and hung off the chandeliers in colorful garlands.

Servers weaved through the tables, alert and on duty regardless of the lack of people. One headed for us and another approached a group of short-haired, ball gowned, diamond-crusted ladies gathered before the stage. He held his tray out to us just as she spotted me.

"Sir. Ma'am. Would you like a stuffed Brussels sprout or cranberry brie hors d'oeuvre?"

"Ember?"

Aunt Violet bore down on me as fast as her heels would take her. Royal slid off my arm.

"Roy— Wait!" I hissed at his back. "Where do you think you're going?"

The ass tossed me a wink, salute, and a smirk as he headed for the terrace.

"Ember, what are you doing here?" Violet grabbed my arm in a painful grip, yanking me to the door.

"Hey, stop!" I cried.

Violet's friends snapped their heads around. She immediately let me go.

"I apologize." Violet collected herself—smoothing her hair and fixing a neutral smile for the wide-eyed waiter. "Ember, step over here with me, please."

We left the waiter behind, moving into the corner.

"What are you doing here?" she tried again. "Harrison told me you and your brother were staying at school."

"I signed myself out for the night. My friends told me about the party. Couldn't miss it." The lie fell easily.

"Signed yourself out?" She sounded like that was the most scandalizing thing she'd ever heard. "You can't do that. Is Eli here too?"

"Eli is at the academy. But I'm eighteen," I reminded. "I'm allowed to leave campus when I choose."

"You don't have a car."

"I got a ride from a friend."

"Which friend? That boy?" She twisted. "Who is he?"

"Just a friend who was coming to the party too and offered to drive me. What's the big deal? I thought this party was for the families." I gave her a sickly-sweet smile. "Like me. Your darling niece."

"Don't get fresh with me," she snapped. "You know exactly what the big deal is. You can't just spring these things on us last minute. We weren't expecting guests at the house. Harrison and I leave for the Hamptons tomorrow and you absolutely cannot stay in our home alone."

Guest. That's what I am. An unwanted houseguest.

I had to give my aunt something, she never pretended to like me. My earliest memory of her was Violet unloosing my pigtails and saying they made my head look big. Unfiltered honesty from day one.

"It's fine, Aunt Violet. I'm not staying at the house."

If possible, her brows shot up even higher, disappearing into her hairline. "Excuse me? Just who are you staying with? Your *friend*?"

"Yes."

I braced myself for denials, lectures, and demands to live under her rules.

Aunt Violet paused, raking me with a shrewd eye. "I should assume your mother took care of this, but are you on the pill? Do you carry condoms?"

I choked. Talking about sex with Aunt Violet did not make it on the list of things I planned to do that day. "I— Yes," I said. "But I never said we—"

"Don't treat me for a fool. I know what eighteen-year-old girls get up to. Someone with such a smart mouth should have a lick of common sense too." She tapped my skull. "Use it. Because I have no intention of caring for a baby."

"Understood," I gritted out.

She nodded, lips pursed. "You may stay. Do not cause trouble and return to the academy first thing tomorrow morning. I will check."

Violet walked off before I agreed. A good thing since I wasn't entirely sure if an agreement was coming or another comment to support my smart mouth.

I escaped the suddenly suffocating room and found Royal leaning against the ledge, rolling a cigarette between his fingers.

"Seriously?"

He tucked it into his pocket. "You look like you'll slap me anyway."

"You took off like she was the cops."

"The key is to not attract too much attention."

"You just didn't want to deal with my screwed-up version of meet the parents."

Royal grinned but didn't deny it. "What did she say that pissed you off?"

"She made it clear she wouldn't raise our baby."

The grin was gone in a blink. "Baby?"

"Don't look so scared," I said. "The three of us have nothing to stress about on that front."

"Okay." Royal squinted at my stomach like he was trying to x-ray my womb. "Good."

"Thinking back to how many times we went bare?" I teased. "Out of curiosity, what would you do if I got pregnant?"

Taking hold of my wrist, Royal drew me in and kissed me. "Shh."

My laugh tickled his lips. "Kissing me is a good way to shut me up. Do it again."

He complied. "I had another reason for ditching you. I tried the key in the locker room. Too big. Don't bother checking the women's."

"Ugh. Great. We can't go to the post office tomorrow either. My aunt wants me back at the academy and she'll call Hart to check I'm there."

"Wow. The way you described her, I didn't think she cared."

"She doesn't. I have no clue what her problem is. It's no doubt punishment for getting up to what eighteen-year-old girls do."

Royal and I killed time on the terrace talking and texting. I texted Cassius and Clay, and Royal didn't share who was on his other end.

"Something up?" I asked.

"It's Rio," he replied, glued to his phone. "He says he's close to finding the dealer."

"What?"

"Not at the academy," he corrected. "I mean the boss. Whoever our dealer is working for. Someone came up to one of our guys on Rainer Street and asked if he was Maurice and how much. They took him out for a talk and he gave up that a friend told him 'Maurice' would hook him up with coke. Someone who lives or hangs around Rainer with a name like Maurice? He won't be hard to find."

I looked away. "I'm all for getting a dealer who sells to kids off the street. I just hate that Rio is the one doing it. He's got cops in his pocket. He should turn the dealers over to them."

"He might."

I didn't ask if Royal believed that. I'm sure he didn't.

"It's getting loud in there," Royal said. "Let's check out the parking lot."

"All right," I replied. Nerves trickled into my resolve. "Are we doing it now?"

"Just looking. We'll do another lap around the party, do what we have to do, and then be back before the cranberry brie runs out."

Ever the cautious one, Royal's description was vague.

Together we skirted outside the building. Royal held me close, walking slowly for the cameras. If anyone went over the security feed, they'd see two lovers looking for alone time.

"—can't anymore. It's not worth it."

We ground to a stop. Tucked away in a pocket of darkness were two figures. I recognized the voice instantly.

"You know what will happen if we're caught," hissed Pomona.

"You don't have to be afraid."

My eyes went round. "Gabriel?"

Royal quickly pulled me back, ducking behind the wall and out of sight of the two. They didn't break their conversation, so they must not have heard me.

"It wasn't a big deal when we started this but now people are asking questions," Pomona said.

Inching closer, I peered around the corner. I could just make out their outlines.

"Just take it." Gabriel handed her something I couldn't see. "If you want out after this, fine. I have to go. I can't be seen here."

I had a moment of panic thinking they were going to walk in our direction.

Good fortune smiled on us and they headed off to the front.

We gave it a few minutes and then we followed in their path. Royal tucked me under his chin, gazing over me at the car thief's buffet.

"There," he whispered. Royal's throat bobbed against my forehead. "Mercedes-Benz toward the back. You already know what to do. It won't be hard for you to get in."

"Okay." My heart was ricocheting around my rib cage and Royal's nearness was only partially responsible. "Can we find the owner? I want to pay them back."

"If you had the money to pay people back, we wouldn't be doing this," Royal said gently.

"One day, I will. Like when I get access to my trust fund. I'm paying them back, Royal."

"Their name and address will be on the registration," he said.

"Good."

"Let's go inside."

Royal steered me past the doormen, holding me close though the cameras weren't a concern. I buried my nose in his jacket, allowing his sweet, tangy scent to calm my jangled nerves.

"Royal? Royal, is that you?"

He stopped dead.

"It is you. Why didn't you tell me you were coming?"

"Royal?" I poked his rigid chest. "What's wrong?"

I knew that voice. We both did. I turned a stiff Royal around and waved to Headmistress Hart. "Hi, Headmistress."

She flapped a hand. "Oh, Ember, we're off school grounds. Call me Gail."

Gail Hart was a knockout. She glided over the Persian carpet in a dress more stunning than mine. A light blue beaded chiffon gown with a ruffled bodice clung to her frame. Her hair fell in a shining wave around her shoulders, drawing every eye to her. A few steps behind, a sulky Julian trailed his mom holding her purse.

"Julian," Hart said. "Look, love. Royal's here."

Julian grimaced like she said, "Look, there's dog shit on the carpet."

"Say hello." My headmistress reared her head in the force of her order.

"Hi," Julian bit out. "Hey, Ember."

Royal wasn't speaking. He wasn't moving at all.

"I didn't know you were coming," I said.

"I don't usually," she admitted. "The school keeps me busy and I have a tradition of carving the turkey for our students who remain on campus." Hart swept the hair back from her son's furrowed brow. "This year Julian's father and I decided it would be good for him if we came as a family."

"Mom," Julian hissed.

I bet your ex is here. No wonder you're dressed fit to cause a mass swooning.

She gripped his chin and planted a smooch on his cheek. Julian glowed neon red. "Go on inside, love. I'll be right in."

He left before she ended her sentence.

"Gail?"

Hart peered over her shoulder. "Oh, Sarah." She stepped aside, gesturing to a younger, shorter Gail Hart. Or at least that's what I thought as I took in the gorgeous woman wrapped in silk coming toward us. "Ember, this is my sister, Sarah," she introduced. "Sarah, this is one of my students, Ember—"

"Bancroft," she said. "I've seen the news. And the dent in my bank account from that missing million dollars."

I had lifted my hand to shake. It fell to my side. "Nice to meet you too."

She dismissed me in a blink, fixing on Royal. "What are you doing here?"

The snap took me aback.

"Sarah," Gail cried.

"We're here for the party," I said, bristling.

"Are you?" Sarah spoke to me but looked at Royal. "I think you'll find you're not on the guest list."

"Sarah!" barked Gail. "Go."

Her sister sniffed. "Come with me, Gail." She walked a few feet and stopped, waiting for her sister to obey the order.

Gail sighed. Her smile was soft as she gazed at Royal. "You stay and have a good time. You're always welcome."

My eyes bugged as she grasped Royal's chin and kissed his cheek much like she did Julian.

"Gail!"

The headmistress walked away, leaving me staring in her wake. "What was that? Can she do that? What if someone—?"

Royal ripped out of my hold. I stumbled, calling his name.

"Royal? Royal!"

He stormed up the stairs. Racing after him, I topped the landing as Royal burst into an empty room.

"Royal, what's wrong?" I raced inside, locking us in. "What—"

"Argh!"

Royal seized an armchair. I screamed as he sent it flying across the room, splintering into wooden pieces and shredded upholstery.

"What are you doing?! Royal!"

He picked up another chair.

I ran to him, grabbing him from the back. "Royal, please!"

He stopped, breaths coming in harsh, ragged bursts.

"Just tell me what's wrong," I cried. "What's up with that woman? Why was she acting like that?"

"That woman. Sarah Joan Ellison nee Hart. That woman is my mother, princess." The second chair crashed into the wall, denting the plaster. "She's my fucking mother!"

I rocked back, shock wiping my mind blank.

Royal dove for another chair.

"No." I dug my heels in, yanking him back.

Growling, Royal pried me off and tossed me on the couch. I bounced off and flew at him, slamming into his chest and bringing us both down.

Royal grabbed my arms, ready to toss me to the side.

"I'm here!" I screamed. "I'm right here."

He stilled—face screwed up in rage, lips peeled back.

I touched his face and he jerked away, snarling.

"It's okay," I soothed. "I'm here and I'm not going anywhere. Talk to me."

I repeated that as I peeled his fingers off and sat next to him. Gently, I placed his head on my lap, dropping kisses on his temple. "It's okay, baby," I said. "It's just you and me."

Slowly his muscles uncoiled, relaxing in the time it took a wild predator to know he was safe. He lay on my lap, breaths easing, and held my hand. His eyes closed as he listened to my voice.

We stayed for a long time. Hours after the party ended.

ROYAL'S SILENT STREAK continued on the drive to his apartment. I tried a few times to get him to talk about anything. School. The key. The last movie he watched.

Royal looked straight ahead and didn't utter a word. It'd be easier to ask the president for nuclear launch codes than it is to make Royal talk when he doesn't want to.

We were a few streets away from his apartment when he spoke.

"I'll give you the money for the next ransom demand." The low rasp from his throat bordered on sinister, if it wasn't for what he was saying. "It was too risky to jack a car with her there. She wouldn't have hesitated to give the police my name."

Her. Royal's mother. The one he said he didn't know.

"I understand," I said. "I want to say no to you paying for me, but I can't take that chance with Eli. I promise I'll pay you back."

Silence descended for another stretch.

"She was seventeen."

I held my breath, not daring to move in case he changed his mind.

"Seventeen and hooked on the coke her boyfriend, Rio, regularly supplied her. Then she found out she was pregnant and her little rebellion with the bad boy from the wrong side of the gate stopped being fun.

"She ran to her sister, Gail, crying and terrified of what their father would do when he found out. Gail came up with a story. The two of them went on a 'gap year backpacking trip' around Europe that was actually Sarah's stint in the rehab facility. She cleaned up, gave birth to me, then returned to Raven River and dumped me on Rio's lap.

"Rio didn't know what happened to her. He didn't know about me. One day he was a coked-up gangbanger, and the next he had a kid. He handed me off to Gran and took off. A sweet fucking game of Pass the Baby."

I slid my hand across and rested it on his fist, keeping quiet.

"Sarah was happy to never see me again, but Aunt Gail couldn't stop thinking about me."

Aunt Gail.

"Rio was bad news. Dangerous. Addicted. Poor. While she was married with her own kid. She wanted to adopt me and raise Julian and me as brothers. Sarah wasn't about to let that happen. She wouldn't have me running around—a constant reminder of her mistakes. Sarah passed me off and warned her sister to leave me alone. If she brought me in her life, she'd drive Sarah out of it. She'd have nothing to do with her."

Royal turned into his driveway and killed the engine. Neither of us made a move to leave.

"She held out ten years before hunting down Rio, and then Gran to see how I was. I didn't know who she was at first. The two of them decided to ease me into it. Let me get to know her first. Eventually she told me she was my aunt and the truth about my mother."

"I'm sorry, Royal." Tears streaked my cheeks. "That's so fucking awful, I don't know what else to say but sorry."

"It is what it is."

"No. Don't do that. Not with me."

The muscle in his jaw ticced, but he didn't ask what I meant.

"Hart changed the admission rules for you, didn't she?" I asked. "So you could go to the academy. Be a part of her life. A big fuck-you to her sister."

"Yeah," he said, dark humor entering his tone. "She's not so bad as aunts go. As my only one, I figure I could have done worse. I definitely lost out when it came to parents."

"You and me both." I trailed a finger along his jaw, willing it to unclench. "I get that it was a time in her life when she felt out of control, but she didn't have to behave the way she did tonight. We were minding our own business."

"It's my fault."

I frowned. "Why would you say that? You didn't—"

"I agreed to stay away from her. I wouldn't have gone tonight if I'd known she'd be there." He cursed. "They never go to these stupid parties. Sarah's always off spending her husband's money all over the country, and Aunt Gail would rather stay at school than watch her ex parade his new girlfriend around town."

"Okay, but it's still not your fault. I'm guessing your aunt put you on the approved guest list, so you have the same right to be there as everyone else."

He tossed his head, bumping my hand aside. "No, Em. I swore to Sarah she'd never see me again... after she gave me the money to pay your ransom."

"She— You—" I stopped, genuinely not knowing what to say.

"I wasn't going to show up at a Ravener's door demanding a hundred grand. He'd have me in cuffs so fast I wouldn't know what happened. I was looking at my life fucked and you dead. I had no choice but to go to her and she made sure it would be the last time."

"You did that for me?"

He carded his fingers through his hair, messing it up as a groan tore out of him. "It's not damn obvious by now that I'd do anything for you? Your ass does have me whipped. Happy now?" He actually sounded a tinge angry asking that. Emotions other than rage and more rage were not what my dark prince did.

Leaning over, I kissed him on the cheek. "You know what," I mused, "I bet if I was pregnant, you'd marry me."

"Shut up."

"Get down on one knee, spouting your undying love." My grin split my face. "You'd whisk me off to New York with Cassius and Clay in the backseat and spend the rest of your life being my sweet house husband—"

Royal threw open the door. Stalking around, he got me out of the car and tossed me squealing over his shoulder.

He avenged my teasing by putting me on my knees and pounded my throat with his cock. I happily took my punishment. Because Royal told me in every way but one how he truly felt about me.

"DID YOU HAVE FUN?"

"Yeah. We sprung for a nice hotel since it was Cam's gift. We met some people on our floor and hung out with them on the beach." Cassius brushed his lips on my temple. "It would've been more fun if you were there."

Cassius and I were ambling through the halls to homeroom. Thanksgiving break ended much too soon and brought Monday on its heels. My brother and I indulged the free time by putting off our homework, playing tennis, and chilling with the streaming service *DoubleFeature*. Our only two interruptions were when we went over the list of the people Mom and Dad defrauded, and exhausted every possibility for what the key might open. Royal drove me to seven different post offices and none of the PO boxes fit the key. My next stop was the lake house.

"We should do it again. All of us," I said. "I can't think of anything better than getting away from this town for a beach vacation. Spring break?"

"Did no one tell you? Seniors don't get spring break. We have senior week instead."

"Senior week?" The phrase tickled my memory. "I remember Hart mentioning it, but she didn't explain."

"We get the week off classes and the teachers take us on field trips, hold events, throw parties. For last year's seniors, they held a concert on the soccer pitch and flew artists in to perform. The rest of us got as close as security let us trying to see."

"That sounds amazing."

He licked just under my ear. "We'll have to put the beach sex on hold."

"But not sex," I twisted and stole a kiss. "Do you have plans during lunch?"

"I was going to eat lunch."

"Not anymore."

"I'd rather eat that pussy anyway."

I giggled. "Literally just every naughty thought that enters your head, comes out of your mouth."

"You like that about me." He put his mouth to my ear. "It's why you picked me first."

Dropping my head on his shoulder, I said, "Picking makes it sound like there was a choice. Everything happened the way it was meant to. My relationship with Royal unfolded slowly and difficultly because everything with Royal has to be. Clay and I connected at our own pace, creating something that is just ours and you..." I pushed him against a locker, brushing his nose with mine. "You were what I needed exactly when I needed it, Cas. Just like you promised you'd be. Keeping promises—there's nothing more important to me."

Cassius's jewel-tone eyes lit with a tender smile. "A thought is entering my head right now," he said softly. "If I'm not careful, I might say it."

My breath caught. "Tell me."

He pecked my nose. "I'm going to hold on to this one for a little longer."

Cassius loped away, drawing ahead though we were going to the same place. I caught up to him in Geske's class. The other Angels were seated and messing around with homework, notebooks, or phones.

Royal held up the prepaid phone. Time to text the dealer.

Forcing the guy to make a move. Would it work? I wasn't sure but they had to do something. The guy, or girl, was covering their tracks too well and asking around was getting us nowhere. I'd seen what happens when Rio runs out of patience.

I pushed thoughts of the gang leader aside as I surveyed my class. Most of them were children of people my parents defrauded. Unsurprising since they told me so in the form of taunts, threats, and violence from the first day. What going through the list did was point me to the underclassmen and seniors that weren't in my classes. It also gave me the exact number of OB kids I needed to focus on because the attackers couldn't be Raveners.

Those from the Estate lost a lot of money and suffered hits to their businesses. But none lost their homes, family, college fund, or everything they worked for in a single night. Someone who did would feel the empathy-deadening rage necessary to put their hands on a defenseless fourteen-year-old kid.

The bell rang, pulling me out of my head.

I survived first period and walked into English literature cursing the amount of physics homework weighing down my backpack.

"Mr. Geske." I slowed down before his desk. "For the final essay, can we do it on one of the books you assigned?"

Geske beamed. "Enjoying *Of Mice and Men*?"

"I am, surprisingly. There's so much I could write about. Mental illness, poverty, or discrimination."

"You certainly could and that's what we plan to discuss today," he replied. "Unfortunately, you must pick a book we haven't discussed for the final essay. I look forward to hearing your thoughts this class."

I continued on to my seat. Bending over, I dropped my backpack behind my desk and glanced up just as Hiro looked away. I lingered, gazing at him since he was looking at me. He turned back and a spark zapped the air and went up the spines of everyone in the room. That's what it felt like.

Hiro and I had been doing that a lot lately. Trading glances in class, in the cafeteria, and when I hung out with Royal in their bedroom. It meant something; however, my mind didn't let me sink too deeply into what. Before he was hurt, Hiro bounced between glares that singed my eyebrows off and ignoring my existence. His expression held neither of those emotions these days.

"Morning, class."

"Morning, Mr. Geske."

"I hope you carved out time to do the reading over your break," he said. "First up, a little question and answer. No tricks. If you read the book, you know the answer."

Geske picked random students, rapid-firing questions about Lenny, Curley, George, Jim Crow, and the Great Depression. We all survived the first portion, so Geske moved on to the next.

"Your assignment is to create a character web," said Geske. "Using proof from the reading to support your conclusions, you'll show

how each character is connected to each other and how that connection influences their actions. I'll pass out butcher paper and you can use the markers, colored pencils, and materials from the back. These webs will be hung up and used as a model for future character webs." He swept his hand back and forth. "Partner with your row."

Clay and Hiro pushed their seats over to mine. We focused on the work. Clay and I tossed the characters back and forth while Hiro sketched out the web, writing in surprisingly sophisticated penmanship.

"Nice handwriting," I said.

Hiro didn't look up from what he was doing. "I took lessons."

"You did?"

"Extra classes after school," he explained. "My English had to be perfect. Reading. Listening. Speaking. Writing."

"You spoke Japanese first."

He nodded.

"How old were you?"

"Six."

Short clipped answers, but he was talking to me. Telling me about the mystery that was his life before we met.

"Fluent in two languages by six. You make a girl feel like a slacker."

The corner of his mouth quirked up. "Says the girl who knows English and sign language."

"And Spanish," I threw in.

He chuckled. "I doubt anyone calls you a slacker."

"Guys, I'll do Curley's wife," Clay spoke up. "Pass me the orange."

Hiro and I reached for the marker at the same time. His fingers grazed mine and I jumped like static shock passed between us. We both pulled back quick.

"Hiro," Clay prompted. "The orange."

Hiro reached for it alone and handed it to Clay. At the end of class, he took off without pausing to push his desk where it belonged.

I watched him go feeling ten kinds of emotions and all of them a variation of confused. Attraction brewed between us, yet Hiro held back. Because of my parents, our history, or his not-girlfriend Mallory, he wasn't going there with me.

Could it be because of the boys? He believes he has to back off?

I dismissed the thought from the boys' end. They got possessive over my platonic friendship with Brandon and Gabriel plucking leaves out of my hair. But Royal didn't blink at me holding Hiro's hand. Clay and Cas were blasé about the growing number of times silent communications passed between me and Hiro. The guys were cool as long as I kept it between the Angels, so what was it?

Just because Clay, Cas, and Royal are cool, doesn't mean Hiro is, I thought as Clay and I walked to lunch. *Pushing it down and moving on is preferable to getting in a relationship you're not comfortable with.*

I bit back a sigh. I could go around and around it all day. The fact remained that it was down to Hiro to tell me what he wanted.

Royal fell in step with us in the main hallway. We joined the line, picked up our food, and headed upstairs. Discovering Julian was Royal's cousin put their entire dynamic in a new light. Julian wasn't only fighting for dominance of the school. He was competing against the other boy who claimed his mother's attention.

Julian and Pomona's table sat empty every day. They permanently moved to the Angels' old table which changed the seating charts. Raveners moved to their side of the loft, and OB kids went to the other.

We didn't go anywhere. The shifting politics earned no attention from the Angels, and underlying the whole ordeal, there was a sense that nothing was happening out of their control. The Raveners sat at their table because they allowed it. And if they changed their minds, they'd go back to where they belonged.

I went to our table to nibble on my food while I waited for Cassius. Gabriel was already half into his meal. We hadn't spoken about what I overheard at the country club. I shouldn't have been snooping and we weren't that close. There was no good way to bring it up.

Royal's pocket buzzed as I sat on his lap.

Pulling out the burner phone, he held it up where we both could see. The screen alerted us to a message that could be from only one person. Royal tapped to open.

My brows snapped together. "What? What is that supposed to mean?"

Staring back at us were two simple words.

555-8546: Nice try.

I kept it vague, aware of the cafeteria full of people. "What are you supposed to do with that? Will he do it or not?"

"Don't know," he said quietly, voice not carrying. "Maybe it's the unknown number. I said I got his from a friend, but it'd be smart to ignore anyone he doesn't recognize."

"What do we do now?"

"We're fine. I'll tell him how much I'm willing to pay and he'll get over his trust issues."

Cassius topped the landing.

"I have to go," I said. "See you after."

After a bout of mind-scrambling sex. Cassius brought me down onto his pillows and sandwiched his face between my breasts.

"It's been too long," he moaned.

"It's been five days."

"Exactly." He kissed my collarbone. "I got you something at the beach."

"You did?"

Cassius got a box out of his nightstand. We rose up, the tiny silver gift between us. Cassius held it delicately as if it would break.

"It's not much," he said. His cocky, self-assured grin faded. "I just saw it and I thought—thought you'd like it and—"

Nuzzling his cheek, I whispered, "And what?"

"And we were there and Clay was texting you and cheesing, and all-around acting like a lovesick bitch, and it pissed me off."

"Why?"

"Because he knows where he stands with you. You guys are dating. He's your boyfriend. While I'm the guy you're still figuring things out with." Cassius grasped my chin between two fingers and raised me to drown in seafoam eyes of sunlight glinting off crashing waves. "I don't want to be just your hookup, Ember."

Cassius removed the lid, uncovering a shiny silver necklace with a rectangular pendant holding browns, ambers, blacks, and oranges inside.

"It's the sand from the beach," he said. "The world outside of this town does exist. You'll get out of here before me, but one day I'll follow you, and it'll just be us."

I clasped his hands and the necklace within them. Longing, love, affection, and laughter bubbled in the piece of my soul that was undeniably Cassius's. The power of one was enough to crumble the façade that I was happy being just his hookup. But all together, it was razed to dust.

I threw my arms around him, delighting in an explosive kiss that stripped us down to our core and laid us bare. Cassius wasn't the abandoned son forced into a harsh life. I wasn't the most hated girl in Raven River—despised by everyone including myself.

It was just us. Two broken people who found each other and would never let go.

"Is that what you were holding on to?" I asked, thinking of what he said in the hall.

"Nah." Cassius placed the necklace around my neck. "That was something even better. I'll tell you one day. If you're good."

"I'm pretty sure I'll be very, *very* bad."

Mirrored grins met in a cheeky kiss. "Then I'll tell you sooner."

ELI WHACKED THE BALL and sent it sailing at my head. I dove out of the way and tripped over my own feet, falling none too gently on my ass.

"*That was on purpose!*"

He howled, falling down midway through running to check on me. "*Total accident.*"

I read his reply upside down. Pushing myself up, I skirted the net and bore over him. "*Liar. I was finally beating you and you couldn't handle it. There's a mean streak in you, Eli Francis Bancroft. A mean, mean streak.*"

He was close to pissing himself laughing. "*There's a sore loser in you, Ember Bancroft. Every time it looks like someone is about to beat you, you make them regret it.*"

"*That's part of my charm, kid. No restraint. No mercy.*" The mantra popped out of my mouth unthinkingly.

"*Intense,*" Eli replied. "*But I like it.*"

Through the chain-link fence, Hiro crossed the lawn and ducked into a pavilion.

"*Done for the day or another match?*" I asked.

"*I've got homework. Can we play tomorrow?*"

I loved that Eli enjoyed tennis. The kid spent so much time inside reading books, getting him interested in anything that required being outside was a struggle. I was the sibling off-roading, hiking, and swimming in the river. He was the one groaning and asking when we were going home.

"*Tomorrow,*" I confirmed. "*Leave the dirty tricks off the court.*"

"*No promises.*"

Eli scrambled up, racing off for a shower, homework session, and at least five chapters before bed. I knew my brother. The person I didn't know sat whole and perfect under a wooden arch.

The sun set on Raven River forest, throwing a myriad of reds and golds over our world. Hiro did not bask in the beauty. Jet-black curtains rudely hid his face, caressing his cheek and dusting his shoulders the way many wished they could. Hiro rose above secret wants and whispered desires. He was right before us but solidly untouchable. Like the single velvety rope that separated you from a museum's priceless masterpiece. It was the easiest thing in the world to step over the line, but the swift, severe consequences that would follow pinned your feet.

I lifted my foot, stepping into the pavilion. "Hiro."

He pulled his head out of the book.

"Eli and I were practicing over there," I said unnecessarily. "And I saw you. Do you usually come out here to read?"

"No, but Royal got a call from Rio and it started getting loud. Clearing out was the best move."

"Is everything okay?"

He lifted one shoulder. "We'll find out."

That did not reassure me, but it wasn't meant to. Blowing smoke up my butt wouldn't shield me when the axe came down.

"We're doing our best to find the dealer. Rio knows that, right? He can't put a time limit on this. If the police could round up criminals on a schedule, Rio would be in Supermax by now."

Hiro chuckled. "Again. Don't let Rio hear you say that."

"I don't have plans to be within hearing distance of that man ever again."

"Good thinking."

"What are you reading?" I asked.

"Manga. My Japanese will get rusty if I don't keep reading and speaking."

I cocked a brow. "Is that the only reason why?"

"All right, I like reading them too," he replied, a smile ghosting on his lips. "You into manga?"

"No. I watch a few animes, but I never got on the manga train. I like my illustrations to move."

"Where do you fall on Korean dramas?"

"Love them."

He scoffed. "Of course. I knew that was SHINee coming out of your earbuds. The over-the-top music, dancing, clothes, and acting is exactly your flavor."

"Hey," I cried, laughing. "What's that supposed to mean?"

"You've got flair, Ban— Ember. Getting revenge with hair removal in the shampoo or itching powder in the jockstrap was too small-time. You violently emptied our insides, got us chucked in the hospital, and created a phantom virus that plagued the entire school."

"Well." I twirled my wrist. "Only the best for the Angels."

"You see? It's all next level with you."

"Don't pretend you have me figured out."

His head tugged back—taken over by laughter that traveled up his long, smooth throat. "No one will ever be able to say they have you figured out. Just when I think I can predict your next move, you prove me wrong. I mean, when you made Royal give you his sketches." He tossed his head. "Royal wouldn't even let me stare at them too long, and you sat there and gave the guy with the knife an 'or else.'"

"It's always nice to be a source of admiration."

"There you go again." The sunset painted his smile infinitely beautiful. "I never know what you're going to say."

Gazing at that rare perfect beam, my tongue tied. It became simultaneously dry and swollen, and I couldn't have used it to lob another quip even if I wanted to.

"Do you know any Japanese?"

I shook my head.

"Come here."

I moved over to him, shoulders glancing off each other as he shifted his manga between our laps. "You see this character." Hiro pointed to a small depiction resembling a twig. "This means tree."

He flipped the pages. "And this one. It's three trees together meaning many trees. Where can you find many trees?"

My gaze swept the wide expanse. "The forest."

"Exactly," he said. "There. Two down, one thousand nine hundred and ninety-eight to go."

I made a strangled noise. "Are you for real? That many?"

"Yep. That's why I have to keep reading manga."

"Of course," I drew out. "I'll help spread that lie if you need me to."

Hiro's laugh was smooth and rich like honey. "I can teach you the character for your name too. Ember."

I sat up, knocking his knee and letting it stay there. "Really? I'd love that."

"The way my name is written, Hiro means forgive. My parents couldn't have picked a name that suited me the least if they chose big, sweet cuddle bunny."

Bitterness ate his sarcasm. My hand lay over his fist. I hadn't noticed it moved.

"But your parents knew what they were doing when they chose Ember. Part of the word literally translates to fire in Japanese, and that's what you are. Wild. Beautiful. Dangerous. Warm."

My head spun under the tide of praise and warnings.

"Unpredictable. Uncontrollable," he rasped. Hiro's fist unclenched under my grasp. "And untouchable."

"I can be touched." My voice was barely above a whisper.

I pressed Hiro's hand to my face. My eyes fluttered shut as his touch skimmed my cheek, and then my lips.

"No." He pulled back. "You can't, Ember. *This* can't. You and me."

I gazed into suddenly hard, smoldering browns. "Why? Because of Cassius, Clay, and Royal? Is sharing me too much?"

"It's not that." He sounded like he meant it. "It's because Hiro—forgiveness—will never be right for me. I'm hard, cold, brutal. I faced the same demons that torment you and they reshaped me too. Fire burns. It feeds and grows and becomes stronger. While ice, it only survives in the harsh conditions that made it, and without, it melts into nothing.

"You and I would be a disaster together, Ember. You'd make me believe in forgiveness and hope, and I'd remind you there is none."

"Hiro," I croaked. "Everything you just said... is a load of crap."

"Amazing." Hiro gathered his stuff and stood. "For the first time, I knew you were going to say that."

I sat in the pavilion long after he was gone. It wasn't every day a guy admitted he wanted to be with you and said you'd be a disaster together in the same breath. The ache in my chest should not have surprised me. I knew only trouble awaited if I crossed the velvet rope.

My phone trilled, yanking me out of my daze.

"Ember," said Royal. "Where are you?"

"Outside in the pavilion."

"Come to my room. Something happened."

The loud phone call with Rio snapped into my mind.

"Oh shit. What is it now?" I thought of Hiro heading back to his dorm room. "Meet me outside or go to my room."

"Your room."

Click.

I hurried to my dorm. Royal waited for me inside, sitting on my bed while he talked to Camila. She was on her laptop like she always was these days. Working on her strike against Leo. No details were forthcoming. She said she couldn't say until there was something to share.

"Royal says you guys need a minute alone." She twisted to the side, waggling her eyebrows at me, and proving the entire Walker trio had raunchy minds. "I'll go down and snag dinner. Text me when your clothes are on."

I waved her out. No point telling her this was not that kind of party.

"Rio called," I said. It was a statement, not a question. "What's wrong?"

Royal shoved off the bed. "I have no fucking clue," he burst out. "Rio lost his shit on me. Yelling and raging about drugs You know that guy I told you about? The one they picked up on Rainer Street asking for Maurice. They had another talk with him and he gave up the friend that sent him into the OB. He said his name was *Royal*."

My jaw unhinged. "I'm sorry. What?"

Royal paced back and forth, puffing and baring his teeth like a caged tiger.

"You heard me. Royal. That's not a coincidence. I doubt there's another guy with that name in this tiny piss-stain of a town. Someone out there is using my name to cover themselves. I got Rio to stop shouting long enough to hear that, and he admitted it's a common trick. Give someone else's name to everyone you do business with, and if they give you up to the police, the cops will waste their time asking people about the wrong person."

"But who? Why?" I cried.

"Their new friend said *Royal* used to supply his cocaine, but he's getting out of the business. He directed him to Maurice who'll give him what he wants."

"I can't believe this," I said, shaking my head. "Do you think it has to do with what's going on here?"

"I hate to agree with Rio after everything, but it's looking like he's right about the main dealer being one of us. A Horseman would know my name was a perfect cover. It'd be a direct hit to me if Rio believed it, and it undermines us both if the police hauled me in."

"It makes sense. Second-in-command and a traitor. While Rio is running around wondering if he can trust you, the real dealer is a phantom, laughing behind the scenes. What are you going to do about it?"

Royal locked my gaze, anger fading under sobering seriousness. "Not me, Ember. Rio's not playing around anymore. He's ditched his marked-bills plan and he's using another approach to find the main dealer once and for all, because it's not a kid locked in this school twenty-four seven. They flooded the OB with their shit and now they've dragged my name into it. It's personal."

"What is he going to do?"

Royal gave me a look. "I don't ask those questions."

"What are *you* going to do?"

"Find who's selling on this campus. He and I have some shit to discuss."

Discuss it while the police are carting him off. When he's locked up and spilling his guts about the main dealer, the cops can get to the guy before Rio does what he's planning to do. This is why I need to be involved to pull you back from the brink, I thought as I stopped Royal's pacing and laid him in bed with me. *I'm your guardian angel.*

Chapter Eight

The next morning, the cafeteria lady served me up breakfast quesadillas, muffins, and yogurt with granola. I carried it up to the loft with Royal by my side. He fell asleep in my room the night before, head resting on my stomach and my fingers still tangled in his hair.

Camila tossed me knowing looks all morning even though she walked in on us fully dressed. I gathered it was a rarity to see Royal snuggled up with a girl.

Our table was packed with the usual assortment of people. Camila and Brandon had their heads together talking. Clay and Cassius bent over Gabriel's textbook discussing the homework.

"Where's Hiro?" I asked.

"Don't know." Clay gifted me a kiss too searing for public but I wasn't about to scold him. "He hasn't come down yet."

He's avoiding me. Hiro tells me about my name, calls me beautiful, sets my face on fire with his touch, and then retreats into his Angry Boy shell. What am I supposed to do with that? My feelings for him are too new to know if they'll grow into something strong, but I'd like the chance to find out.

I dug into my quesadilla, forcing myself not to think about long-haired bilingual boys with calloused hands.

Royal brushed my arm fishing his phone out of his pocket. A frown crossed his features as he read the message.

"Cas. Clay."

Royal tapped the screen and then the triplets glanced down at their own phones. They nodded to him and went back to homework.

"What is it?" I whispered to Royal.

He showed me the message rather than answer.

Hiro: Random dorm and locker search. They're already through the first floor.

Good ole Mallory, I thought.

Maybe that was the real reason. Hiro couldn't be with me while he and Mallory had their arrangement. If he can't get product in, he can't pay the pot. His first priority was avoiding giving Rio another reason to shoot him.

Royal made to pull back and stopped. His phone hovered over my lap.

"Nice try," he said under his breath.

"Royal?"

A darkening cloud passed over his face. Royal's cell creaked under his tightening grip. "Nice try."

"Royal? What—"

He shot up, startling me into dropping my fork. I didn't get the question out before he grabbed my hand. "Ember, we need to go. *Now*!"

I chased him without a thought, tripping down the stairs, and racing outside.

"What's going on?" I cried.

"Nice try! He knows, Em. It's a fucking setup!"

I wasn't following a thing he said. Royal ran faster, near carrying me around the food hall to the dorm building. He took the back staircase two at a time. My lungs burned staying on his tail.

What the hell is going on?!

Royal burst into the boys' side and threw open the door to his room. Startled, boxes of pills flew out of Hiro's hands.

"Shit, man! You scared me. I thought you were security."

Royal didn't hear him. He yanked out his drawers, tossing everything out and pawed inside. I goggled at him, chest heaving, shirt clinging to my sweaty back.

"The dealer knows we're on to him," Royal rasped. "Nice try. That's what it meant! This random search isn't random. Neither is that guy showing up in Horsemen territory dropping my name. I'm being set up."

"What the fuck are you talking about?!" Hiro shouted.

Darting to his bed, Royal flipped the mattress in a single heave.

"I'm talking about this!" Over the leaning mattress, Royal held up a small baggie of white powder.

Stunned, I could only stare as Royal ran into the bathroom and flushed the vile stuff down the toilet.

Holy shit. It's true. Someone did this! Who?!

"Hiro, quick," he ordered. "Check the triplets' room. They want the drugs found, so all the obvious hiding places. Ember, your room too. We all left during break and everyone knows you're with us. Security must be on the second floor by now and we have to check everything, put it back, and be out long before they get here."

I jerked like I'd been slapped. My room? It's not possible.

"Ember, go!"

I took off running.

Cam's and my room was neat, clean, and seemingly undisturbed. I tore the place apart. Under the mattress, in the drawers, the bathroom cabinet, the toilet tank, our shoeboxes, and even in our tampon stash. I searched every possible hiding place and then put it all back with hands that shook so badly I dropped Camila's pen cup and broke it.

Someone planted drugs. This was serious. Bigger than silly feuds with the Raveners or Rio's pathological need to control his territory. This was the people I loved being expelled, arrested, slapped with records, and their entire future thrown off course. Yes, in my cold bathroom as I flushed the baggie of white powder I found in Camila's shoebox down the toilet, I could admit that I loved them.

They were the family I made when mine deserted me. Another shadow man was after them, and he wasn't messing around.

"Ember!" Royal ran inside and scooped me off the tile. "Did you look everywhere?"

"I— I think so," I croaked. "I mean, yes. I did. I found it." I looked into his eyes. "I found it, Royal. In Camila's stuff."

"They got Cassius and Clay too." Royal carried me outside and down the stairs. "They didn't try with Hiro. Every place he can hide something is used for his products. He couldn't risk Hiro stumbling on it himself."

"Why would they do this? How did they even know it was you?"

Royal reached the pavilion. He set me down and took what might have been his first breath since he read that text.

"I took a gamble asking Destiny about the dealer, and another when I texted him with an unknown number." Royal leaned over me, arms on either side of me, hair brushing my forehead. I saw through the gap in his shirt to the sheen of sweat covering his chest. "I assumed he'd have enough people sliding his number around that he wouldn't notice. But I was wrong." A harsh laugh tore out of him. "Or maybe it was Destiny. I don't know anymore. This could have ruined us, Em. Kicked out in our senior year. Arrested. Cam loses her acceptance. We weren't even close to finding him. He did this just to show us he could."

"Royal, sit," I whispered. "Breathe."

Royal dropped to his knees. His head fell on my lap, muscles unbinding as adrenaline leeched out. "We have to be careful from now on. Protect our lockers, our bags, and our dorms. And, Em, we will find him."

I stilled. The adrenaline did not leave him. It collected in Royal's eyes, transforming into a harder, colder promise.

"And when I do, you won't hold me back."

"When you do... I won't try to."

Royal nodded. Once. We understood each other.

Both of us stayed in the pavilion until our sweat cooled and calm returned to our limbs. The bell rang forcing us inside. Royal walked me to my locker, the two of us silent, consumed by our thoughts.

I unlatched my locker to an unwelcome sight. A note from the blackmailer topped my sociology textbook. I read the demand for another thousand dollars and flung it across the hall. A seed was taking root in my soul. Torn apart by seeking tendrils that twisted, entwined, and knotted as they burrowed too deep to be removed. I didn't know what this seed was or how it would come to matter, but I knew something had changed, and I welcomed it.

Royal and I stepped into Geske's classroom. Our teacher's conversation with Officer Ramadi and her partner ended.

"Royal Cruz?"

"That's me."

"Come with us, please." Her hand moved to her cuffs. Her partner's moved to his holster. "We have some questions for you."

Royal touched my arm, sensing I was ready to blow.

"I don't answer questions. I'm known for that around here. Call up my lawyer. He loves that shit."

Lines tightened around her mouth. "No need for lawyers. This is a simple, painless conversation. Let's not make it more difficult than that."

"Handcuffs for a simple, painless conversation?" Royal almost sounded like he was enjoying himself.

"It's procedure."

When you're dealing with Horsemen went unsaid.

The kind, caring officer that swore she'd punish Eli's attackers, cuffed my smirking Angel and marched him out of class.

"I CAN'T BELIEVE THIS." It was Camila's turn to pace the carpet. "Someone put drugs in our rooms. They pawed through my stuff!? What the hell?!"

"It's awful."

I clutched my phone in my lap, willing Royal to call. Classes relentlessly plowed on but Royal did not make an appearance. At lunch I went to the office to ask Headmistress Hart where he was. Mallory turned me away saying she was in a closed meeting and would not be disturbed. It was a safe bet to say Royal was in there with her, but what did that mean?

Why did Ramadi come for him? Did Royal miss a hiding place? Were they in there discussing the process of arraignment?

I would not let them take him. If it came to it, I'd spill everything including the order from Rio that started us down this path. Losing Royal after just getting him back was not an option.

All day Hiro, Cassius, Clay, and I waited for him to stride through the door. The end-of-class bell finally forced me to my dorm to wait with my phone.

"Why would anyone do this?" Camila asked. "I would've been kicked out. Lost my acceptance. And my brothers... The law doesn't go easy on poor guys covered in gang tats. This was beyond cruel, Ember. This is the act of someone who hates you." She came to a standstill. "Do you think it was Leo?"

I broke from my screen. "I didn't... until now. Leo would take it to this level. I don't underestimate that guy for a second."

"We should tell the police." Camila closed on the handle.

"Tell them what? They let him off a charge when there were witnesses. This time we have nothing."

"Ugh," she cried. "Whether there is proof or not. Whether Leo is behind this or not. His free days slinking around the halls are over."

"What you were working on," I began. "Are you finished?"

"Yes."

"That's great, Camila."

"It'll be great if it works."

A knock interrupted us. Camila opened the door on Royal leaning against the doorframe. Alone. Relaxed. Uncuffed.

"Royal!" I vaulted off the bed and threw myself in his arms. My head stuck out the door and I saw Clay, Cassius, and Hiro behind him. Royal brought me inside and we sat down on my chair.

"I had you worried," he said.

"Of course you did." I whacked his arm. "Why didn't you call?"

"I just shook Hart loose."

"What happened? You were gone all day."

"He was right about a setup," Hiro said. "An anonymous call hit the police saying that he was dealing drugs."

"They found nothing," Royal confirmed, "but they couldn't let the day go to waste without questioning me. It took so long because I refused to speak until a lawyer got here and Hart backed me up. When they both came—Hart called one too—I told them I was framed."

"You did?" I asked.

He nodded. "They don't know about the presents we found in our rooms. I dropped that we keep drugs off the campus to protect the OB kids. Someone who doesn't want to worry about us getting in the way would call in a tip and hope they tripped over something that would get us out. The lawyers shared all of that with Hart, but just told the police the tip was fake and they didn't turn up proof showing otherwise. They also accused them of harassment. Hart's lawyer said a lot of nice stuff about discrimination and suing the department for cuffing and dragging me off after their search turned up nothing."

"Nothing?" I pressed.

"Nothing. We've been doing this for years, princess. We know how to hide our shit."

"We got lucky," Clay said. "We were twenty minutes away from matching silver bracelets and a parade across the lawn. This will not happen again."

"It won't," Cassius agreed. He put an arm around his sister. "I'll come up with a way to keep this guy out of our rooms for good."

"How?" asked Camila.

"Trust me."

Four days later, Cassius and Clay presented their solution.

"Personal door wedge alarms," said Clay. "Used by solo female travelers around the world."

"You use it like you would any other door wedge, but if a sneaking fuck opens your door and presses on this, the alarm will go off."

Camila and I examined the tiny triangular contraption with interest.

"Its genius is in its simplicity," said Cassius. "Perfect if you're in a dorm room with weak security."

"Will we get in trouble for using these?" I asked.

"If Hart has a problem with it, she should come up with something better."

"What happened to the cameras she was going to install?"

"She's working on those," Camila piped up. "I stopped in to ask after... you know. She said it's taking time because she must choose an approved vendor that has passed background checks on all its workers. She can't have just anyone walking around a dorm full of kids. The one she hired is backed up on jobs, but they'll be in to install them in a few weeks."

"That's something at least."

"Ember." Clay tossed me the second alarm in the pack. "That's for Eli. The alarm is insanely loud. We tested it in the forest. If anything, it'll alert his entire floor if they try his room next. The guy will either be scared off or someone will come running."

I clutched the small chunk of plastic, metal, and wires to my chest. I loved him so much at that moment, I bordered on the edge of blurting it out. "Thank you. This means a lot to me. We've been freaked out for days."

"We can't have that," Clay said. He stepped back, dusting his hands and admiring his handiwork.

"As a reward," Cassius threw in. "Blowjobs all around? Cam, go to the library or something."

Camila saved me a reply and smacked him over the head with a pillow. Although, I did follow them back to their room and showed my appreciation.

The next week brought the first days of December and the ticking countdown to winter break. Two weeks off for those going home to presents, lights, trees, movies, and families looking forward to seeing them.

"Are you going home?" I asked.

Falling in behind a group of students, Camila and I lazily tromped to breakfast. We were quite a pair in plaid pants and thick sweaters. Winter was making a fool of the sun and dropping temperatures to stay-inside-and-watch-Christmas-movies weather.

"No, my brothers and I stay on campus every year. Hart makes it fun, so I don't mind."

My eyes flicked off her face, catching the peeking glance from one of the girls ahead of us. She saw me and turned around.

"Eli and I will be here too. I'm going off campus next week to buy mini trees, presents, and lights to make it— What are you staring at?"

The girl jerked. She whispered to her friends and the group picked up the pace.

"They're staring at me," Camila said.

"You? For what?"

"I forgot that you deleted your social media accounts. You remember what I was working on for Leo?" She took out her phone and handed it to me. "It worked."

I paused to read... and read... and then scrolled down and read some more.

"Oh my gosh, Camila. This is amazing."

"Thank you." She smiled—not politely or strained or in amusement. But a smile that reflected her strength more powerfully than she knew. Camila swore she would see Leonardo Tremaine held accountable for what he'd done, and she made it happen with nothing but a laptop.

"Leo is going to lose his mind," I said.

She shrugged. "Let him. He can't hurt me anymore."

Inside the cafeteria, the stares she received were revealing. Some students looked curious. Some shocked. A few angry. And, it could have been wishful thinking, but I swore a more than decent number of kids were approving. Perhaps proud.

We picked up our trays and went up the stairs. Cresting the landing, I spotted Cassius, Clay, Gabriel, and Brandon seated at our table.

"There she is! Lying bitch!"

I twisted around, nearly tripping on the step.

Leo streaked up the stairs. The hate warping his face struck real fright in me—for Camila. I grabbed her arm, knocking the trays from both our hands and sending it and our food tumbling down the steps. Leo jumped over a tray and stumbled, falling hard. His roar ripped through the chatter in the cafeteria.

I yanked Camila the rest of the way, running for the boys as they ran for me. "Ember, no." Her wrist was abruptly gone from my grasp. "I'm not running from him. Cas! Clay! Stop!"

Her brothers skidded to a halt. Camila faced Leo as he charged at her.

"Somerset revoked my acceptance pending a review!" He crumpled up a paper and threw it in her face. It was me who grabbed her brothers and held them back. "You made your last mistake, slum trash. My father is on the phone with our lawyers right now."

Camila stood tall, resolve squaring her shoulders and stiffening her spine. "What do you think they're going to do, Leo? I put the truth in those letters. Somerset revoked your acceptance because of what you did, not me."

What Camila did deserved a ton more credit. Those long nights on her computer were spent emailing the admissions board of every prestigious, mid-class, and local college a letter detailing what happened the night of the party. She didn't embellish. She didn't even call him all the names he deserved. She simply stated what the video and witnesses supported. She was drugged, Leo brought her to her room, and they were found with his pants down and Camila unconscious with her dress around her waist. She shared the details of the investigation that went nowhere and Leo's return to school. She ended the letter with a simple signoff:

There wasn't enough evidence for the police. Is there enough for you?

Camila didn't know which worker in which admissions office decided to put the letter online, but it was trending on every social network I didn't have.

"I didn't touch you," Leo snarled. "You think you won something? I got accepted to five other colleges. I'll be out of this fuck town in six months, and you, those thugs, and your drunk daddy will be sued out of your shithole. I give you a year until you're hiding your track marks and selling your pussy—"

Clay got free of me. He rushed Leo but someone got there first.

Brynn shoved through the crowd, marched up to Leo, and smashed her fist in his face. He staggered into the arms of the nosy onlookers who saved him from falling down the stairs.

Face flushed and jaw clenched tight, Brynn turned on Camila. Shocking everyone watching, she took Camila's hand, parted the crowd and walked her to our table. She left the loft, stares, and her shouting ex-boyfriend and escaped outside.

"I WISH I COULD EXPLAIN, but I was as surprised as everyone." Camila spoke to me from the bathroom. She combed her hair in the mirror, preparing for bed. "Brynn didn't say a word to me about Leo before or after."

"She acted like she believed him," I said. "I saw her nodding along when people called me a liar."

Pajama-clad and tucked into my sheets, I considered my day over. Between Leo's confrontation, Brynn's punch, a flurry of gossip, and another visit from the police, I welcomed the peace sleep would bring.

"Maybe she wanted to believe him," Camila replied. "Only Brynn knows what was behind that punch, I hope she talks about it one day."

I nodded. "How'd it go with Ramadi?"

"Good." Camila shut off the light and climbed into her bed. "The station has gotten calls since the letter went viral. One of them from Leo's parents. She came by to reassure me they don't have grounds to sue. I didn't make anything up or defame his nonexistent character. Everything I wrote is backed up in the official police reports."

"I'm glad Somerset did something," I told her. "Hopefully, the rest of them follow suit."

"Even if they don't, his name is out there. People know what he did. He can't silence me after I've spoken."

"I love that. Are you majoring in inspirational speaking by any chance?"

"Early childhood development, but I'm open to minors."

We shared a laugh, indulging in a good, triumphant moment. Tensions were high, the dealer was still out there, and the future was uncertain. But that day was a victory.

I snuggled into my pillow, allowing sleep to take me.

My phone vibrated on the nightstand.

Snapping my eyes open, I picked it up and tapped the message from Clay.

Clay: We're outside on the bottom staircase. Come outside. We have something for you.

The clock read ten minutes past midnight. I was up for whatever we were going to get up to, but did I have to go outside? It was fifty-something degrees out there.

Sucking it up, I shoved my feet into some boots and pulled a hoodie over my head. Clay and Cassius ceased talking as I came down the steps.

"What's going on?" I gave them both a kiss. "Why are we out here?"

"Because there's something we have to do in the forest," Clay replied. "Will you come with us?"

"Guys, I'm all for forest sex, but it's freezing out here."

Cassius chuckled. "I told you she'd think it was about sex."

"Put those dirty thoughts away," said Clay. "It's a different surprise."

Cassius held out his hand. "Come with us. Please."

I don't know if I could've refused him when he asked me like that. I didn't try.

Together the three of us crossed the grounds, though not in silence.

"Cam was amazing," Clay began. "She taught a lesson that will last longer than a beating. That letter will follow him for the rest of his life. The colleges considering him. The employers looking him up."

"She needed to see him deal with the consequences and she had to do it her way," Cassius added. "Cam was right to tell us to step aside. We've looked out for her for so long we forget Camila can take care of herself."

We arrived at the gap in the fence. Clay widened it to help me through.

"She can." I ducked down, passing from campus to forest. "I imagined a bunch of things when she said she was working on revenge against Leo, but this was better."

Darkness rushed to swallow us. The triplets beat it back with their flashlights, lighting the path as we continued through the forest.

"There's just Nolan left," Clay said. "He told my sister he loved her and then he watched his friend drug and pour alcohol down her throat. He called you his girlfriend and he abandoned you alone in the dark miles from home."

My fists balled. "I remember what he did."

Cassius held my hand and helped me over a fallen tree. "It's not right that he gets away with it. Someone that hates women as much as he does can't run off to be the university golden boy basking in his riches without learning a single lesson."

"I agree with everything you said."

"Cam is done with him," Clay continued. "She doesn't want to think about him. She told us that if we wanted revenge, we should go after it with her blessing."

I nodded along. "What are you going to do?"

"That's just it," Cassius said. "We can't make the same mistake twice. Pretending like it's our revenge to have when those things didn't happen to us. They happened to you and Cam."

"What do you want to do, Ember? Do you care to make Nolan pay for that night in the woods?"

Memories tumbled through my mind one after the other. Nolan's severity as he ordered me out. The biting chill of whipping winds tearing through my thin fabric. The glowing brake lights disappearing in the distance. Icy tears seeping into my skin and shredding my childish beliefs in love. Oozing, painful blisters marring my toes days after the five-hour trek.

"Yes." The word was said so softly the wind almost snatched it away. "I care."

"It's up to you, Ember," Clay said. "Whatever you want to do to him, we'll help, we'll follow your lead, or we'll stay out of your way."

The triplets guided me over the final mound. Lifeless limbs fell out of their hands.

In the tree's crevice that was Clay's favorite spot, Nolan Ives knelt bound in the dirt. He saw me, and desperate muffled cries leaked past his gag.

"It's your choice, Em."

Moonlight glinted off the blade's serrated edge as Cassius presented it to me.

"It's your revenge."

Nolan crawled to me and was pulled up short by the rope tying his hands to the tree. His bulging eyes begged to be set free.

"Cassius. Clay…" I trailed away.

What could be said to this? They snatched a man from his bed, carried him into the woods, and held him against his will.

And the knife.

My gaze drifted to the weapon in his palm. Why would they do this? Why would they believe *I* could do this?

"What do you expect me to do?" I whispered.

Clay's response slipped inside and burrowed deep. "Whatever you want to do."

Whatever I want to do.

What do I want to do to the person who made a bet over my virginity? Who pretended to like me, date me, and made me feel special. Who showed me just what kind of trash he thought I was when he discarded me without a second thought.

What do I want to do?

My hand closed over the knife.

The distance between Nolan and me was no more than twenty feet. Those feet stretched into miles as I stepped off the mound and approached the thrashing boy.

A seed took root in me. Implanted by the callousness of my parents, fed by the cruelty of Eli's attack, and growing strong on my helplessness to the mercies of the blackmailer and drug dealer who came within twenty minutes of destroying our lives. I didn't know what that seed provided for me... until then.

Nolan stopped his shouting. His sickly pallor shone under beams of moonlight and eyes that were more white than brown latched on to what I held in my hand.

I bent down and released his gag.

"Ember, don't do this." A hoarse rasp struggled out of his throat. "They're fucking crazy. Violent. Dangerous! But you're not." He lunged forward, lurching within a hair's breadth of my face. "This isn't you. Let me go and no one has to know about this. We'll forget this ever happened."

"Why did you do it, Nolan?" I didn't recognize the person speaking. But it was me. "Why did you go through all of that to get me to sleep with you? Have you ever asked yourself that? Why you, who could be with anyone, would put so much effort and maliciousness into tricking a girl into believing you like her, just so she would have sex with you? Serious question, Nolan. At any point in the last two years, did you ask yourself what the fuck is wrong with you?"

Nolan's head snapped this way and that, searching for a way out. "Ember, that was years ago!"

I twirled the blade's tip on my finger. "That's what you have to say for yourself?" I asked, tone light.

"No, I— Sorry." Nolan spoke to me, but looked at the weapon. "I'm sorry! It was wrong. I never should have made that bet."

"But it went further than the bet, Nolan. You weren't satisfied with lying and using me. You then had to humiliate me for daring to say no to you." I leaned in, pressing my face to his and feeling his cold sweat on my forehead. "You left me in these very woods in the middle of the night because a person who denies you is no longer of any worth."

"That's not true—"

"It is true! You can save your lies for someone who doesn't know you, Nolan Ives. Your mask doesn't work with me anymore!"

"What do you fucking want from me?!" he roared. "I did it! I made the bet! I left you in the woods! You had two years to do something about it!"

Nolan swung with his bound hands. The blade flew from my grip, landing on the riverbank.

"But you didn't because you moved on," he said. "You didn't care about me either until *them*. This isn't about you, Ember. They hate me. They've always hated me and threatened me to stay away from their sister on our first date. But I loved Camila. I treated her right. I don't deny that I should have stopped Brynn and Destiny and their stupid joke, but believe me I didn't think for a second that Leo would do what he did.

"This is not you, it's the Angels. And they want you to be just as low and twisted as them!" Spittle flew from his mouth, dotting my cheek. "They're using you. Manipulating you. Untie me, Ember. I swear if you do, we'll forget this ever happened."

There was one interesting part of his speech. A statement I could not let go. "You loved Camila?"

He bobbed his head roughly. "Yes, I loved her. And she wouldn't want this either."

"Those fuckers don't know they're the reason we've been together this long," I said slowly, watching his jaw slacken with shock. "I get to screw her as much as I want and, for once, I don't have to pay for it. The perfect girlfriend."

I raised a brow. "Who said that, Nolan? Wasn't it you? Kind of a nasty thing for a loving boyfriend to say about their girl."

Nolan didn't reply. He didn't give another speech. He didn't breathe.

"But this isn't about Camila, Cassius, or Clay." I held out my hand and Clay pressed the handle into my palm. "This is about you and me." I shook my head. "No, it's completely about me and how fucking exhausted I am with people hurting, abandoning, and lying to me. I can't change what my parents did. I can't stop the blackmailer. But I can make sure right here and right now, that the next time you get it into your head to manipulate and degrade another woman, you'll think twice."

Gripping the handle, I lofted the knife over our heads.

"Ember, no! No!"

I stabbed with all of my might, his screams a distant echoing in my mind.

The blade stuck in the dirt between Nolan's legs. I stood up, dusting myself off.

"It's your turn to be left alone and vulnerable in the woods," I stated. "That knife will cut you out of those ropes but I'm betting it takes a few hours when your wrists are bound. Better get started."

I stepped around him, untied him from the tree, and gave him my back. Clay and Cassius fell in behind me, the three of us leaving him behind without a backward glance.

Nolan's shouting began anew—laced with vile threats, promises of revenge, and merciless consequences if we didn't come back and untie him.

I took Cassius's and Clay's hands as he faded in the distance. "I love you."

"We love you too."

CASSIUS UNHOOKED MY bra in the hallway. He flung it over his shoulder, smacking it square on some guy's doorknob.

Giggling, I twisted out of Clay's arms and ran to get it. I picked it up just as Cassius took hold of me and threw me over his shoulder. He carried me unceremoniously into their bedroom.

The triplet tossed me on his bed and Clay was on me before I caught my breath. Drawing up my hoodie, untying my hair, removing my bottoms in one swift tug.

"Say it again."

His order was a deep, husky whisper that made my toes, hairs, and fingers curl.

"I love you."

A screech interrupted my undoing of his belt. Cassius pushed the beds together, gazing at me as he hopped on top and came closer.

I couldn't believe this was happening. I joked about it. Fantasized. Dropped hints. But I didn't let myself believe the night would come that Cassius, Clay, and I would share in all that we felt together.

Clay kissed the tip of my chin. His sweet lips caressed a trail to my breasts. I fisted the sheets as he blew hot air on my nipple. The poor thing was already harder than a pebble. Teasing was unfair.

Clay seemed to agree. He took me into his mouth, licking and flicking the pebble into submission while the other stood to attention under his tweaking fingers.

My moans were loud and wanton. Wildly I pushed on my underwear, desperately trying to get it off and without stopping what Clay was doing.

Cassius watched the show, slowly taking off his shirt, then unbuckling his belt as his ridge hardened in his jeans.

Noticing my struggle, Clay gripped the lace and ripped it off my body. I gasped as my favorite panties landed in tattered strips on the floor.

"Is destroying my underwear going to become a habit with you, Clay?"

His chuckle rumbled my sensitive nub with tantalizing vibrations. I instantly forgot what I was mad about.

Cassius pulled off the last sock. He was wonderfully naked before me and I reached for him, wanting to touch him. Wanting him to touch me. Desiring to melt into the men I loved like a raindrop becomes the sea. Joining in something bigger and more powerful than myself.

Our mouths connected in a hungry clash of warring tongues that lit a blaze in my lower belly.

Both boys released me at the same time. I made an angry noise, vision blurring under my pleasure-addled brain.

"C'mere, baby."

Cassius leaned against the headboard, a sinful portrait of beauty and sex with his legs open, one bent and his arm draped over it. The other hand stroked his length with slow, magnetic movements. I crawled toward him, licking my lips and knowing what he wanted me to do without asking.

I swallowed him to the soft skin of my fingers, cupping his cock and tugging in time with my bobs. Cassius hissed rough, guttural noises that increased my fervor. My bare ass wiggled in the air, begging for Clay.

If he's watching, I should give him something to look at.

Bracing myself on Cassius's thigh, I plunged two fingers past my folds as bold as I pleased. A sharp grunt said my bid for Clay's attention was successful. It felt nearly as good as the gentle removal of my fingers and the replacement of his.

Cassius tangled in my hair. "Fuck, Ember. You're incredible."

This was incredible. My blood sang with the literal translation of my name: Fire.

My skin burned like flames licked at me. Beads of sweat popped all over my body and my nerves thrummed with heat, arousal, need, Clay, and Cassius.

Clay picked up the speed, hitting that spot with relentless determination. My cries spurned Cassius on and his grip on my strands tightened.

I pulled back just in time. Cassius exploded on my neck and chest. I came seconds later, screaming Clay's name.

Cassius caught me as I collapsed on his thigh. "Who told you not to swallow?"

I laughed—happy and warm. "You mad? Do something about it."

He dragged me up and kissed the shit out of me. Biting and nipping my lips and tongue until they were just as red and swollen for them as the rest of me.

Reaching behind, I drew Clay in. I broke apart from Cassius and kissed Clay just as fiercely.

Hair tickled my stomach. Cassius was moving down between my legs. "Say it again."

"I love you." I'd say it as many times as he wanted. I'd say it as quickly as my name, birthday, and favorite candy. No hesitation. No pausing to question. I loved them.

His expert tongue found its home, tasting my arousal and drawing more. High off of one orgasm, my core was ready for another.

Clay drew away to reach in the nightstand. My nails scraped tiny chips in the headboard. If Cassius was the rough, hard, pounding jackhammer, then Clay was the nail gun. Every pump was knowing and deliberate, sliding inside of me with perfect ease. I loved both for the simple fact that every time I was in their arms, it was all about me. My needs and my pleasure came first though I was far from selfish. For a brief moment in time, their world centered around me and only me.

The boys guided me onto my back.

I sank into the pillows. My hand linked with Cassius and my legs wrapped around Clay. "I'll take mine now."

They didn't have to ask what I meant.

"I love you, Ember," Clay said. "Possibly since the first day I met you and stole a kiss that wasn't mine."

"And I love you," said Cassius. "Since the first time we had sex and you said three more times." He accepted my swat with a grin. "And the night I looked into your eyes and saw that you and I were the same. Meant to find each other. Meant to heal the other."

I bit my lip, heart cracking with so much love I was on the tip of crying.

Cassius's mouth found my breasts as Clay positioned himself at my entrance. Cassius scraping my nipples with his teeth was my weakness, so of course, he set on the tiny nubs with no mercy. The cries were already building in my throat as Clay pushed in a single smooth thrust. He started pumping and that was the end of me.

I was powerless against one of them. Both together and I came apart like a frayed sweater—screaming and clawing the sheets, begging for more until speech deserted me completely.

I came in a shower of bursting explosions, showering sparks on me that awakened each memory of their touch on my skin.

Riding the wave down, I grinned, reaching for my boys. "Don't stop. I've got at least three more times in me."

THE NEXT MORNING, NOLAN glared a hole in my head from two tables away. The boy survived his night in the woods and returned to school in time for breakfast, but he didn't look as happy with his sweet potato and kale frittata as the rest of us.

"Why the hell is Ives looking at you like that?" Hiro snapped. "Is he trying to start something?"

I hid a smile at his protectiveness. His mouth said he didn't want to be with me but every other part of him said differently. "No, he's angry because I finished something. Forget about him. He's not important anymore."

I twisted and kissed Royal's cheek. "I'm going back to my room. See you guys in homeroom." I shared a private smile with Cassius and Clay.

"Hey," Royal said. "I put it in your locker. And don't say you'll pay me back. That piece of shit will when we find him."

I kissed him again—slow and savoring. "Thank you."

"There's another party on Christmas Eve. The Raveners just can't help themselves. We'll take care of business then."

"Okay."

Royal's timing was scarily good. The blackmailer was on my mind and the reason I dragged myself from my breakfast early. I told Nolan I couldn't do anything about the attack and the ransom. But I did not believe that. I couldn't.

There was a way to track them down. I had to find it.

The list of victims was in my nightstand drawer. I got it out, rested it on one knee and propped my laptop with the other. Eli said his attackers were boys that were both taller and heavier than him. That was something. Actually, it was more than something. Families with daughters or no children were eliminated. Short boys I could ignore. Somewhere in this list were the guys who hurt Eli and forced me to steal to meet their demands. They were begging to be found. I would oblige.

THE REST OF THE SCHOOL week passed in a blur of homework, lectures, two exams, and uncomfortable looks from the boys I stared down in the halls, mentally comparing them to the information Eli gave me.

Saturday morning, I said bye to Eli outside the gate. Royal leaned on the hood of his car waiting for me.

"*I want a new bookcase,*" he signed. "*A tablet too.*"

"*I love you, dear sister. Drive safely,*" I corrected. "*That's what you meant to say, right?*"

No one rolled their eyes at me more than this kid. "*Yes, that too. I also want sneakers. My pair has a hole in them and Aunt Violet bought me nothing but leather dress shoes.*"

"*I'll see what I can do. By the way, how long is your gift list for me?*"

He grinned. "*Look at that. Royal wants you. Better get going.*"

The stoic boy hadn't twitched or moved a face muscle.

"*See you. Text me when you get to the lake house.*"

I waved goodbye.

Royal beeped his car open for me. We slid in and made our escape, turning onto the road that led us into town.

"Where to first?" Royal asked.

"Christmas shopping first. Might as well get Eli's presents and my gifts for you guys while we're off campus."

"You don't have to get me a gift," Royal said.

"Are you saying that because you think *you* don't have to get me something? Let me tell you right now that's not going to work. I have high expectations for this Christmas, Royal Cruz. If you don't deliver, there will be serious consequences."

"Oh, really?" It was an interesting part of our relationship that Royal liked it when I threatened him. "What are you going to do?"

I flicked his chin. "Don't find out."

"About the list." He suddenly grew serious. "You've checked out every guy in the school by now. What do you got?"

"I'm glad you asked." I retrieved the well-worn, scribbled-on list from my backpack. "I'm assuming some things," I admitted. "Like that they're not Raveners and they're directly related to the people on this list. Another grandson with a different last name and I'm screwed."

"True."

I sucked in a breath. "Okay, here's what I got. Kyle Casen, Luis Riviera, Adrien Miller, Harley Donovan, Craig Howell, Royce Lamb, Yuki Watanabe, Ken Han, Amir Blake, and Jasper Crown," I said. "Ten guys in this school whose families lost a lot of money. A few of them have told me to my face how they feel about me, so I'm thinking I'm on the right track."

"How do you want to handle it?"

"Direct approach. Get up in their faces and say that I know it's them and I'm going to the police. The ones who crack are the guys."

"These guys have proven they don't have a problem beating on someone smaller than them. You don't think you're getting in their faces alone, do you?"

"Nope," I said easily. "You can join as long as you leave your knife behind."

"Nope," he replied, mocking me.

"Royal, I'm serious. Why do you even carry that thing?"

"It's easier to hide than a gun."

I gaped at him. "You did not just say that."

He took his eyes off the road to meet me head-on. "You're surprised? After what happened in Caesar's garage? I walk around with this angel on my arm, Em. People know what it means. Guys have tried to jump me four different times. Either other bangers or folks with a grudge against the Horsemen. I don't go around with protection like Rio does and they think I'm easy game. They quickly find out they're wrong."

"Royal, holy shit." I squeezed his arm. "I had no idea."

He shrugged like we were talking about gnats flying in his face and not people trying to beat or kill him.

"If it makes you feel better, I wasn't serious about the gun. You dig out enough bullets from guys screaming and pissing themselves and it changes your mind about them."

My heart squeezed painfully in my chest. Royal's time with the doctor ripped at me every time I thought about it. Rio exposed that sweet, smiling boy in the photograph to horrors no teenager should see. Hell, adults shouldn't see it either.

"By now people know not to mess with me." Royal stroked my cheek. "I hang on to the switchblade for the stubborn ones."

"I think there was a compliment in there somewhere," I murmured. "Buried under your usual messed-up shit."

He chuckled. "It was in there. The woman to tame me had to be a fighter. Which means she had to be you."

I cheesed like a lovesick puppy. "That was so damn sweet, I might make you pull over this car."

Royal hit the brakes.

EVENTUALLY, WE GOT on the road and put Raven River in our rearview. The lake house was five hours out of town, and the trip granted us stretches of vibrant forest, rolling mountains, and the city of Easthaven three hours into our ride.

Trips to Easthaven were a rare occurrence in my life. Closest mark of civilization to our town, but Mom and Dad only visited for a special treat. A trip to the zoo. Theater tickets. A high-end shopping day.

I pressed my nose on the window, following the skyscraper to the very top. Easthaven was alive with people, color, sounds, and smells. Banners hung from telephone poles announcing events. Trash spilled out of overflowing cans. Mothers chased after kids on leashes. I loved every bit of it.

"I used to get so excited when Mom and Dad brought us here. Put on my best clothes and did my hair nice. City people were fancy in my head. I had to look the part."

"This is my first time here."

"Really?"

He nodded.

"You'll love it. There's an art store in the mall we're going to. You should check it out while I'm Christmas shopping." I bopped my eyebrows. "That's also your chance to get me something nice. Hint, hint."

Royal didn't grin to my bait, though he seemed entertained by it. GPS directed us to the mall and bad luck made us drive up, down, and around three blocks to find a parking space. We finally got one and headed inside, splitting up at the entrance and then meeting an hour later in the food court.

Royal took one look at my bags and called me out. "You got Eli everything he wanted, didn't you?"

"You know I did." Plopping down, I brazenly took his gyro off his plate and snagged a bite. "Tablet, bookshelf, three of his favorite books, and new shoes. It's our first Christmas without our parents and we're spending it in a school because our aunt and uncle don't want us home. Fulfilling his wish list is the least I can do."

"What's on your wish list?"

"Hmm." I draped his arm over my shoulder, snuggling in. "There's a collection of Berenice Abbot's photographs I've wanted for a while. She took pictures of 1930s New York architecture. Also, I used to have posters of my favorite K-pop bands.

"The Child Protective Services lady said we could only take what we could fit in one duffle bag. The FBI agent was breathing down my neck the whole time, checking that I didn't take anything valuable, that I got flustered and left without them. I'd love to replace them. And candy," I said. "Always a good choice."

"Good to know."

I pestered him asking if he planned to fulfill my wish list. He kept his yes or no close to the vest because he wasn't Royal if he wasn't masking human emotion under ten layers of anger, raw masculinity, and a pathological need to wind me up.

After finishing our food, it was back on the road for the final leg to Earnshaw Lake. Memories unfolded as my surroundings became familiar. Happy memories because I blocked out the rest. Eli and I paddling on the lake. Dad teaching me to fish. Me wandering aimlessly along the bank. The Thanksgiving celebrations with kind neighbors looking for more family like we were.

Pavement gave way to dirt road. We were almost there. The trees closing in and the familiar scent of pine left me certain.

I pointed out community mailboxes sticking up at the bend. "Turn there. Our place is forty-six."

Royal turned off as directed, rumbling up the incline to the home near the end of the road. The police tape made it easy to spot.

We parked in my old driveway. The lake house was just how I remembered it. A river stone chimney stack rose half as high as the trees. The screened-in porch wrapped entirely around the house, basking in remembrance of little socked feet running around. Windows made up most of the structure. Looking through, I saw the old armchair Dad used to watch television in and the kitchen where Mom taught Eli to make blueberry pancakes.

"Ember?"

I shook myself. "Sorry. Did you say something?"

"Where do we start?"

"There's a shed in the back. Also, the attic and crawlspace."

"Those places scream hiding spot," Royal said. "The feds would have been all over them. Your parents were smart. They'd have known that. They put that line in the note. They left the key at the cemetery. They're not making it obvious, so think like them, Ember. Where would they hide something that they know only you would find?"

"Only me," I whispered. "Only me."

My gaze traveled up to the second floor. "My room. There was a loose floorboard under my bed. I wrote notes and hid them in there, imagining that a hundred years from now another little girl would find and read them."

"Your parents knew about this?"

"Yes. Dad bought me pretty stationary so the letters would be nice. This key is small. Maybe what it opens is small too."

"Let's check it out."

The front door lock was replaced. A minor issue as I didn't have the key for the old one either, so we knew we'd have to deal with this. Royal picked the lock with such ease I seriously wondered if my two-year no-sex streak was because my lady boners only got it up for bad-boy criminal types. I lost my virginity to a car thief and all of my boyfriends were in a gang, so the evidence was strong.

"Where would I be if I had regular, buttoned-up boyfriends who held my doors open and gave me flowers on our two-week anniversary?" I asked as we walked inside.

"Bored out of your skull."

I inclined my head. "Fair enough."

Royal looked around. "Nice place."

He was being sarcastic. The authorities that blew through our home clearly never heard of putting things back or closing a drawer after opening it. Our board games were scattered on the rug. Mom's hutch where she kept her antiques was bare and one of the doors hung askew off a broken hinge. A thick layer of dust coated everything.

Royal followed me upstairs to the second door on the left. My room was simple. A full-sized bed, armoire, desk. Everything else was carted out with the rest of the valuables. The walls were warm wooden panels painted white, and decorating them were a few of my favorite bands.

Royal immediately began taking down the posters. Hugging him from behind, I buried my face in his back. "Thank you for being here with me. I couldn't do it without you."

"I doubt that. You don't need me. You're stronger than that."

I hung on a little longer, soaking in his warmth.

Royal finished with the posters. I let him go to grab the bedpost and push it back.

This was it. My bed wasn't moved. The rug beneath was undisturbed. The feds didn't look under my floorboards like Dad knew they wouldn't. Eli was right. Whatever they wanted me to find was here.

Dropping to my knees, I threw back the rug. I took a deep breath, held it long and deep as I lifted the board and—

My breath whooshed out in a flood of disappointment. Tucked beneath the wood lay a dozen pink envelopes, dusty and curled by age. I pushed them aside looking for something—anything.

"There's nothing here," I said.

"Doesn't mean it's not in the house. We'll look through everything like you promised Eli." He held out his hand to help me up. "If it gets too late, we can sleep here."

"We won't have electricity or water. We'll freeze our tails off and smell stinky doing it."

Royal laughed. It was the most beautiful music.

"We better hurry, then," he said. "Where do you want to start?"

"Up here. See if there are more loose floorboards."

We swept through the lake house pawing through every nook and cranny. We looked in the appliances and behind them. We moved the furniture to look underneath. I got on my hands and knees searching for loose floorboards. Royal picked the lock on the shed and we examined the tools like they were potentially more than metal and plastic. As the sun set, we finally accepted the lake house did not hold a clue for me.

I hefted a fallen lawn chair, righting it before the firepit. *This is the chair Eli sat in while we roasted marshmallows.*

Marshmallows. That's what our Christmas needs. Hot cocoa and marshmallows.

I'd have to get some on another trip off campus. This one was over.

"Let's go," I said. "It's getting late."

Together we went in through the back door, locking it behind us, and passing through to the front.

"This is a nice place," Royal remarked. He carried the rolled-up posters under one arm. "For real. I was thinking what's the point of leaving one riverside town in the middle of the forest for the same thing by a lake. But this place is nothing like Raven River."

"No," I murmured. "The people are nice here. They don't care about silly things like which side of the gate you're on. And Mom was different here too. She was softer. Freer. Happy. Because she was away from... the memories."

Royal and I climbed off the porch. I pointed to the flowerbed lining the house. "See? Someone's been taking care of them. I bet it's Mrs. Henderson. She planted these flowers with me one summer when I told her how much I loved her garden. She and I..."

I trailed off, eyes bulging and trained on a tiny black insect scuttling over a flower petal.

"What?" Royal prompted. "What did you do?"

"Royal," I croaked. "Holy shit, Royal. I've got it." I smacked at my pockets, rushing to grab the key. "The message. The key. I've got it. I know what it opens!"

"What?" he asked. Shock, excitement, and anticipation lighting his handsome face.

"Mrs. Henderson!"

"It opens Mrs. Henderson?"

I grasped his bicep, running to the car. "Come on. We're driving back. I'll explain on the way."

Royal didn't waste a second. We hopped in the car and he gunned it, peeling out of the driveway and kicking up a shower of fallen leaves in our wake.

"Mrs. Henderson is from Easthaven. She retired here ten years ago and filled her house with toys, games, and even had a tree house built to encourage her grandchildren to come and stay with her. They rarely did.

"When Eli and I were here, she'd invite us over instead. We'd hang around for hours playing and eating cookies in the tree house. Mom and Dad got close to her and every Thanksgiving she was the first one they'd invite over."

"Okay," he said slowly. "She's friends with your parents. Do you think she knows what the key opens?"

"*I* know what the key opens." I rolled the innocent hunk of shaped metal on my palm. "It was fricking obvious. I should have known the second I saw it."

I shot forward, pointing out the window. "Stop here. Next to the mailboxes."

"Mailbox?"

Nodding, elation bubbled up, straining the limits of my excitement as I showed him the key. "This is a mailbox key, Royal. And Mrs. Henderson lives on Earnshaw Drive, house number twenty-two."

"Holy shit," he breathed.

We dove out of the car at the same time, leaving it running and doors wide open. My hand shook as I fitted the key in the lock, turned, and drew it open.

I found it. I can't believe I was right. Eli was right. They didn't just leave us.

Yanking out the stack of mail, I roughly pawed through flyers, coupons, bills, and personal letters.

"Lisa Henderson, Lisa Henderson, Lisa Henderson—"

I froze having reached the bottom of the pile and the final letter.

"Ember Bancroft," I read.

I raised my head, latching on to round, chestnut eyes holding the same feelings as mine except for one.

Fear.

"This is it," I said. "What if their location is in here? What do I do?"

"You open it, Ember. Whatever is in there you'll deal with it, but right now, you need to know."

Taking a sharp lungful of air, I held on to it till my body made me let go, reminding me that it wanted to live, fight, and change.

I opened the letter.

A single white slip of paper was tucked between the folds. I drew it out, and my face crumpled in confusion.

"What the hell is this?"

Royal bent over me for a look. Typed on the paper we drove hours to find were three letters and a string of random numbers.

CMB

440059765985664128645

"What am I supposed to do with this?" I asked. "It doesn't mean anything to me."

"It could be a code," he offered. "And the letters are a clue to help you break it."

Groaning, I fell back against the mailboxes. "Come on, Dad. I got here to where the feds wouldn't think to look. Couldn't you have just given me the answer instead of another flipping question?"

"I'm guessing they were being careful in case Mrs. Henderson got curious."

"No, wait," I said, straightening up. "Mrs. Henderson left mail in her box that wasn't hers and she would have given them her key. She knew I was coming for this. Mom and Dad must have told her why."

"Think she's home?"

"She's always home."

Just like that, we were in the car and racing up the street.

Mrs. Henderson's home was a short drive from the main road. She built a gorgeous retreat back on the property. As we rumbled up her twisty drive, lights peeked through the trees. She was home.

Royal parked and let me out. "I'll wait here. Rio called me twice. It could be about the dealer's boss."

"Okay. Be right back."

I bounded up the porch, nerves jangling like her wind chimes.

My parents must have given her an explanation. Please, let me end this search here.

Mrs. Henderson opened up just as I lifted my hand for a third knock. Her powdered, wrinkly cheeks stretched into a smile. "Ember, oh my goodness. What a lovely surprise."

"Hello, Mrs. Henderson."

We hugged like long-lost siblings who found each other again. Mrs. Henderson smelled the same as I remembered—gardenia, flour, and hair spray.

"Come in, come in," she said. "I was just about to sit down to dinner. Who is your friend? He can come too."

"We can't stay long."

I let her hustle me inside. Lisa's home was as inviting, warm, and lived in as I remembered too. Her grandchildren should've visited. They would have loved it here.

"I came because of this." I presented the letter.

"Oh, good. I'm so glad you found it," she said over her shoulder, shuffling to the couch. "I worried you weren't coming after all this time."

"You knew about this," I confirmed. "What did my parents say about it?"

"Say about it?"

She sat and pulled a blanket over her lap. Mrs. Henderson patted the cushion for me to join her. She was relaxed and slow for a normal catching-up chat.

I sat, allowing her to drape the blanket over me too. "Did they explain when they asked for your key? It took me so long because I didn't know what was going on. I still don't."

"I see," she crooned. "How awful. I'm afraid I can't help in that case. Frank and Nora didn't explain much. They said that a lot would be said about them in the news but that everything would be okay once you had this letter. They told me you would know what to do."

"Me? But I don't understand what this letter means. How could I know what to do?"

Her shoulder rolled in a half shrug. "That's all they said, dear. We've been friends for a long time, I trusted them." She squeezed my knee. "And I trust you. You will figure this out."

We talked for about twenty minutes. I asked for every detail of her last conversation with my parents. I even showed her their clue to see if she could make sense of it.

Mrs. Henderson had nothing more for me except for two containers of Tuscan chicken and garlic spaghetti. My empty stomach refused to turn them down.

"Thank you." I kissed her leathery cheek over the threshold. "I promise to visit more often. Next time, I'll bring Eli."

"Sweet girl. I would love that."

"Bye."

Royal was done with his phone call. He started in before my butt hit the seat. "What'd she say?"

"Nothing. They didn't explain. She doesn't know what the weird letters and numbers mean. But she did supply dinner."

"Not in my car. We'll eat in your place."

We broke in for the second time and ate her warm, delicious meal in the cold, dark living room. Afterward, we got on the road for home.

"Say it."

I dragged my gaze away from the window, frowning at him. "What?"

"Say what's bothering you."

I considered him. "Do I have to?"

"Yes."

"Do I have to tell you that my head is wrecked too?" I drew my feet onto the chair and hugged my knees to my chest. "Not for a single second did I believe there was another explanation. That they hated me and left Eli because he'd put up a fight was my cold truth and I accepted it. But now... What's true, Royal?"

"They were selfish bastards," he stated blunt and hard as a man for me had to be. "That's true. They lied, cheated, and stole. That's true too. They did not treat you the way you deserved. All of that is true, Ember." He cupped my chin with a gentle touch. "But it can also be true that deep down they loved you, and that part of them couldn't leave you with nothing."

"You truly believe that?" I whispered.

"You're not the kind of girl that you can easily let go of."

I reached for his hand. "You don't talk much, but when you do, it's always to say the right thing."

We didn't talk much on the rest of the five-hour drive. I sat there with my phone and the letter, typing in random things and looking up possible codes. We passed the *Welcome to Raven River* sign and I was no closer to deciphering the letters and numbers than I was at the start.

"CMB," I said aloud. "I've tried three different codes with the numbers and get gibberish when I replace them with letters. There are more I have to try, but I have a feeling I have to figure out what CMB is to know what the numbers mean."

"So far these clues have been connected to you." Royal slowed to make the final turn into the forest and on to the academy. "Do you know anyone with the initials CMB? Or is it a place you've been?"

"Someone's name..." I repeated. "There are one or two people I know with the initials CB. I overheard Hart call Mrs. Blanchett, Cecilia. I'm pretty sure my parents never met her though. And Grandpa's house manager's name was Charles Bernadetto but I haven't seen him since the funeral and I bet my parents could say the same. We— Wait. What is that?"

Headlights blotted out the horizon. Squinting in the high beams, I raised an arm to shield my eyes.

"What's wrong with this guy? Royal, flash your lights."

"It's more than one guy."

"Wow. Are they for real?" I made out three or four cars blocking the road. "Academy kids thought the middle of the road was the best place to party?"

"No."

"Wha—"

"Ember, hide the letter!"

His shout made me jump. Royal hit the brakes—his pale-knuckled grip strangling the steering wheel.

"What's wrong?"

Just as the question left my mouth, I saw him. Elegant and impassive, a man of equal beauty and savagery stood lone before the pack. The headlights illuminated him to mocking effect, encompassing his body like a halo.

"What is he doing here?!" I cried, scrambling to hide the letter.

"He called me. Said to come see him." Royal rolled to a dead halt inches before his father. "I fucking told him I was out of town and coming back late tonight."

My nails ripped through his leather seat. "But why is he here? What does he want?"

Maybe Rio read lips too because the question no sooner left my mouth than he smiled. The handsome black-suited devil gestured to us, telling us to get out of the car.

My heart raced erratically out of control. The gun. The office. The look in his eyes as Rio promised we weren't done. All of it flashed through my head in the time it took Damien to advance on us.

"Get out," Royal said softly. "Let me handle this."

I gripped the latch as the brute made to do it himself. Damien moved back, letting me pass, and flashed out to grab the door, preventing me from shutting it.

"Dad," said Royal. He strode up to his father—shoulders loose, hands in his pockets, irritation etched in the lines on his brow. "What's up? I told you I'd swing by your place tomorrow."

"So you did," he replied, almost pleasantly. "But I forgot to mention it's not just you I needed to see. Since you two were out together, I saw the perfect chance to speak to you both." Rio's gaze slid to me. "How are you, sweet Ember? I swear you're lovelier every time I see you."

I plastered on a smirk. "Let's get this out of the way. It's not going to happen between us, Rio. I don't have a daddy kink."

The gangster laughed uproariously, shoulders shaking with true mirth. "Oh, I did miss that fire. Our first Horsewoman."

I tensed. I hated when he called me that.

"Though you are tempting," he continued, "I confess you're not my type either. I prefer honest, loyal women."

"Did I lie about something?" I flicked between Rio, his men, and the blockade. "What's with the welcoming party? If you wanted to talk, a phone call would do."

"A phone call wouldn't allow me to look you"—he snapped to his son—"and you in the eye when I ask where's the money."

"The money?" I repeated. Behind me, Damien rooted through the car. There was a thud and I feared he'd gotten to Eli's Christmas presents.

"I have an understanding with an accommodating woman in the administration that I'm to be informed whenever my son leaves the academy."

Shock flickered in Royal's eyes. He did not know about this.

"I hoped you'd be kind enough to let me know of your progress tracking down your parents and the money, but just in case, Damien's been keeping an eye on you. You two led him on an interesting chase the day before Thanksgiving. Gyms, the bus station, and the storage units." He clasped his hands in front of him, the picture of polite curiosity. "What were you looking for?"

"Not the money," said Royal.

"No? Because it occurs to me the one thing those locations have in common are locks that need opening. Searching for something stashed, Ember?"

Holy hell, he was smart. Why was he so fucking smart?!

"That's right," Royal said.

My throat closed, panic seizing me. *Royal, no. What are you doing?*

"Our dealer has been using random empty lockers to deliver the drugs," he continued. "We figured that's something he picked up from the boss, and we drove around to check it out. You told us to find him. It's what we're doing."

"Really?" Rio arched one perfect brow. "And what did you find out?"

The letter singed my backside. I was highly aware of it in my pants.

Rio and his pets didn't get handsy with me the first time I was at their mercy. It was a desperate gamble that Damien wouldn't search me too.

"The gyms are out except for one possibility. Rocco's gym. Random people can't go in and out of the other ones without being noticed but Rocco's is a dump and no one mans the place. The storage units are no good too. They have cameras and guards. If they're using the same trick, it's got to be the bus station. No cameras. No security. All they have to do is stick it in a locker and leave it for someone else to pick up."

"Hmm." Rio lifted his chin, staring his nose down at Royal. "There is a logic to that. Why didn't you mention it before?"

"It's just a hunch," he replied. "We don't know enough to get our guys to watch the place. All I know is that's how I'd do it."

Rio twisted ever so slightly and nodded to one of his men. "We'll look into it. As for today, tell me what prompted the trip to Easthaven. Damien followed and then lost you on Brookes Street."

I spoke up. "Christmas shopping. Damien is seeing that for himself. The Easthaven Mall is three blocks away from Brookes Street."

"It's true, boss," said Damien. "Got the receipts too. They were at the mall."

"The mall. Should I look up what time it closes?" Rio pressed. "Why are you getting back close to midnight?"

"Because we stopped for a fuck," Royal shot back. "Dad, are we done with this? We weren't looking for the money."

"If that's the case, we have an entirely different problem. I made myself clear." Temper leaked through Rio's mask. "I want that money. You're telling me it's been a month and you've done nothing."

"I have been looking," I said. "Mom and Dad went after most of their friends and the list told me who exactly. The ones they hadn't got to might've helped them escape."

"And?"

My options were limited. I knew without a doubt there was a gun in the folds of Rio's coat. He was angry and impatient though his face hid it well. And he drove here to get answers one way or another. If Royal and I wanted past him, I had to give him something.

"And the day they ran, they went to the lake house."

"Lake house?" Rio stepped toward me and Royal moved with him, edging between me and his father. Rio hardly registered him. "What lake house?"

"Ours. On Earnshaw Lake. One of our neighbors spotted them," I said. "I didn't tell you because the feds have already been through the place. I figured it was nothing."

"It's not nothing."

Rio moved in closer. He pushed Royal out of the way and snarled when he jumped back, refusing to let him near me.

"Move aside, boy. You're testing my patience. I have no intention of hurting her."

I touched Royal's back, silently communicating it was okay.

"It's not nothing," Rio continued, sidestepping him. "Twenty-five million dollars in their pockets and a short window to get away. They wouldn't make a stop unless it was absolutely necessary. They went to that lake house for a reason."

I did say the man was intelligent.

"What reason could that be?" I asked. "And what does it matter? The FBI searched it. If there was something, they would have found it."

"A search is only as effective as the searchers, and they are completely ineffective against a smarter target. Give me the address."

I rattled it off without hesitation.

"Damien, let's go," Rio ordered.

Cold fingers wrapped around mine and brought them to his lips. "Thank you for your help, Ember. If this information doesn't pan out, expect us to have another conversation."

"Call next time. We'll do it somewhere warm. Lit. Maybe a café. Do you like chocolate scones?"

His chuckle turned to frosted air on my knuckles. "Love them. It's a date."

Rio and his men retreated to their cars. Only when their lights were specks in the distance did I fall to the ground, knees giving out.

Chapter Nine

❝ *What does it mean?"*

Eli scrutinized the paper backward and forward. He even flipped it over.

"No clue. Do you have any ideas?"

The two of us were in my room the next day. Eli showed up first thing to grill me on what went down at the lake house. Smug didn't begin to explain his smirk when I told him what we found in the mailbox. He loved me enough to spare the "I told you so."

"No. It's three letters and nineteen numbers. It's not a phone number. If it's in code, it's a short message."

"I'm hoping it's simpler than NSA code-cracking. Mom and Dad knew I didn't mess around with that stuff. The other clues were kind of easy for me to follow," I muttered. "Ciphers and secret-book codes are too hard."

Eli twisted side to side in my desk chair. He fixed on the note like staring at it hard enough would reveal the answer.

"What if they're done leaving you clues and this is it?" Eli offered. *"They couldn't put this letter in a vase outside. The rain would've destroyed it. But the feds weren't about to dig through Mrs. Henderson's mail. It was safe in there, so they could tell us what they needed us to know. Somehow, this is it."* He shook the paper. *"This is where they are."*

"Could be," I reluctantly agreed. My plan to avoid getting his hopes up was dying a quick death. Those hopes were up. Eli's baby blues were shining like Christmas, Hanukkah, Kwanzaa, and Boxing

Day were rolled into one, and Mom and Dad were coming home for the massive celebration.

"I looked up countries connected to those initials." The words tugged out of me on a hook tied to my promise to tell him everything. "CMB is the airport code for Colombo, Sri Lanka, and the United Nations country code for Cambodia."

"*Cambodia.*" Eli bounced in the chair. "*Em, Cambodia is a non-extradition country. That's it!*"

"And those numbers are supposed to be an address? In another language? How would I figure out what it is? I have nothing to go on."

He was far from deterred. "*I'll find out what it means. I'll start looking now.*"

Eli got up, marching off paper in hand.

"Whoa, no."

I plucked it from his fingertips. Eli spun with "What up?!" written on his face.

"I'm hanging on to this. Mom and Dad left this for me. They believed I'd find out what it means and I will."

"*I can help you,*" he protested. "*I knew about Rory and Mrs. Henderson. I could've found the clues. This is connected to me too.*"

"It's too dangerous. The FBI calls what I'm doing obstruction of justice. The nice man who turned the town against me repeated it over and over."

"*Who cares about him? How would he even know?*"

I care about you, I thought. *And Rio knows.*

The man had me followed. He ambushed me in the forest in the middle of the night. He nearly killed me for the money the first time.

Eli was fine as a silent figure on the sidelines, but looking up non-extradition countries and booking tickets to Phnom Penh was out of the question. My parents' actions ultimately led to him being attacked. How much more danger was his family supposed to get him in? When was he allowed to just be a kid?

"This is my responsibility," I told him. "Trust me. You will be the first to know when I find out what this means and we'll decide what to do about it."

I crossed to my desk, put the letter in my top drawer, and firmly closed it shut.

"Want to watch a Christmas movie?"

Eli was not pleased and his flat no and walking out of the room told me as much.

I let him go without a fight. He didn't need to understand everything I did to keep him safe. He would come around eventually.

ELI DID COME AROUND. By Wednesday he broke down and apologized. By Saturday he joined in my Christmas movie marathon. The Bancroft siblings were happily humming along if not for the little blip of his constant pestering to help me decipher the note.

Monday morning, I woke and dressed early. I planned to hit the library and tackle some books on numbered codes. Those nineteen numbers meant something. I would find out what that is.

I walked out of my dorm and saw Hiro just as he pressed the button for the elevator. I hurried and slipped in before the doors closed.

"Hiro." I leaned against the wall, adopting his stance.

Hiro looked me up and down warily. "Ember."

"What's up? Have a good weekend?"

He shrugged. "Read. Did homework. Watched TV."

"Are you staying over winter break?" I asked.

"Yeah."

"Nice. I'll be here and so will Cassius, Clay, Camila, Royal, and Eli. All of us should do something together to celebrate. It doesn't have to be big."

He shrugged again.

"Do you know what I think?" My tone was soft. I rolled on my shoulder blades, rocking side to side on the wall.

"What?"

"I think everything you said in the gazebo was bullshit, except for the part that you want to be with me. I think you can't move forward because of Mallory. You need her to pay the pot and I've seen firsthand that Rio isn't a guy to be messed with. Being with me is no good if Rio sees that it's a short relationship. I understand. I truly do.

"But I also think you need to talk to her and work out another deal. Cut her into the profits or remind her that her job is on the line. Anything because—"

I gripped his collar and jerked him toward me. Our lips collided in an explosion of pent-up desires and desperate frustration.

Kissing Hiro was nothing like I imagined. And wow did I imagine this day until I lost count. His lips were softer than melting butter. His hand tangled in my hair and tilted me back, opening me up to all of him. Unrestrained. Free.

Hiro backed me up to the opposite wall, trapping me between his body and the elevator. Every inch of him molded to me, our thrusting hips grinded, pulling moans out of both of us.

Our tongues danced playfully. Teasing and tasting the delicious sweetness of lingering looks, accidental brushes at the lunch table, and shared smiles we couldn't hold back. My very requited feelings for Hiro reached a fever pitch and this kiss tipped me over the edge. There was no going back now.

We broke apart panting—lips swollen. Eyes cloudy.

"Because after a kiss like that, I'm not buying your bullshit anymore," I finished. "You want me, Hiro, and I want you. Make it happen."

"You don't understand!" he burst out. "It's not that simple."

"Yes, it is." I pressed *open*. The sliding doors released me. "Find me when it's done and we'll enjoy our Christmas together."

Hiro didn't stop me walking away. I pictured his look as I left. Half pissed, half bored, all annoyed, but in his eyes, raw, naked want... of me.

I entered the main building, heading to my locker. Geske's class was closer to the library. I'd grab my textbooks and save myself the trip.

I rounded the final corner and pulled up short. Nolan Ives leaned against my locker.

"What do you want?"

"Ember, there you are." Nolan peeled off, closing the distance. His relief at my arrival confused me. "I was hoping to catch you before homeroom. I need to talk to you."

"No, you don't." I went around him to my locker. "Go away."

"Please. Can we just go somewhere and talk?"

"And again. No."

"I want to apologize."

My hand froze on the dial.

"I've thought a lot about what you said... that night," he said softly. "And I owe you one that's long overdue, don't you agree?"

"You know I do. Say what you need to say and then go."

"Not in the hall. Mrs. Gardener's class is open. Please, just for five minutes."

"Why?" I scoffed. "Because you're afraid someone might overhear and discover just what kind of person you are? How you treated Camila gave that away a long time ago."

"Fine. Never mind."

His footsteps retreated.

My fist dug the lock painfully into my skin. *He can't just walk away after everything he's done. I am owed that apology.*

"Wait."

The footsteps paused.

"Five minutes."

"Thank you, Ember."

Mrs. Gardener's class was the nearest to my locker. Nolan rushed ahead to hold open the door. The kind, charming smile of the guy I once dated tinged with nerves and hope.

I propped myself on her desk, arms folded. "I'm listening."

"Okay." Nolan paced in front of the door, wringing his hands. "The other night was crazy. Waking up to their hands on my mouth, ripping me out of bed before Julian knew what was going on. Over and over I've thought about what you three could've done to me, and I realized it should have been much worse."

I nodded. *Amazing. His night in the forest did teach him something.*

He took a deep breath. "I owe you an apology, so here goes." Nolan planted his feet, looking at me directly. "Ember, I'm sorry that..."

"... after two years you're still bitching and whining about me leaving your ass in the woods."

I blinked. *What did he just say?*

"I dated you for three months and you were shying away from my cock like the stuck-up princess you really were under your blue hair and fake tough act."

The pleasant mask peeled away. The one used to trick me before and done so easily once more.

"I'm sorry I wasted my time with you. It only seemed right to teach you a lesson."

"Get the fuck out of my way!" I barreled for the door.

"Ah ah." Nolan shoved me back. "Believe me. You're going to want to hear the rest of my apology."

I dove at him, fist raised. Nolan seized it, twisting my arm behind me. Bones crunched under the assault. I cried out, pain almost blotting out his words.

"Leo tells me you've got a mean hook," he hissed. "You fight for real, and if you try that again, I swear I will too. A pair of tits won't stop me throwing you over those desks."

"Let me go!"

He did. I stumbled away, putting as much distance between us as possible. I wasn't afraid to fight him, but Nolan had a foot and fifty pounds on me. If we went at it, I wasn't walking away unscathed.

I glared at him across the room, cradling my sore arm. "You're fucked up, Nolan. In your head. Deep down in the pit of your soul where human compassion and empathy should be. There's nothing. *You're nothing,*" I spat. "Just an empty shell in a pretty wrapper. You think you can go through life like this and there'll never be consequences? Trust me, bitch. It's going to catch up to you."

He laughed—a cruel, grating sound that ran up my spine. "I thought it finally did the night those disgusting thugs grabbed me out of bed. They tied me to the tree and then left. The whole time I was thinking they went back for Royal and that long-haired shit. I figured that was it. They knew what I'd done and I was looking at a knife between the ribs and a deep sleep in the river.

"Then they came back with *you.*" Nolan looked like he would piss himself laughing. "A-and you didn't do shit! After everything I've done to you, the weak, pathetic little girl you are couldn't pull the trigger. I cut out of those ropes and was back in my room two hours later."

My nails pierced my forearm. A physical fight wasn't the smart play, but damn was he pushing it. There was a single statement I latched on to amid his taunting.

"You thought they knew what you'd done? What does that mean?"

He shrugged, smirk unfolding in horrifying delight. "I thought they pulled me out for a midnight chat because I'm the one who planted drugs in their rooms."

My hands went limp at my sides, muscles unraveling like my strings had been cut. "You did what?" I rasped.

"I almost got them expelled. Almost!" Anger bleached his glee. "I'd been waiting for the perfect time to make a move. And then Vera tells me Royal asked Destiny for my number and I knew this was it."

"Your number? You're—"

"Keep the fuck up," he snapped. "Yes, I run a little drug business on the side. You can blame the Angels for that too."

"How the hell is it their fault?!"

"Because it was the only way to take him down!" Nolan came at me. I leaped and snatched a pair of scissors off the desk.

"Stay where the fuck you are," I snarled. "You don't want a fight, don't ask for one."

He put up his hands, smirk returning as he backed away. "Easy now. We're just talking. This part is important. You need an explanation."

"Damn right, I do. You were the dealer the whole time. You sold to the freshmen. *Your drugs* were used on Cam. Were you gift-wrapping her for your rapist buddy?!"

He bared his teeth. "Don't put that shit on me. I didn't know what Leo was going to do. And don't bother with the 'what about the children' crap either. They're the demand, I'm the supply. Everyone who bought from me knew what they were doing. Whatever happened to them is their own damn fault."

"You—"

"It's also not important," he broke in. "This is about Royal. He's a fucking disease! A cancer spreading from the Horsemen and I will exterminate him"—he thumped his chest—"because someone has to. Someone has to make it right!"

My head was spinning. Make it right? What was he talking about?

"Royal didn't make it easy," he plowed on. "I couldn't get him on the poker game, SAT scam, or running Hiro's store. He stays out of all of it. It had to be something I could pin on him that no one would question. Hooking up with my new dealer friend was perfect. I supplied his drugs, quietly spread the rumor the Angels were behind it, and when that text came from an unknown number, I knew he was ready to play.

"I could've planted the drugs and tipped off a room search any time but I needed him to know in some way that it was me. That I got to him, and for all his tattoos, thugs, and Horsemen, he couldn't stop it.

"That's what got me in the end, isn't it?" He tossed his head. "That text was a step too far. Royal realized something was wrong, and saved Cassius, Clay, and that trashy bitch. Shame because those three deserve everything they get for backing him up and inking that angel in their arm."

"You're crazy," I whispered.

"You think so?" Nolan dropped his chin, humming. "Good. Believe that, Ember, because I'm telling you all of this for a reason. I want you to know what I've done. You have to see that I'm serious, so in the back of your mind while I'm telling you what happens next, you'll think 'if he's already gone this far, how much farther will he go?'"

I held the scissors higher, recoiling on the look in his eyes. "What is that supposed to mean?"

"I've been watching you with them. I assumed at first that you were just a fuck. Royal doesn't care about anyone. Why would he care about you? But after that night in the woods and Cassius and Clay risking federal prison to get you revenge, I held off getting those cunts hauled off and took a closer look."

Nolan took a step and so did I, passing behind the desk and putting two hundred pounds of wood, papers, and more sharp objects between us.

"It's the real thing. The way Royal looks at you. Touches you when he thinks people aren't watching. He loves you."

He flung the beautiful statement like an accusation.

"And I'm betting he's told you things he's never told anyone else." He leveled a finger at me. "You're going to tell me, Ember. That guy is as innocent as a child-diddling priest. He's into shady shit and you're going to spill and help me take him down."

"The fuck I will!"

"You will," he stated, "because if you do, I'll tell you who attacked your brother."

The world tilted sideways.

No, I did.

I fell hard against the chalkboard, physically smacked by his reply.

"Eli? But how— Who—" The amusement on his face penetrated. "You're lying! You don't know who they are and I wouldn't tell you where the hose was if you were on fire! Get out of my way. Royal is going to love this story."

Nolan pasted himself on the door, not even looking at my scissors. "I do know who they are. I know where they eat. Where they sleep. I know what they like on their pancakes. I know everything about them, Ember, and you don't. If you're any kind of sister, that must burn you up inside. Knowing they're still out there and could hurt him again whenever they wanted."

The scissors shook in my hand, inches from his chest.

"No tricks. No games. I'll tell you exactly who they are if you tell me what I need to know." He placed his hand over his chest—where a heart would be for a normal person. "I swear. We both get what we want."

"I. Said. Move."

He tsked. "Are you serious? Eli is your little brother. You're picking Royal Cruz over your own flesh and blood? And you think I'm cold?"

I bristled. "That's not what I'm doing. I don't need to make a deal with you, Satan. I know who attacked Eli." The list of names was tucked securely in my backpack. "They're waiting their turn for my *full* attention, but right now, you have it, and you'll wish you didn't."

Nolan shook his head, a slow smile curling his cheeks. "Oh, Ember, trust me. You don't know who it is. If you did..." He whistled. "You wouldn't have waited a second to make him pay."

That smile pierced my confidence, doggedly chipping away. His confidence, on the other hand, was unshakeable. He was absolutely sure I didn't know who the attackers were and he did.

"I know where they eat. Where they sleep. I know what they like on their pancakes."

"Julian and Leo," I croaked.

The smirk didn't twitch. "Are you asking me or telling me?"

I pressed my lips together, trembling.

"That's what I thought," he said. "You don't know, but if you think you do, I'll give you a chance just to show I'm a fair guy. I'll give you until Friday to find the real attackers and hand them over to Hart. Then I'll have nothing on you and you can tell Royal the truth.

"But if Friday comes and goes and they're still here, I'll give them the money that they were so desperate for that they beat up your brother. The full amount your parents stole plus extra if they jump him again, and this time, they stomp his hands."

The scissors slipped through numb fingers, clatter echoing in my ringing ears. My lips parted but no sounds came out.

"Break all ten fingers to get my money's worth," he pressed. "And you could tell Hart or call the police, but it won't change the fact that you could've protected him, but you chose Royal instead."

"You wouldn't do this," I whispered. "Eli's innocent."

"I won't do it," he agreed, "if you tell me how to take down Royal."

Panic rose in my throat like bile as my mind scrambled for something. *Anything* to stop this.

"I'll go to Hart right now!" I cried. "I'll tell her you're a drug-dealing psycho threatening my little brother."

Nolan cracked open the door. "I'll take that chance because we both know you don't have a clue who attacked Eli, and if Hart so much as gives me a funny look, I'll tell them to do it." He motioned to the now bustling hallway. "Go on."

I shoved past him, not sparing Nolan another word. He was wrong. I had ten names and five days to find the children-beaters in the haystack. I'd confront them, throw them at Ramadi, and then Nolan was next.

Kyle Casen, Luis Riviera, Adrien Miller, Harley Donovan, Craig Howell, Royce Lamb, Yuki Watanabe, Ken Han, Amir Blake, and Jasper Crown.

I didn't waste a moment cornering them.

Harley I grabbed on the way to sociology. The kid was confused, babbling that he didn't know what I was talking about, and finally owning up that he was smoking weed with Major and two other guys behind the soccer stands when Eli was attacked.

"Ask them! I swear I was there! Just ask them."

I asked and they confirmed it was their daily ritual. It wasn't Harley and that was my Monday gone.

Tuesday, I cornered Craig on his way out of lacrosse practice. He dismissed my accusations and tried to walk away.

"He was jumped by two tall, big guys with a grudge against my parents. You've got one to the tune of thirty thousand dollars," I shouted at him.

"Was one of those guys over six feet and pummeling him with brown fists? Because the only guy who fits that description in this school is me and I didn't do it!"

That snapped my mouth shut. I texted Eli to be certain and he confirmed. Neither of the guys were that tall nor were they Black. After that, I was forced to take Amir Blake, Jasper Crown, and Royce Lamb off the list.

Tuesday was gone and I had five guys left.

Wednesday, Ken Han, the youngest son of Mr. Han, blinked owlishly at me in the library, appearing genuinely stunned.

"Why would I attack your brother?" he asked. "Did he make your parents rip off my dad?"

"You did it to force me to pay back what they took," I said. "Don't bother denying it. I'm telling Hart what you did."

"Tell her whatever you want. It wasn't me. I walk my girlfriend to class every day after lunch. And no, we didn't stop to beat up a fourteen-year-old on the way."

Ken's girlfriend backed him up.

Yuki was next and the guy was so offended that I accused him of jumping a Deaf kid, he threatened to go to Hart himself if I tried to pin it on him. That was Wednesday gone with no results.

Thursday, Luis Riviera asked who the hell my brother was and Adrien showed me pictures of the brace he was wearing for his dislocated knee around the time the guys hit Eli. He challenged me, asking if one of the attackers hobbled away, and if not, to get out of his face.

I got out of his face.

That night, I lay awake, tears soaking my hair and pillow.

I had one name left. One was not two. Two guys attacked Eli. One guy could refuse to give him up. One guy was enough for Nolan to send after Eli. They've shown they'll attack my brother over money. And Nolan has shown he's an icy bastard.

I could convince Uncle to transfer Eli out of this school.

He'd send him to another boarding school where he didn't have to deal with him, my internal voice reminded. *And he wouldn't do it in time.*

Hart and Ramadi. Tell them what's going on and they'll make sure he's safe.

That option was better, but still not enough. Eli would be safe and Nolan brought in for questioning—where he'd lie his cold-blooded ass off, fed every bullshit response by his dad's lawyers. I accused Leo of being an attempted rapist and they kicked him loose. I accuse Nolan of being a drug dealer and framing Royal and the others with no evidence, our battle of he said, she said would end with police swearing to keep an eye on him as they walked him out of the station.

But Eli will be safe, the boys will be on their guard, and the world will look twice at Nolan Ives.

And he'll get away with it. So will the boys who beat Eli.

I wanted a choice.

I would have taken any other option that spared all the people I loved. Even if it meant I was hurt in their place. But Eli was my brother and he was the only one counting on me to protect him. There was never truly a choice when he got involved.

Friday morning, I knocked on Nolan's door and fought not to heave when he smiled triumphantly.

"I'll do it."

Chapter Ten

I shoved past him into the room. It was an unholy mess of strewn laundry, crumpled sheets, and a smell like something had gone stale under the bed. It twisted my already roiling stomach.

"I tell you how to get to Royal and you give me the name of Eli's attackers. Right now. Today. Two milliseconds after I'm done talking," I said. "That's the deal."

"No."

I rocked back. "What? Then why the hell—"

Nolan put up a hand. "You tell me what I can use against Royal, and *after* I've gotten rid of him, I tell you their names. Right then. Two milliseconds after it's done. That is the deal. Take it or take it. Remember who holds all the cards."

I gritted my teeth till my jaw cracked. "How do I know you'll tell me the truth after you've gotten what you want?"

"How do I know you won't run to Royal and warn him the second you get what *you* want?"

We stared at each other. The worst battle of wills in history.

My history—because again there was no choice.

"Fine," I said. "Royal is a car thief."

Shock blew the arrogant mask to shreds. "He's what?"

"You heard me. He's a car thief and his favorite target is Raveners."

His forehead scrunched up. Eyes darting around as he made sense of what I was saying.

"Prove it," he demanded.

I said three words. "Leo Tremaine's car."

Nolan's jaw went slack. Seeing him like this—flinty greens delighting with malice. Spiteful edge to the quirk of his lips. Hard set of his chin as he callously held Eli over my head. I asked myself why I ever thought he was handsome. Nolan Ives had to be the most hideous person alive.

"Royal stole Leo's car? I can't believe this," he said mostly to himself. "This is perfect. Forget expelled. He'll do real time in jail." He snapped to me. "He told you he did it. You're a witness. If you go to the police—"

"You don't want me in that interrogation room, Ives," I said. "If I get in there, a lot more is coming out than what Royal did to Leo. Besides, I'm sure Camila's softened the nation up enough that Royal would get a sympathetic jury."

"If you don't—"

"Do not open your mouth to threaten me again. There's no point anyway. Leo's car is in a million pieces and sold to buyers I don't know about. How will you prove he stole a car that doesn't exist anymore? It's another game of he said, she said."

"Then what do you suggest?" he snapped. "What about his car? Did he steal it?"

I shook my head. "Royal's not stupid, Nolan. He's not driving around in a stolen car. He bought his fair and legal. No, if you want to prove he's a car thief, you have to—"

I stopped. My betrayal was a living force, churning my stomach. Poisoning my soul. I sucked in hard, deep breaths, compelling myself to get through this without vomiting.

"If you want to prove it," I continued. "You have to catch him in the act."

"How? Do you know what car he's going after next?"

"As a matter of fact, I do." It burned coming out. "The Christmas Eve party at the Estate Country Club. Royal's going to jack a car from the lot while everyone is getting drunk on plum wine."

"From the parking lot?" His eyes narrowed. "Impossible. You're fucking with me, aren't you? Royal's going to steal a car out from under the valets and security? And in less than two weeks? What convenient timing."

"There's nothing convenient about it, jackass. It has to be during the party because stealing a car from a parking lot is a lot easier than a locked-down Estate mansion. All your precious guards are inside watching over the partygoers, and what is a valet going to do? Risk himself over someone else's car?"

Nolan's surety was taking a hit.

"As for why. He's doing it for me," I croaked. "We couldn't pull it off on Thanksgiving, so we're trying again Christmas Eve. It's all to get the money to pay off the blackmailers you're protecting."

"Thanksgiving... Julian did say he saw you two there," he said slowly. "And you said we. Royal expects you to help him."

"Yes."

"All right, yeah," he said to himself. "I can work with this." He began pacing, back and forth as he muttered to himself. "Catch him in the act. He can't wiggle his way out of that."

Nolan turned on me. "Okay, this is what we're going to do..."

I left Nolan's room an hour later. Returning to my dorm, I closed the door, walked into the bathroom, and vomited until there was nothing to choke on but bile.

THE FINAL WEEK UNTIL winter break was the hardest of my life. I was so out of it my friends took notice. Multiple times a day they asked me what was wrong. Brushing off their concern was almost as horrible as avoiding the boys. I couldn't look them in the eye and that's exactly what Nolan wanted. He drilled a hole in my head from across the cafeteria, intensifying when I got too friendly with the Angels.

The end of the week should have brought relief. But this was my life. Fate did not have gifts for me this holiday season.

"I don't understand," said Camila. She sat on her bed watching me pack. "I thought we were all staying and celebrating together."

"Change of plans. My aunt and uncle want us home. They've softened their hearts to their little orphaned niece and nephew."

"Okay. Well, I hope you guys have a good time."

"We will," I managed to say with a straight face. "It'll be a blast."

Camila hugged me as I picked up my things to go. "I'll call you on Christmas."

"Bye."

Eli waited for me on the first floor. We tramped through the grounds and met our aunt at the front gate. She sniffed.

"You two look fine to me." She whipped around. "Let's go. I have a nail appointment at three."

Nope. This was not going to be a blast. Too bad I didn't have a choice. Nolan had to go home for the break and he wasn't leaving me on my own with the Angels until his vile plan succeeded. His first thought was to make me come home with him and tell his parents we were dating again. I almost threw up right there on the spot.

As a compromise, I agreed to stay with my aunt and uncle. Blanchett witnessed the best performance of my life. I burst into her office crying and wailing about being depressed, homesick, and missing my parents more than ever. I laid on thick my wish to get away from this dreary school.

She suggested I leave for break and I asked if she would call my uncle because "he won't let me leave." She was on the phone with him in five minutes impressing upon him the hard time I was going through and needing my family more than ever. That was that. Appearance over everything.

There Eli and I were. Forced to stay in that mansion cold of temperature and spirit.

We made the most of it. I put on movies every night. Ran out to get marshmallows and cocoa. I even got us a mini tree and we decorated it in his bedroom. He perked up seeing all the presents I got him under the tree.

Christmas Eve morning, I was awoken by a lump on my back. I fell asleep in my brother's bed after the movie and he made me pay for it.

Eli lay flat on me, head bent over mine and big blue eyes coming into focus as I blinked blearily.

"Ugh. Come on," I groaned. I stuck a finger between us, holding up one.

Eli made an excited noise and tumbled off the bed. One for the single Christmas present he was allowed to open.

He picked up the biggest present of course. Eli pumped his fist at his newest bookshelf.

"That one comes with a bonus present," I signed. *"Open the blue one too."*

Eli tore off the paper and found himself holding *Harry Potter* bookends. Hedwig flew on one end and Dobby held his sock on the other.

Eli ran over, I thought to hug me, but he dropped at my feet and reached under the bed. A flat rectangular gift was placed in my hands.

"What's this?"

He was cheesing wide like a kid who knew he nailed it.

I unwrapped the gift and gasped.

Berenice Abbot's photo collection.

"Royal spilled what you wanted and Hiro helped me buy this."

"How did you pay for it?"

"*I asked Uncle for money to buy Christmas presents.*"

"And he gave it to you? Wow."

"*Mr. Johnston held the phone up to my mouth when it was my cue to cry.*"

I burst out laughing. I laughed and laughed and laughed some more. There with Eli holding our perfect presents and laughing our heads off, it felt for the tiniest, briefest spell like a happy Christmas.

Until nightfall brought our aunt into the room. I was standing over Eli doing his tie.

"Are you two ready?" Aunt Violet took one look at me. "Heavens, Ember, what are you wearing?"

I glanced down. "What? It's a formal dress. It fits the dress code."

"It's the same dress you wore to the Thanksgiving party," she cried with way more outrage than I felt the situation warranted. "What will people think?"

"Uh... that I own a washing machine?"

"Don't be ridiculous," she snapped.

Yeah. I'm the one being ridiculous.

"Go change. Now," Violet ordered. "I'll finish with your brother's tie." She removed my hands and steered me out the door. "I bought you the cutest red gown before school started. Wear that."

I considered fighting her and changed my mind. The party would be terrible enough. I didn't need to add Violet's disapproving stare trailing me the entire night.

I changed into my red satin ball gown adorned with crystals on the bodice and an empire silhouette. I never said my aunt didn't have good taste. This dress just wasn't my style, though it'd look perfect on the Violet clone she wanted to turn me into so she'd find me tolerable.

My mismatched family waited for me at the bottom of the stairs.

"Ember, honestly," said Violet. "Would it have hurt you to put some lipstick on at least?"

"Very possible."

She whirled on my uncle. "Just listen to her, Harry. Every reply a smart-aleck remark. Do you see what I endure all day? You're at work and I have to put up with this behavior."

"Ember, apologize to your aunt!"

Neither of us were in a good mood as we piled in the car and set off for the country club. We rolled to a stop next to the valet stand and I tapped Eli's arm for his attention. He lit up as I pulled out my tablet.

"Find an empty room and enjoy yourself. I'll bring up a plate."

Eli split from us in the lobby. Skipping out on this party was basically another Christmas gift.

I watched him go with regret, worry, that steel-rooted protectiveness, and a wish I could change what was going to happen.

Gliding into the ballroom was like melting into a snow globe—almost literally. Fake snow fell from the ceiling, dusting the silver tablecloths and Christmas tree centerpieces. All around me a picture of wealth, class, and grace reflected in the gorgeous gowns, bright smiles, and gushing conversations of trips to Aspen and the Seychelles.

I wanted to take a hammer to it. Shatter the glass and expose the snow globe for what it held. A fantasy.

All eyes flew to me, the vision in red, but my eyes were on him. How did Royal convince himself he was someone who could blend in? Women lingered on his chiseled features and raven hair even softer than it looked. Men watched him move with power and authority and flashed jealousy they couldn't hide. And when he saw me through the sea of people and grinned, the impact knocked everyone within ten feet of him on their asses.

He set down his glass and headed toward me. A silver suit and tie suddenly blocked my view.

"Remember," Nolan hissed. "You find out which car he's going for, tell him you'll distract the valet and then meet me upstairs."

"I remember, but feel free to tell me for the thirty-fifth time."

Nolan walked off muttering something about sarcastic bitches.

Royal took his place. He jerked a chin at Nolan's back. "What did he want?"

"Nothing important," I said. "You look very dapper."

Royal's hair was slicked back and his crisp black suit hung on tight.

"Never been called dapper before."

"Keep strutting around looking like that and you'll hear it all night."

He laughed. "Come on. It's a good time now that it's packed."

I took his outstretched hand. We parted the party, collecting curious and appreciative looks as we passed through to the terrace.

"Just like last time," he said. "Stay close to me. Head low. And—"

"Royal, you don't have to do this," I blurted. "Not for me. Not for my brother. You're risking too much."

"It's the same risk I've taken many times," he said. "It's a risk I'd take if I had a good reason or not. This time I do." Royal cupped my chin in the way I loved. "It'll be okay."

"I'm scared it won't be. Just in case..." I swallowed hard. "I'll distract the valet while you do it. Angle him away so he doesn't notice a car leaving the lot."

He raised a brow. "If I do most of the work, I get most of the pay."

"Distraction is plenty of work. That's got to cut me in for a good chunk."

Royal responded to my joke by putting his arm around my shoulder and leading us off. We made our loop, walking close and intimate like lovers.

"There," he whispered. "The Infiniti. Second to last in the back. I'll give it another twenty minutes. Do one more loop. Then I'll take it."

"Okay."

Royal and I returned to the party.

Twenty minutes.

That's how long I had.

Dancing wasn't on the menu for me. The waiters may as well have been carrying actual slow-roasted feet. The sight of food was turning me off.

I found a table in the corner and texted Eli. I'd prefer to run down the clock with him in person, but orders were I stay in Nolan's sight.

Twenty minutes on the dot, Royal passed by my table. "It's time. Let's see how much your distraction game is worth."

I rose from my seat and exited the ballroom. Striding past the front doors and the valet, I texted Nolan.

Me: It's time.

I went upstairs and blew past room after room until I found the right one. It was a smaller, cozier space. A half a dozen armchairs formed a semicircle on the carpet and a fireplace dominated the majority of one wall.

This is a place to hold a book club.

I brushed aside the curtains, peering through the window at the Infiniti squarely in view.

Not a place to help a twisted psycho lay a trap for the man I love.

Nolan arrived minutes following my text sharing where I was.

"Which car?" he asked without skipping a beat.

I pointed through the window. "That one second to last on the end."

Nolan took out his phone. "Yeah. Second to last on the end. The silver car. He has dark hair and a black suit." Nolan turned on me. "When is he coming out?"

"Now."

"He's coming now," he repeated, pushing me aside. Nolan pressed his forehead against the window searching for him. "Where are you hiding? If he sees anyone, he'll run. Also— There! I see him."

I pushed in, straining to look. A dark figure materialized out of the shadows. He walked with deliberate steps to the car—perfect in the way he blended in.

Nolan gazed in palpable excitement as he walked around the car, peering in the windows, and trying each door handle. He stopped at the driver's side door. It was hard to see from our angle and the weak light coming from the light post, but he seemed to be pushing the window down as far as it would go. After that, he walked away.

"Where is he going?" Nolan growled. "What the hell happened? Did you do something?" he flung at me.

"What did I do while I was standing right next to you?"

"You—" He cut off. "Wait. He's back and— What the fuck?"

He came back all right and, in his hand, he hefted a large stone from the garden border. In paralyzing slow motion, he heaved the rock over his head and swung, smashing the window.

"Holy shit," Nolan cried over his laugh.

Everything happened at once. Security jumped out of their hiding places and swarmed him. Their shouts and orders to put down the rock reached us through the window. I snapped the curtains closed, not able to bear it any longer.

"There," I exclaimed. "You got what you wanted. The deal was you tell me their names the millisecond it's over."

Hollering, Nolan pushed the curtains back. He feasted on the sight of him on the floor, the top half of him blocked by the car as security wrangled his hands behind his back.

"You did hold up your end, didn't you?" He tsked. "Which kinda makes me feel bad that I have to tell you I lied."

The blood drained from my face. "You what?"

Nolan lifted his shoulder, eyes only partially on me as he watched.

I ripped the curtains closed. "You lied to me?! You don't know who attacked Eli!"

"Yes and no. I know one of the guys who attacked him. Couldn't guess who the other is but I'm sure he'll tell you if you ask nicely."

"Who is it? Tell me!"

"Hmmm," he hummed, screwing up his face. "I don't know. Seems like a better idea is making you help me take down all of the Horsemen trash that's invaded our school. Maybe I'll tell you after that."

He was enjoying this. The bastard was so obviously getting off on my rage, the threads snapped on my self-control.

"I knew better than to trust you," I said. "That's why I didn't."

Nolan's grin faded as mine grew.

"I lied too, dumbass." Raising my voice, I called, "Royal."

Creaky hinges sounded in the space and in he walked. My dark prince. Perfect and untouched.

"Wha— How?!" Nolan shot to the window and the man still face down in the asphalt, most likely pleading his innocence. "What did you—"

"My fault." Cassius strolled inside and threw himself in an armchair. A step behind him, Hiro entered the room.

"I hung around for half an hour waiting for some guy with Royal's hair and build to make an appearance," said Cassius. "I lifted the poor guy's keys, locked them in his car, and then came out of nowhere saying I noticed an Infiniti with the keys on the seat and if it was his. Took the cellphone too, so he couldn't call for assistance." He winked at me. "How'd it go, baby?"

"Amazing. He broke the window. It was so perfect, it could have been scripted."

Harsh lamplight fell on Nolan's bloodless lips.

"Did he give you the names?" Royal asked. He stalked closer, slinking through the gloom as he, Hiro, and Cassius spread out.

"No," I said. "He's claiming now that he only knows one name and he won't give it up unless I help him with another failed revenge plot."

"I'm sure we can change his mind, princess."

"Me too."

That was all the warning Nolan got. I swung and buried my fist in his gut. The boy doubled over but didn't drop.

I leaped onto the window ledge, placed both feet on him, and kicked. He flew into the back of an armchair and they both crashed to the floor. I was on him in a heartbeat. Kicking the chair aside, I jumped on him and grabbed his collar. Nolan howled as I smashed my knuckles in his face.

"Tell me who they are!" I roared. "Or get the beating I saved for them."

I punched him again.

"Tell m—"

"That's enough!" Something cold and hard jammed beneath my ribs. "I said that's enough!"

My body went rigid—fist in the air and poised to strike.

"Hey!"

"Don't move!" Nolan shouted as the boys surged forward. He hauled us both to our feet, arm encircling my neck as he pressed the gun to my temple. "Nobody fucking move."

The expressions on the boys' faces were night and day to the smirking victors that walked in. Icy terror stiffened me in his hold.

"You think you got me?" Nolan flung. "Huh? You think I don't have friends too?"

Nolan felt for his phone with one hand and the other trained the gun on me.

"Yeah," he said. "Last room on the left. Come join the party."

He hung up and freed my body to put the phone away. Royal took a step forward.

"Don't move!"

Nolan kicked the back of my knees. I dropped, crying out as the muzzle bit into the back of my skull.

"If one of you gets too close, I might get twitchy. Too hard on this trigger and pretty little Ember is splatter on the carpet."

"Calm down, Ives," Royal said. "There's no need for this. Put the gun away."

"It depends on you if I put the gun away." He chuckled. "It was a gift, you know. From my supplier. Did you also know your old man was spot on about a traitor in the ranks? The boss is none other than a Horseman himself and"—he whistled—"boy does he have plans for your dad."

Royal glared. "What the fuck do you know about my father?"

"I know so much more than you think," he replied. "Rio Cruz. Your father. Leader of the Horsemen. Lying, cheating, thieving piece of shit."

Footsteps sounded in the hall.

"I'll tell you what else I know," he said, "as long as everyone plays by the rules. You don't come near me and you don't open your mouth. If you obey, the gun stays in my pocket. Understand?"

Stiff-jawed and silent, the boys nodded.

The pressure on my scalp disappeared just as the door opened.

"Cassius? Hiro?" Julian's smooth voice leeched into my brain. "How did you get in here?"

The boys didn't answer. They couldn't.

Through a gap between chairs, I saw Leo turn the lock.

"They came because they've realized all the damage they've done," said Nolan. "They're ready for their penance. And we're happy to provide, aren't we, guys?"

Leo and Julian hooted their agreement.

"Teach them a lesson." His hand clamped on the back of my neck. "They won't put up a fight."

The last command was undoubtedly for my Angels. Helpless at his feet, I choked back a sob as the first punch landed on Cassius's jaw. He fell out of sight and all I could hear were his grunts as they beat him.

"Stop it," I shouted.

"Shut up!"

Nolan yanked me by the hair. I screamed, my neck wrenched back, and hands grabbing for his wrist.

"Ember?"

"Ives!" Royal yelled. "Fucking do that again and this won't end the way you want!"

"Ember?" Julian repeated. His head rose above the chairs, finally spotting me. "Nolan, what the hell are you doing? Let her go."

I made to get up and he shoved me down. "No, she's fine where she is," he said through gritted teeth. "She's keeping these bastards in line, so they can finally get what's coming to them. The Angels," he spat. "Your mother should have kicked them out the second they showed up in school with that tattoo. They've taken over our academy and have everyone too afraid to do something about it. Now it's our turn!" Fervor made him shake me. "They're going to see what it's like to be afraid!"

"Sounds good to me," said Leo. He ran at Royal, a metal flask in his grip to deal a brutal blow.

Royal ducked the swing, snapped back, and laid him out with a punch that knocked Leo into Julian.

"Hey!" Nolan shouted.

"I'm not following your rules, Ives," Royal said, "and you're not going to kill her. We both know you won't get out of this room if you do."

"Kill her?" Julian jeered. "What the fuck are you talking about? No one is going to kill her."

Short, rapid pants rattled my chest as I watched Julian advance on Royal. He truly did not know what was going on here.

"But you are going to learn a lesson. Raven River is our school." Julian shoved him. "Built by us, for us." He shoved him again.

Royal snarled, fists balling up. I had a feeling their family connection was the single restraint staying his hand.

"Things are going to change from here on. We're taking back our school and all the slum trash"—he sunk a fist in his gut—"are going to learn their place."

Royal rocked back, the barest grunt escaping him. As he straightened, a grin laced with madness twisted his face. "Your mommy doesn't agree about where my place is."

"My mom feels sorry for you! Poor little bastard that nobody wanted! After I'm done, you and the OB trash will be looking for a new school."

"Fucking right!" Leo said. He came for Royal. Cassius and Hiro jumped on him, wrestling him down.

"Get off!" Nolan ordered.

"Are you going to drive them out by any means necessary, Julian?" I cried. "You willing to beat them? Frame them? Flood the campus with drugs and hide baggies of coke under their mattress?"

"Ember, shut the hell up," Nolan snapped.

Julian looked at me like I was crazy. "What the hell are you talking about?"

"Exactly," I said. "You wouldn't do those things because even though your friends are the worst fucking people ever born—"

"I'm the worst?" Nolan's mirthless laugh set my teeth on edge. "You may want to take a closer look at the guys you're fucking."

"—you're not like them, Julian," I plowed on. "You harassed me but you never forced yourself on me like your buddy Leo, and when you have a problem with someone, you say it to their face. Unlike Ives who sneaks around like a little bitch!"

Nolan grabbed my neck, choking a gasp out of me. "You just can't shut your mouth, can you?"

Royal and Julian lurched at us. "Nolan, ease up," Julian said.

"Why do you give a shit about her? She's the same stuck-up bitch we swore off."

"Just let her go."

His grip tightened, drawing me away as Julian, Royal, and Cassius and Hiro holding Leo edged closer. He was losing control of the situation and that's when he would reveal his true self. Julian needed to see it.

"You see?" I croaked. "This is who he really is. A monster. A drug-dealing, blackmailing monster who threatened to have my brother's hands stomped!"

"I'm the monster?!" He shook me. "Your boyfriends are the monsters! You don't— You have no idea the things they've done or just how little of a fuck they give for your brother!"

"Nolan!" Julian shouted.

"Why don't you ask them?" Nolan hauled me to my feet.

The tight grip he had on my neck, and the gun in his pocket, kept the boys inching forward but slowly to not spook him.

"Ask what they've done for the Horsemen," he demanded. "Those thugs run Raveners who dare to enter their slum off the road to jack their money and cars! Ask them if they were one of the guys that ran my mother into a tree!"

His bellowing battered my eardrums.

"Ask them if they gave her a concussion, stole her purse, car, and phone, and then left her injured and alone on the side of the street!

"Ask them how many people they've hurt. How much blood is on their hands. The Horsemen toss their kills in the dumpster and spray-paint angel wings above their heads! When you dump their bodies, who takes the feet and who takes the arms, Royal?"

"They would never do those things!" I shrieked.

"You can't be this naïve. Do you know anything about his father? The things he's done. Rio Cruz is a ruthless, sadistic animal. He's a demon! And he raised his son to be the same way!"

"And what kind of son did your father raise, women-hating drug dealer?"

He barked a laugh. "My father was a heartless bastard, Ember, so I'll give you that. But he wasn't stupid. When Viviana came home with Dante Gallo on her arm, gushing about true love and getting married after five weeks, he saw right through him."

Viviana? The older sister Nolan never talked about?

I remembered seeing pictures of her in the house and the subtle subject changes when I asked about her.

"Dante didn't have any friends or family or anyone from his old life to back up a thing he said. Dad ran background checks and found out *Dante* came out of nowhere five years ago. Dad warned Viviana he was using her for our money, and if she didn't get the marriage annulled, he'd cut her off. She refused. She didn't believe a word he said and accused him of using his money to control her life like he'd always done. Dad lost it and threw them both out of the Estate."

His stale breath washed over my face. "Guess what happened then, Ember. Guess what Dante/Rio did!"

I didn't need to guess. That this story didn't have a happy ending was inevitable with the mention of one name: Rio.

"He left her," I said tonelessly.

"That's right." Nolan laughed though there wasn't a trace of humor left in his soul. "Dumped her like week-old trash in an OB motel. Said he was coming back and she never saw him again."

"I'm sorry for your sister, Nolan. What he did was awful."

"We haven't gotten to the awful part," he hissed. "The part where she was too proud to crawl back to Dad. She swore she'd make it without him or his money. You know the part where Mom drove around the OB for weeks looking for her and ran into the Horsemen ins-tead!"

Nolan's voice cracked, and with it, the seal on the true suffering behind his jeers and malice. His chest heaved wildly against me and the hand holding my neck loosened as his trembling palm slicked with sweat.

"Nolan," I began. "Please—"

"She had nothing! She went to a pawn shop to sell the last of her jewelry and walked out when the guy lowballed her. He followed her, pushed her into an alley, and bashed her head into the fucking wall over and over and over! All for two necklaces and a ring! She bled to death on a pile of trash because of his father!"

Spittle showered the back of my neck along with something that could not be mistaken. Tears.

"I'm sorry," I said, and I meant it. "Viviana deserved so much better, and Rio needs to pay for what he's done. But Royal and the Angels are innocent—"

"Innocent? They must be slipping you drugs too, if you still believe that. Although, the real problem is that like my sister, you refuse to see the truth. So, forget that you tricked me, I'll tell you who attacked Eli—"

Royal lunged. He reached for me, ready to tear me from his hold, and Nolan's gun was between us in an instant.

The boys threw themselves back.

"Nolan, what the fuck!" Julian cried. "Why do you have a gun?!"

"I had to protect myself if they tried to pull something," Nolan said. "And they did. The three of them came up here to jump me. Kill me! Wanna bet Royal's got his switchblade in that tux?"

The cold breath of unease fed my terror. That wasn't just bullshit. It was the rehearsed lines you fed the police to support your self-defense plea after doing the unthinkable.

Royal roughly turned out his pockets. "The only one with a weapon is you, Ives. The only one holding a hostage is you. The only violent, dangerous thug everyone is staring at is *you*!"

"I'm a violent, dangerous thug?" he repeated. "Do you agree, Ember?"

"You are giving a really good impression of one."

"If that's what you say about me, what do you think of the guy who jumped your brother?" He swung me around. "Go on. Tell me he's innocent. Defend the Angels. Defend Hiro after what he's done."

"Hiro? What are you talking about?"

"It's him, Ember. He attacked your brother. He blackmailed you."

The words rapid-fired out of his mouth, ripping me to shreds, and I stood there, the hapless prey with nowhere to run.

"I don't know the other guy who helped him, but I wouldn't look much farther than Cassius, Clay, or Royal."

"Lying shit," Cassius bellowed.

"You're desperate, Ives," said Royal. "Hiro never touched Eli and you sure as hell wouldn't know if he did. You're looking for a way out of this. Drop the gun and we can all walk away."

"Put it away, Nolan," Julian said.

"You said we'd tune them up," Leo threw in. Sweat soaked his collar and his shuffling feet showed he was desperate to get away. "I didn't know the truth about Vivi and it's messed up, but I don't want any part of this."

Everyone had something to say except for me... and Hiro.

I stared at him. At the curtain of hair that obscured his eyes. At the rigid line of his shoulders. At the sealed lips that once said—

"You and I would be a disaster together, Ember. You'd make me believe in forgiveness and hope, and I'd remind you there is none."

There is no forgiveness.

"Hiro," I whispered. "What did you do?"

"Baby, don't listen to him," Cassius said. "Ives is lying through his teeth."

I barely heard him. "Hiro. Look at me and tell me you didn't do this."

His head lifted slowly like every muscle in his neck fought him. Hiro trapped my gaze and I knew before he spoke.

"Ember... I'm so sorry."

I would have dropped if Nolan wasn't holding me up.

"You can't be sorry." Wetness collected in my eyes that I wouldn't let fall. "Real men know seven letters don't fix anything."

"You see?" The triumph in Nolan's voice was unmistakable. "They are the real monsters, Ember. Everything I did, it was only to stop them and the Horsemen from hurting anyone else."

Nolan dropped the gun.

"You said you were saving that beating for the actual sack of garbage that jumped your brother, well, there he is. Don't let me stop you." Just like that, the hand holding me back was gone.

I lunged at him, screaming my rage and pain and so much more for everything he destroyed between us.

Hiro didn't try to defend himself. We went down in a flailing heap.

"Why?!" I grabbed his collar and shook him, knocking his head on the floor. Hiro flopped limply, eyes dead. "Why did you do this?!"

Cassius pulled me off. "Em, stop! It can't be true. Just give him a chance to explain. Hiro, tell her it's a lie!"

In the confusion, Leo slinked away and bolted out of the door. His thundering footsteps faded down the hallway.

"She knows it's true," Nolan said. He sounded like his old self—calm, relaxed, self-assured. "This is what the Horsemen really are and it's why they have to be stopped. As soon as I turned eighteen, I hired someone to track down Dante Gallo and take care of him, but he returned with the name Rio Cruz and the truth of the man I was dealing with. For weeks he gathered information on the gang and Rio's weakness, and he found two.

"The son he keeps tucked away, grooming for the day he'll take over, and the traitor among his men, setting the dominoes that will topple the Horsemen and free our town. Because it's them that make this place hell on earth."

"Argh!" Cassius swung me around. I was fighting furiously to get to Hiro. The long-haired boy stood there awaiting punishment.

"I've been helping him," said Nolan. "Funding him. Rio Cruz is going to lose everything he cares about"—Nolan leveled the gun on Royal—"starting with his son."

Royal! No!

I struggled with Cassius for an entirely different reason.

"Nolan, stop it!" Julian cried. "You're not shooting anyone!"

"Listen to your friend," Royal said. "You'd be wasting a bullet. Rio doesn't care about me. Just look at me." He put out his hands. "Look at what he turned his own son into. I'm a means to an end. A pawn. And if I'm gone, he'll find someone else to take my place." Royal stepped toward him, brimming with more fearlessness than a person should have. "You want to avenge your sister, I respect that. It's exactly what you should do."

"Royal!" I shrieked. *What the hell was he saying?*

"But this isn't the way," he continued. "You've got a gun and one traitor, Ives. Rio's got a gang, cops in his pocket, another sixty years on his life, and witnesses who'll tell him exactly who he'll be hunting down for the rest of it."

Nolan's expression gave nothing away, though I prayed Royal was getting through to him.

"You won't accomplish a thing by shooting me."

Nolan shrugged. "Won't know until I do."

"No!"

"Nolan!"

A bang ripped through our screams.

Julian leaped in front of Royal. The bullet struck him, spinning him into his cousin, and both boys collapsed to the floor.

Cassius, Hiro, and I raced to them, screaming and shouting in an overlapping, unintelligible mess.

Julian was loudest of all. "Fuck!" he cried, clutching his shoulder. Blood oozed under his fingers, a growing stain on his shirt. "He shot me!"

"You're going to be okay." Royal pushed out from under him. I dove for him, feeling him over for a scratch. "I'm fine, Em." He gently removed my hands. "You need to call an ambulance now and—"

Royal shot to his feet. "Where's Ives?!"

I spun. Nolan was nowhere to be seen. I didn't so much as hear his retreating footsteps.

He was gone.

"What's going on up here!?"

Security broke onto the scene. The next half an hour was a whirlwind of questions, flashing lights, tears, hushed whispers, and my first hug from Uncle Harrison. He squeezed me to his chest—a more painful embrace than anything—as the party spilled out of the lobby.

"I can't believe it," he breathed. "Nolan Ives is a good kid from a good family. Why would he do this?"

Eli pushed between us and hugged me even tighter.

It took me a while to slip away from them and join Royal where he stood beside a tree, silent and alone as he watched the ambulance drive off with his cousin and crying aunt.

"Julian saved my life," he said mildly.

"He did."

"And Ives got away."

That much was certain. Security searched the entire place and found nothing but the oil stain in the parking space where his car had been.

"What do we do?"

"Ives is coming for me and there's a traitor among the Horsemen." The flashing lights lit the night purple as we watched them go. "It's war, Em. This means war."

If you'd like to read the final book in the series, The End, click here.[1]

---

1. *http://mybook.to/TheEnd*

The End

It doesn't feel like the end.

It feels like all of my problems are just beginning.

There's more happening in my town of Raven River than I knew.

More lies. More secrets. More pain.

Enemies seen and unseen are circling and not even my guardian angels can protect me.

There's a war coming and I'll fight because this time my Angels...

My Horsemen...

My loves...

... are the ones who need saving.

ABOUT THE AUTHOR

Ruby Vincent is a published author with many novels under her belt but now she's taking a fun foray into contemporary romance. She loves saucy heroines, bold alpha males, and weaving a tale where both get their happy ever after.